THE TRUTHSEEKER

BOOK TWO THE SOULWEAVER SERIES

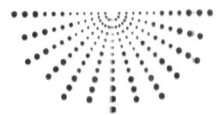

HEIDI CATHERINE

SEQUEL HOUSE

For Nathan.
My star.

PART I

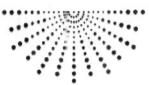

NAX

CHAPTER ONE

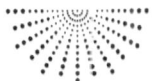

*N*ax threw his body from the jetty and landed in the cold ocean. The gills on his chest flared in response to the water and he propelled himself downward, forcing his head under the surface. Water flowed through his gills and he fought the urge to breathe through his mouth.

There was something about this that didn't feel right. He couldn't do it. He wasn't like everyone else. He was going to drown.

The water in his gills stalled as if sensing his panic and he kicked his way back to the surface. He took several deep gulps of air, the oxygen soothing his fears. Hauling himself up a rusty ladder, he stood once again on the jetty, hands on hips, surveying the huge expanse of water before him.

The secret world that lay beneath the surface would still be there tomorrow. He didn't need to see it today. He didn't even need to see it tomorrow. It could wait.

Nax picked up his carefully folded day-suit and stepped into it, stretching the black fabric over his torso and finally his head. He checked that every inch of his skin was covered, including the soft grill that protected his face.

Glancing to the sky, he noticed the sun was sinking to the horizon. Soon it would disappear, and the world would wake. People would emerge from their homes feeling safe under the gentle light of the moon. The jetty would be crowded with parents pushing strollers, people hurrying to their jobs under the ocean or teenagers taking detours on their way to school—all with bare arms and legs, soaking in the freedom of the night.

Nax had risen early and come to the jetty before moonrise. He'd wanted it to himself. Most of the students at his school already considered him strange. He didn't want to provide them further evidence with his failed attempts to do what they seemed to find so easy—breathe under water.

The fact was that he *was* strange. That is, if being strange means to be unlike everyone else. He resented having to hide away from the sun and live his life at night. It didn't feel natural. It wasn't how humans were intended to live.

Hundreds of years ago people hadn't been afraid of the daylight. They'd slept at night and actually baked themselves in the rays of the sun, trying to darken the color of their skin. They'd been able to lie on the grass and watch clouds float past without the fear of death.

And they hadn't had gills. That was the bit Nax couldn't get past. How he envied these ancient ancestors with their smooth chests. They weren't forced to try to breathe under water. They weren't ridiculed for believing life should be lived on land with your eyes open at day and closed at night. At times he wished he could glue his gills shut and pretend they weren't there. He may as well. They didn't work anyway.

When the first faint lines of gills had started to appear on babies, humans should've been horrified, not excited. Evolution had gone too far. Instead of leaping into the ocean and exploring a new world safe from the sun's harmful rays, this new generation of gilled freaks should've been banished from the water. Maybe then the human body could've had a chance to be restored to its original form.

He began the walk home, knowing his mother would worry if she woke and he wasn't in his bed. He was her only child, which meant he occupied all the space in her heart.

Nax didn't have a father. He knew there must be a man out there somewhere who was responsible for half his genetics, but that didn't make him his father. A father was a man who celebrated your successes and picked you up when you fell. A father was a man who loved you. No, he didn't have a father. The only person in the world who loved him was his mother and she poured so much love over his soul that it almost made up for it.

If only she'd tell him who his father was. All he wanted to know was what he looked like. Did he look like him? Did he share the same green eyes and mass of dark curls that insisted on growing upwards instead of making their way to his shoulders? Was his skin olive despite having been hidden away from the sun? Was he tall?

When he was younger, Nax had been the tallest boy in his class. Now, at the age of sixteen, he'd been overtaken by several of his classmates. He'd watched them sprout like weeds while his growth had stunted. Maybe it was the swimming that was making them grow, as if defying gravity for hours at a time was stretching them out.

This was the thought he'd had in mind when he'd headed for the jetty earlier that afternoon.

It was a stupid theory, he decided, as he pushed open his front gate. Swimming didn't make you grow. Besides, he was still taller than most boys his age. He didn't need to be the tallest. He could find something else to be the best at. Something he could control.

"Naxan. Where have you been?"

He jumped at the sound of his mother's voice. She was standing at the front door wearing a wide-brimmed hat in case one of the sun's rays decided to jump the threshold and bite her on the nose. Her orange hair stuck out the sides of the hat. No matter how hard she tried to tuck her hair away, it always managed to find its way out into the world.

"It's Nax," he said, avoiding her question. He'd been telling her since he was a child that he preferred the shortened version of his name. He didn't really expect her to start listening now.

"Quickly, get inside," she said. "You shouldn't be out in the sun."

"Yes, I should. We all should." He felt defiant. "Besides I'm wearing my day-suit."

"You know I don't trust those things." She closed the door behind him and scowled.

"So why did you buy it for me then?"

"You're being very rude this evening. Where have you been?"

"Sorry, Mom. I've been down at the jetty." He headed down the hallway to the kitchen, hoping she'd follow. There were more distractions in there. Maybe she'd forget to be angry with him.

"Were you trying to swim again?"

"I can't do it, Mom. Why can't I do it? What's wrong with me?" He sat down and ripped off his day-suit, letting it hang from his waist. His naked torso prickled with cold.

"Don't be like that, sweetheart. You just need more time. There's nothing wrong with you."

"Then why am I so different to everyone else? Why doesn't anyone like me?"

"I like you." She ran her hand lightly across his shoulders as she headed for the kettle and turned it on.

"You don't count."

"That's not very nice. I should count more than anyone."

"I don't mean it like that. Why doesn't anyone my own age like me? I'm not a bad person. I've never hurt anyone."

"You're a beautiful person, Naxan. The most beautiful person. People will see that one day."

"Not until I learn to use these stupid things," he said, poking at his gills. "How can I make any friends when I can't go where they go? They talk about Aquatica all the time. I can't join in with those conversations. I don't know what they're talking about."

Aquatica was the underwater world that the first of the gilled humans had created. Nax had seen photos of its brightly colored theme parks, movie theatres and sporting fields. In its early days, people had spent hours down there, only coming to the surface to eat or sleep. Then huge airlocks had been placed on the ocean floor to house restaurants, bowling alleys and hotels. More and more people were choosing to live under the ocean where they were safe to roam the world at any time of the night or day. It seemed it would only be a matter of time before the entire world moved to the ocean floor. And what would Nax do then?

"Well, you're not the only one who's never been there," his mother said. She insisted she had no interest in going to Aquatica. He knew that wasn't true. She was just being protective of his feelings. Forgoing yet another pleasure in her life for the sake of her son.

"What's for dinner?" he asked, keen to change the subject.

"The same as always. Toast, cereal or eggs. Which would you prefer?"

"Eggs, please."

"All right. You go and get dressed for school while I get it ready for work." She switched on the light. It was getting dark outside now.

He blinked as artificial light filled the room. Was this

what it looked like in Aquatica? The sun didn't shine down there either. It must be awfully dark deep down in the ocean. No wonder electricity consumption had reached record highs recently. It was all those lamps lighting up a world that should never have existed—a world that wouldn't have existed if humans hadn't used so much electricity in the first place.

Humans shouldn't live under water. They weren't fish. Although with their gills, maybe that's exactly what they were evolving into. He imagined a man covered in green scales, his legs growing together to form a tail as a fin sprouted from his back. He shivered.

"Go on. Get dressed." His mother woke him from his thoughts, and he rose and headed for his bedroom. That was another reason the other kids at school didn't like him. He'd get lost in thought and miss entire chunks of what was going on around him. It was just that the world of his imagination was often a place he'd prefer to live in.

He sat on the edge of his bed and rolled his day-suit down over his legs, slipping his feet out of it and wiggling his toes. How long until babies were born with webs of skin between their toes?

He pulled on the gray shorts and shirt that were his school uniform, resenting their dull color as he did every day. At least his school had remained on land. He'd heard some schools were starting to take their classes under water. He only had a year left, so hopefully he could finish before his school made the same decision.

Maybe the whole world would move below the surface and he'd be the only person left on the land. It wasn't an entirely unpleasant thought. He wouldn't be able to feel the stares and hear the giggles from his peers if they all went away.

"Dinner's ready," his mother called.

"We should call it breakfast," he said, plonking himself back down at the table.

"Don't be silly." His mother shook her head at him. "We eat breakfast in the morning before we go to bed."

"But that's what I mean. It's called breakfast for a reason. You know… *Break. Fast.* You break your fast when you wake up after a long sleep. That's what our ancestors used to do."

"Not this again, Nax. You need to let all this nonsense go. We're not our ancestors. We haven't slept at night for generations." She set his plate of eggs before him. "Now, eat your dinner."

"It doesn't feel right, Mom. We should be out in the sun."

"Of course, it feels right. This is how we've lived our whole lives. Anyway, look what happened to your beloved ancestors in the sun. They all fried just like the eggs on your plate and died from cancer."

"Not all of them. We wouldn't be here if all of them died."

The population of the world had drastically diminished as the strength of the sun increased. Skin cancer spread like a plague, forcing people into their homes during daylight. Even those blessed with darker shades of skin were affected. Cures that had been developed over the years had ceased to be effective, the cancer reinventing itself and finding new ways to attack each time it seemed to have been beaten. Gradually, the world had accepted defeat and changed their routine so that night became day and day became night. It was safer that way. Everyone thought it made sense. Everyone except Nax, although he wasn't around in those days to voice his opinion. And it was clear that nobody was interested in hearing it now. Not even his mother.

He ate his dinner, kissed his mother and began his long walk to school. There was a bus that could take him, but he avoided it. He didn't like to be in confined spaces with people who'd made it clear they thought he was a fool. Hopeless. Pathetic. Unable to use his God-given gills.

He looked to the moon and wondered if there was a God. There had to be something more out there than the small green planet he lived on. Surely this couldn't be the only planet in the universe to contain life? He felt a familiar tug from the sky. Maybe that's why sometimes he felt like an alien.

Nax sat on the edge of the jetty the next day after yet another failed attempt to force his gills to work. He flexed his arms in the sun, enjoying the way it warmed his skin. He knew he should put his day-suit on. His mother would have a heart attack if she could see him.

He decided he didn't care. He felt good. He felt human.

He stretched out his legs and watched the beads of water run across his skin and drip back into the ocean from where they'd come. Humans were like that, he thought. All huddled together in clumps, afraid to break away on their own. Then there were humans like him who walked alone, not by choice, but by circumstance.

The fabric of his swimming shorts started to dry. He needed to get out of the sun. He would. In just another minute or two.

He thought about the vitamin D tablet he begrudgingly swallowed each day. Humans weren't supposed to obtain one of life's basic ingredients through a tablet. They were meant to synthesize it directly from the sun as they soaked up its warm rays each day.

There wasn't much about life today that was how it was meant to be. Perhaps it was time he started getting used to that.

He stood up, having risked his skin in the sun for far too long already.

"You know you're fully mad, don't you?"

He spun around. It was the voice of a girl, although the figure standing behind him looked more like a woman. It was hard to tell who was under that day-suit. He didn't think he knew her, but there was something familiar. Not so much in the way she looked, but in the way she felt. It was the energy she radiated.

"Who is that?" he said, straining to see her face through the mesh of her face guard.

"Put your day-suit on and I'll tell you."

"What if I don't?" Who was this stranger to tell him what to do?

"Please yourself. See you at your funeral." She turned and marched away down the jetty.

He hadn't meant to scare her off. In fact, he'd been enjoying their extremely short conversation. Had he just messed up his first chance to make a friend?

He picked up his day-suit, rushing to put it on. But for all the good these suits did at protecting them from the sun, they were useless when it came to dressing in a hurry. His legs got tangled and he tripped, falling with a thud on the splintered timber.

He cursed and rubbed his rear end. He'd get a nasty bruise out of that.

"Wait," he called, running down the jetty with his day-suit in his hand. He wasn't sure why, but he had to catch up to the girl. He suddenly felt as if his life depended on it.

She turned, saw him, and continued to walk away.

"Please wait," he called again, as the gap between them closed. He was fast. Faster than she was.

"Then please put on your suit." She paused, placing her hands on her hips. "Why do you care if I put on my suit?" he asked, as he tried for the second time to squeeze himself back into it.

"I'm not into horror movies," she said, tapping her foot impatiently.

"I don't think death is that instant," he said, finally getting his legs safely into the suit. "I should have at least a few months to live. Besides, it's nearly dark. I'm only going to have to take this off in a minute." He threaded his hands through the armholes, pulling the suit up his back and over his head.

He stood to face her, noticing for the first time the blue of her eyes reflecting through her face grill. He wondered what she looked like. He'd bet she was pretty. So, what was she doing talking to him?

"Do you really care so little about your life?" she asked.

"Actually, I care a lot about my life." He did. He hadn't risked his life lightly. He'd needed to feel the sun on his skin. How could he explain that to this stranger? She'd never understand.

"You know you're fully mad, don't you?" she said, repeating the line she'd used when she first approached him. The way she said it didn't sound like an insult. She sounded amused. Maybe even a little impressed.

"That's what all the girls say." He blushed, glad to have his face obscured. It was true. Plenty of girls had told him he was mad. Although in those cases they most definitely hadn't been impressed.

The sun slipped below the horizon, shrouding them in darkness.

"It's late. I have to go," she said, running away down the jetty.

"You didn't tell me who you are," he called after her, knowing she wouldn't reply.

She'd been right. It was late. He'd look pretty stupid if

anyone saw him standing there under the light of the moon wearing his day-suit. He'd better get to school. He ducked behind a tree where he'd left his bag and got changed into his uniform. Shoving his day-suit back into his bad he silently apologized to his mother for not taking the time to fold it.

His mother worked at the factory that made the day-suits. She sat at a machine six nights a week, sewing suits she wasn't sure she believed in. The boss of the factory had been worried when people had started living under water, thinking demand for the suits would plummet. The opposite had occurred. People were getting used to moving around at any time of the day or night and wanted the same freedom when they returned to the surface.

Regardless of Nax's mother's beliefs, she'd bought a day-suit for Nax. She knew he liked to sneak out of the house while the sun was still high in the sky, so thought it was worth the chance—just in case they actually worked.

The girl on the jetty had seemed to think they did. She'd been quite upset with him for not wearing it. It felt strange for someone to worry about him. Someone who wasn't his mother.

He arrived at school almost an hour later to find a huddle of students in the courtyard. They were looking at something and giggling excitedly amongst themselves. The glare of the floodlights that lit the courtyard sent reflections bouncing off the small crowd, making it impossible for Nax to see what they were looking at.

He wished he had the kind of easy relationship with his classmates where he could wander up, join the huddle and find out exactly what was so exciting. He knew if he tried, they'd either ignore him or turn their attention on him. He wasn't sure which was worse.

The school bell rang, and the students began to move

away, slowly revealing the source of their fascination. A new student.

She was facing away from Nax and he noticed immediately how her blonde hair floated down her back in soft waves. He took a step toward her, fighting a strong urge to reach out and touch her hair.

The trend for most girls was to cut their hair short, as they found it easier to handle underwater. But there were still a few who chose to wear their hair long, so it wasn't as if he'd never seen long hair before. He'd just never seen hair quite like this. It looked almost as if it was glowing.

"Put your tongue back in your mouth, loser," said one of the other boys, shoving him firmly on the shoulder.

He barely noticed the shove. The sky could fall on his head and he was unlikely to notice. He couldn't tear his eyes away from the girl.

She spun around and he knew immediately she was the girl from the jetty. The blue of her eyes was even more brilliant without the grill of her day-suit. Her curvaceous figure was unable to be disguised by the drab uniform she now wore. But those weren't the features that gave her identity away. It was the aura surrounding her.

He felt himself being pulled toward her and fought his every instinct to close the small gap between them and wrap her in his arms. He wanted to breathe in the scent of her hair, hold her face in his hands and study each fleck of color in her irises as he felt the softness of her skin pressed against him.

The huddle of students had reformed, only this time it was to laugh at him. For once he didn't mind. They were so far away from him in this moment. The only other person who existed was this exquisite creature who'd somehow appeared in his life.

"Nax is in looove," one of the girls teased, stretching out the word like a bow on a violin.

The crowd cackled and shrieked.

"Keep away from him," a boy called Morko warned. "That freak can't breathe under water."

"Sure he can," said the new girl, taking a step towards Nax. "I saw him swimming this morning. Maybe he just doesn't want to swim with freaks like you."

A hush spread through the crowd. Mouths dropped open before spilling over with giggles and hoots. It seemed someone as beautiful as this girl could say what she liked.

Morko scowled and scurried away, clearly deciding he wasn't having as much fun as he thought he'd been.

A wave of delicious warmth raced through Nax's heart. The girl had stood up for him. Not only that, she'd lied for him. Nobody had ever done that before.

The final bell for school rang and students began to hurry towards the main entrance. The girl hesitated, studying Nax for a moment before deciding to follow the others.

"I'm Maari," she called back to him over her shoulder.

He would've told her his name, if only he could speak. Instead he stood planted to the spot.

Soon he was alone in the courtyard. He knew he'd be punished for being late, but it seemed worth it. One detention in exchange for a few precious minutes in the cool night air to imprint the last moments of his life in his mind forever. These weren't moments he ever wanted to forget. When he was the last man left standing on the land after all others had disappeared under the sea, he wanted to remember what it felt like to have a friend—a beautiful friend with hair that glowed like an angel.

Nax waited all week for a chance to talk to Maari. It was impossible at school given the week of detentions he'd been handed out for being late, so instead he'd come to the jetty every afternoon hoping to see her again.

He yawned, swinging his legs off the edge of the jetty as he waited. He was exhausted getting up so early every day. He'd started falling asleep after school before the sun had even risen. His mother was worried. Despite her complaints, she'd been willing to overlook him sneaking out in the day occasionally. But this was too much. He was putting his body at unnecessary risk.

The risk seemed worth it to him. It frightened him to think how much he was willing to risk for a few moments in Maari's presence.

He'd never been in love before and wondered if that's what this was. Nobody had told him it would be like this. Was the feeling this strong for everyone? He couldn't imagine his mother feeling this way about his father, whoever he was. Wherever he was.

His feelings were obviously not reciprocated. Otherwise Maari would've come to the jetty. She must know she'd find him here.

Today looked to be no different to the ones that'd gone before. She wasn't coming. He may as well give his gills one more try while he was here and nobody was watching.

He glanced at the sky. It was overcast with gray clouds rolling in. A storm was coming. He'd have to be quick.

Before he could change his mind, he tore his day-suit from his body and plunged into the water. He paddled about for a few minutes trying to delay the feeling of uselessness that would drown him when he failed yet again.

He pushed the water upward with his hands, propelling himself under the surface. His gills sucked in water and he concentrated on repressing his instinct to breathe through his mouth.

Panic wrapped him like a blanket and soon his heart was beating so loudly he thought he'd wake the humans who slept in their air-locked crypts on the ocean floor.

He fought his way to the surface and sucked air into his lungs, coughing and gasping for life.

"You know you're doing it wrong, don't you?"

It was Maari. He hadn't wanted her to see him like this. He'd been sure she wasn't coming today, or ever.

"Obviously," he said between gasps, noticing the easy way she treaded water to keep herself afloat. He hadn't seen her slip into the water. How long had she been there? Perhaps she'd come from under the surface.

"Can I teach you?" she asked in a way that made him feel he'd be doing her the favor by saying yes. Her golden hair was damp, turning it several shades darker.

"Why would you want to teach me?" He was genuinely perplexed.

"I like you. The others were right. You're so weird."

"And weird is good...right?" Now he was even more confused.

"Weird is great. Ready for your lesson?" She swam toward him until they were close enough to touch and looked into his eyes. He felt sparks of electricity tingle his soul. Her pupils widened and she smiled.

He suddenly felt self-conscious and looked away, diverting his eyes to the thin black straps of the swimsuit that hugged her shoulders. He quickly realized this was worse as she'd likely think he was staring at her chest. He drew his eyes back to hers.

"I'm ready," he said.

"Give me your hands." She reached out for him and he froze at the prospect of touching her. He'd yearned for nothing else since he'd met her and now that he had the chance, it seemed beyond him.

"I won't bite." She found his hands and laced her fingers through his.

A dull pain shot into his stomach. His fingers took on a life of their own in response to her touch and closed themselves around her delicate hands. He gripped her tightly. She felt exactly as he'd thought she would.

Warm.

Soft.

Exhilarating.

She drew in a sharp breath and for a moment he though she was about to pull away. There was a flash of hesitation in her normally confident face.

That was when he saw her true self. She wasn't the self-assured, assertive girl he'd seen take strips off Morko on her first day of school. She had doubts about herself as much as he did. Weakness and sorrow were embedded in her soul, alongside strength and joy, weaving the fabric of who she was. She was complex yet simple, vulnerable yet powerful, pure yet flawed.

In that small moment of hesitation, she reached out and won all the corners of his heart that he'd kept protected. She knocked down his wall of fear of being rejected—of being abandoned by someone other than his father.

"One, two, three," she counted, lowering herself under the water, pulling him down with her.

His gills flared as panic inched its way down his spine. His eyes opened and he saw the blurred figure of Maari before him, still holding his hands. She smiled, her eyes begging him to relax.

She released one of his hands and placed it on his gills. They were motionless. Useless. Water had begun to flow into them, then stopped.

She took his hand and placed it on her gills and for the first time he felt what it must be like to breathe using your body instead of your mouth. Her gills waved back and forth like a field of wheat in a summer's breeze. Water flowed through them at a gentle yet constant rate, feeding her lungs with the oxygen she needed.

He understood instantly what he'd been doing wrong. He'd been trying to suck air through his gills in the same way as he did through his nose or mouth. Breathing under water wasn't like this. There was no rhythm of air coming in and out. It was one constant stream.

He relaxed his gills and resisted the urge to fill them with oxygen. Instead he filled his mind with the idea of water flowing gently into his body, feeding him and flowing out again. The more his lungs screamed for oxygen, the more he visualized what he needed to do.

Maari lifted his hand from her gills and placed it back on his own. He felt them shimmer to life as if waking from a deep sleep.

He was doing it. It was working. He was breathing under water.

He drew in a breath of surprise, immediately choking as saltwater filled his lungs.

He kicked to the surface and coughed, expelling the water from his body.

Maari surfaced next to him, laughing.

"What happened?" she asked.

"I did it," he said, his eyes ablaze with excitement.

"You did what? Swallow half the ocean?"

"No, I did it. Only for a second, but I did it."

"That's brilliant." She seemed genuinely happy for him. "Let's do it again."

A flash of lightning lit the sky, followed only moments later by a loud clap of thunder.

Maari flinched. "I hate storms. Let's get out of here."

She began swimming for the jetty.

"Aren't we safer under the water?" called Nax, keen to give his gills another chance.

She didn't answer. She was already hauling herself up the ladder. He saw her climb onto the jetty, scoop up her day-suit and take off. She didn't say goodbye or even turn to wave. She seemed to move faster than the lightning that'd spooked her so much.

Nax treaded water and watched her. So, she hadn't come from underwater. She'd left her day-suit next to his and joined him in the ocean. She must've seen his first pathetic attempt to breathe. No wonder she wanted to help him. She must feel awfully sorry for him.

He was mad with himself. He didn't want her sympathy, much preferring her admiration. He could never hope for her to fall in love with him if he kept this up.

Ignoring the storm, he prepared himself to go below the surface one more time. He needed to get this right before he saw her again.

He took a deep breath only to hear a loud crack pierce the air. A bolt of lightning hit the ladder Maari had climbed up only moments before. It splintered away from the jetty and dangled over the water, held by only one bolt as it swung back and forth.

The bolt couldn't take the weight and soon the ladder came crashing into the sea. Despite being a safe distance away, Nax flinched. Water turned to steam as the ladder sank into its depths.

Thank goodness Maari hadn't been on the ladder when the lightning had struck. It would most certainly have killed her. What a difference a few moments in time could make. Her number didn't seem to be up.

He wondered if he actually believed that. Was life predetermined or did it strike as randomly as that lightning appeared to have? Whatever the case, he was glad Maari was safe.

Now to get out of the water. Without the ladder he'd have to swim to shore and walk back up the jetty to retrieve his day-suit. It was either that or use the regular entrance to the sea at the far end of the jetty where a shiny metal ramp sloped into the water. He'd never used the ramp and didn't intend to start now. There were far too many people there. He preferred the rusty ladder that had hung to the side of the jetty for decades. Until today.

There was no way he'd make it to school on time. It looked like he'd be having another week of lunchtime detention.

Maybe he shouldn't bother going to school at all. He could explain what happened to his mother and she could write him a note. He'd have to be dramatic and convince her that his life had been in danger, but that shouldn't be too hard. She seemed to think his life was always in danger. Today it wasn't even a lie.

By the time he reached the shore, the storm had blown over and the sun fallen below the horizon. People had started to emerge from their homes. He decided to leave his day-suit where it sat on the end of the jetty. He didn't want anyone to see him. Knowing his luck, he'd be halfway down the jetty and would run into Morko who'd take one look at his damp skin and know exactly what he'd been up to. He didn't need hassles like that.

He'd tell his mother his suit had torn and use his meager savings to buy a new one. Hopefully she wouldn't get too mad. With any luck the suit would still be there the next time he went back.

By the time he reached his front door, the moon was high

in the sky and his mother had left for work. He'd need to talk to her when she returned.

After letting himself in, he flopped down on his bed, exhausted. A short nap would do him good.

He closed his eyes and filled his mind with Maari, quickly becoming lost in the world of his dreams as slumber took hold.

He was floating on his back in the water, the sun shining down, warming his belly and his soul. The sun wasn't harming him. It never did in his dreams. And he wasn't trying to use his gills for the simple reason that he didn't have any.

When Nax's eyes were closed, the world was different to the world he lived in when his eyes were open. It was exactly how he'd always longed for it to be.

He wondered how long it'd be before the woman appeared in his dream. She was always there. Sometimes in the background, sometimes standing before him, smiling and reaching out for him.

As a small boy he'd sometimes seen her when he wasn't asleep. Then she'd disappear and he'd search for her, looking under tables and in the broom closet.

"What are you looking for?" his mother would ask.

"The lady," he'd say, his eyes wide with innocence.

His mother would nod as a small frown crossed her brow. She didn't need to ask what lady he spoke of, for he spoke of her often. She'd asked a doctor about it once and he'd told her it was normal for children to have imaginary friends. She hadn't pushed the issue and Nax now knew that was because of her fear that he'd be taken away from her. It was obvious even back then he wasn't like other children.

Deep down his mother had known this was no ordinary imaginary friend. Nax was too specific and consistent in his descriptions of her.

He'd talked of her dark, shiny hair that floated around her face and her even darker eyes that looked both happy and sad at the same time. He'd been particularly fascinated with the way she glowed.

Now he only saw her in his dreams.

Tonight was no different. He saw her in the distance, sitting on a raft with a mast made from a living pine tree. She waved at him.

"Hello," he called out, knowing she wouldn't reply. In all the years he'd been seeing her, she'd never once spoken to him.

Her raft floated closer and he saw her face light up.

Then Maari was beside him in the water. He swam towards her and she wrapped her arms around his neck.

Her skin was heaven. Her touch was bliss.

He encased her in his arms and brought his lips to hers. But the kiss wasn't what he expected.

Her lips were icy and the moment he touched her the air was torn from his lungs. He tried to pull away but couldn't. The grip she had around his neck had tightened. He couldn't breathe. He couldn't move. What was she doing to him?

His eyes blinked rapidly, and he saw the lady on the raft behind Maari. The joy had been wiped from her eyes and instead they were brimming with fear. It wasn't an expression he'd ever seen on her face before.

He felt the life slipping from his body.

The lady on the raft opened her mouth and cried out to him, speaking her very first words to him.

"Matthew! Keep away from her."

Nax plunged into a world of darkness.

CHAPTER TWO

*M*ax's sheets were soaked with sweat. His heart was racing.

He sat up and sucked air into his lungs, certain he'd been deprived of oxygen in more than just his dream. He wondered what would've happened to him if he'd died in his dream. Would he have died in real life, too? It seemed like it.

He got up and looked out the window. How long had he been asleep? The sky was still dark. It couldn't have been that long. He checked his watch, surprised to learn he'd been sleeping for several hours.

He lay back down and attempted to retrieve the details of his dream before they slipped beyond his grasp.

He'd been in the water. He'd been happy. Then Maari had tried to kill him. Why would he dream that? So far, she'd proven herself to be his savior, not his killer.

Perhaps it was just his fear of falling in love that'd brought this dream to life?

Then he remembered perhaps the most unusual part of the dream. The lady had spoken to him. She'd told him to keep away from Maari. And she'd called him a strange name.

Matthew.

He'd never heard that name before. It sounded foreign.

"Matthew," he said aloud.

Something lit within him. It felt like a switch in the center of his brain. What exactly it was lighting, he wasn't sure. Nor did he have any idea what it meant.

"It means you overslept," he mumbled, getting up again and pulling on a singlet to hide his gills. He was still wearing the shorts he'd worn in the ocean and he brushed away the fine layer of salt that had dried on them.

It was a stupid dream, he decided. Meaningless. If that lady were real and she did care about him like he'd always believed, then the last thing she'd be telling him was to keep away from the only person his age who'd ever been nice to him.

Perhaps she was jealous of Maari?

He heard a soft knocking at the front door.

"Coming, Mom," he called out as he walked to the door. She was always forgetting her key. Lucky for her, he was home this time.

But it wasn't his mother.

It was Maari.

She was panting and tears were streaming down her face. Her school uniform had twisted into bunches around the strap of her schoolbag and her silken hair was flying away in all directions.

He still thought she was the most beautiful girl he'd ever seen.

"Thank goodness you're okay," she gasped, throwing her bag to the ground and stepping forward to slide her arms around his waist.

The physical contact took him by surprise, and he stood frozen for a few moments. Then the sweet, salty smell of her hair reached a place deep inside him and he enveloped her in his arms. He held her close, deciding to skip school more often if this was the kind of response it evoked.

"You'd better come inside," he said, noticing the sun casting long shadows on the ground as it made its journey into the sky.

She broke away and his heart sank at the loss of contact. She picked up her bag and followed him to the kitchen.

"I thought you'd drowned," she said, taking a seat at the table.

He slid into the seat next to her and wondered how it was possible she knew what he'd dreamt.

"I don't understand," he said.

"The storm. Remember? The last time I saw you, you were in the water with the storm overhead. Then you didn't show up at school and I started to worry. I went back to the jetty as soon as school finished and the ladder had gone. All that was left was the charred timber where it had once been bolted. Someone said they saw it get hit by lightning. Then I found this." She reached for her bag and opened it to pull out some dark fabric. His day-suit.

"You thought I was hit by lightning?" He wanted to laugh, but the serious expression on her face told him that was a bad idea.

"Of course that's what I thought. Why else would you leave your suit there and not turn up at school? You'd either been hit by lightning or you'd drowned."

"How did you know I didn't finally get the hang of how to use my gills and spent the day at Aquatica?"

She raised her eyebrows.

"Okay," he said. "Fair enough. I wasn't at Aquatica. I saw the lightning strike the ladder and had to swim to shore. By the time I got there it was so late I decided to ditch school. I ditched my suit, too. There were so many people around by then."

"Well, I wish you told me."

"How could I? You ran away. Anyway, you weren't really worried, were you? Why would you care if I drowned?" He was fishing for a compliment and he knew it. He would have to tell her how he felt soon, and it'd be so much easier if he knew she felt the same.

"I don't know why, but I care. I care so much I've just spent the day feeling like I was the one who drowned." She looked away.

"Thank you." He reached for her hand and held it gently. He ran his thumb across her fingernails, noticing she'd bitten them down to the quick.

"I know they're ugly," she said, pulling her hand away. "I bite my nails when I'm nervous."

He reached for her hand again. "Maari, there's nothing ugly about you. Every part of you is so beautiful I lose my head around you. I don't know what's going on here, but ever since I first saw you, I haven't been able to get you out of my mind."

She leaned towards him. Did she want him to kiss her? He hoped so, as that was exactly what he was going to do.

As he bent towards her, he remembered his dream. Her lips of ice that'd almost stolen his life. It was only a dream. He didn't even care if it was real. One kiss would be worth it.

He pressed his lips to hers and groaned softly with relief when he felt her warmth. Her mouth was made for kissing. It welcomed him, caressed him, seduced every fiber of his being.

He deepened the kiss. This wasn't a girl he could keep away from. This was a girl he'd spend his life doing everything in his power to be by her side.

"Good morning, Nax." It was his mother. He hadn't heard her come in.

She placed some shopping bags on the table and smiled at Maari. "I'm Lorarn. And you are?"

Maari leaped to her feet, her face a dark shade of purple. "I'm Maari."

"Nice to meet you. Nax has told me nothing about you." She started to unpack the shopping. Her face was blank. That wasn't a good sign. Her face was always blank when she was upset. "Will you be staying for breakfast? I thought I'd roast a chicken."

"No, no thank you, Lorarn," said Maari, picking up her bag. "I need to get going. It was nice to meet you."

Nax glared at his mother and walked Maari to the door.

"Meet me at the jetty tomorrow?" he asked, leaning on the doorframe.

"No ladder, remember?" she said. "Unless you want to meet at the ramp?"

"Meet me on the shore. We can wade in."

"Okay. As long as you don't bring your mother," she whispered. "She's scary."

"You know what they say about redheads. They're a fiery bunch. Besides, you're scarier." He meant it. She was the most frightening girl he'd ever met. She had the power to destroy him if she wanted to. He was under her spell. And he'd never felt so good.

"I'm not scary," she said, standing on her toes and reaching for his lips. He kissed her lightly, afraid of being caught again.

As soon as their lips met, his good intentions deserted him. He slid his hands around her back and pulled her to him, enjoying the way she felt tucked up against his chest.

"Goodbye, Maari," his mother called down the hallway.

He let go and watched his love scurry away into the dawn.

"Thanks, Mom," he said, taking a seat again in the kitchen and scowling at her. "That was terrific. I really appreciate it."

"What are you talking about?" She looked at him with innocence she didn't possess.

"The first friend I make, who also happens to be the first girl I ever fall in love with, and there's you trying to frighten her away."

"In love? Please Nax, be serious. You've never even mentioned this girl. How serious could it be?"

"Serious." He crossed his arms.

She put down the can of tomatoes she'd been holding and sat next to him.

"I'm sorry," she said. "I didn't think…"

"I didn't mention her because I wasn't sure how she felt until today. I haven't known her very long."

"Well, you look like you've made up for lost time."

"Mom. Not that it's any of your business, but that was the first time I kissed her. The first time I kissed any girl. And wasn't it romantic with you interrupting."

"I said I was sorry. I was just surprised. I didn't expect to see that when I came in the door, that's all. She seems…nice."

"She is nice, Mom. More than nice. She's amazing."

"Why aren't you wearing your uniform?" she asked, getting up and opening the fridge.

"I got caught in the storm at the jetty. It freaked me out a little, so I came home and went back to bed."

"You mean you didn't go to school? Are you okay?" She came over and pushed a stray curl off his forehead so she could feel his temperature.

"I'm fine, Mom. I was just shaken up. The lightning came very close. I was right near the ladder when it was struck. I couldn't have coped with school after that. I just needed some time out. You'll write me a note, won't you?"

She studied him for a moment, deciding whether she

believed him. "Sure, but I don't want you going back to the jetty tomorrow."

"Come on, Mom. It's the weekend. I'm meeting Maari tomorrow."

"Stop putting those big, green eyes on me. I said no."

"Please," he said, batting his eyelashes theatrically and grinning. "The weather will be fine. The storm's over."

"I have a feeling it's just beginning," she said.

He waited to hear her laugh, but she didn't.

Nax sat on the sand in the shade of the jetty. He'd stripped off his day-suit, hoping the shade would offer him enough protection from the afternoon sun's rays.

He'd already been there for two hours, having given up on sleep. The long nap he'd had the night before had thrown out his body clock.

The little sleep he'd had was anything but restful. The woman with the dark hair had haunted his dreams. Bothered him. She wouldn't leave him alone.

She hadn't spoken to him. She just shook her head and he'd known what she was saying. She was disappointed in him. He hadn't listened to her. Instead of keeping away from Maari, he'd drawn her closer.

He'd turned away from the woman and she followed, imploring him with the depths of her eyes to heed her warning. He wasn't interested in her warning.

"I will not keep away from her," he'd screamed at her. "Why don't you try keeping away from me? I don't want you here."

She'd looked horrified. Hurt. Then she left and now he wasn't sure how to feel about it.

Had she really gone? He knew it wasn't normal for an

imaginary friend to stick around past your sixteenth birth-day, but that had never bothered him. There wasn't a day of his life that he'd ever have used the word normal to describe himself.

The woman had always been there. Like a security blanket or a well-loved teddy bear. She loved him. He knew that. And he'd always felt like he loved her. She was like a second mother. He'd secretly wondered if the universe had sent her to him to make up for him only having one parent.

But she wasn't real. She couldn't be. She was a figment of his imagination and it was way past time to let her go. He had Maari now. He didn't need the friendship of a woman made from dreams instead of flesh and bone.

Life would be strange without her though.

He looked down the beach, hoping to see Maari. It was dark now. She should be here soon. Soon she'd be by his side. Would she kiss him again? He longed for another taste of her lips.

"Boo!" Maari leaped at him from behind and threw her arms around his shoulders.

He laughed. "I thought you'd come from the other way."

"Just keeping you on your toes." She kissed him on the cheek. He liked the casual way she did it. It made him feel like they'd known each other for years. She was wearing a pair of denim shorts and a pink tee-shirt that hugged her body in a way that made his heart race.

"I'm glad you're here," he said.

"How long have you been waiting?"

"Not long," he lied. She didn't need to know about his sleeplessness. Nor did she need to know about his dreams. She'd said being weird was good, but that might just tip the scale beyond acceptable levels of freakiness.

"Was your Mom okay after I left?"

"She was fine. Don't worry about her. It's just been the

two of us for so long I guess it's going to take her a while to get used to the idea of you."

"Your father doesn't live with you then?"

"No. I don't know where he lives."

"I'm sorry."

"What about you? Do you have a big family?"

"No, I'm an only child, too. Except my parents are still together. Dad just started a job down there as an engineer, which is why we moved." She pointed out to the ocean.

"So, you've been to Aquatica?"

"Yeah, I've been there. Don't worry, you're not missing out on much. It's so tacky. All bright lights and loud colors. I much prefer it out here."

"You don't really mean that, do you?"

"Of course, I mean it. Look around you. It's beautiful here. The trees, the ocean, the sky. I think that's the part I like least about Aquatica. There's no sky. I've always loved staring into the sky." She lay down on the sand and looked to the heavens.

He flopped down beside her. "What do you think's out there?"

"Who knows. Something amazing."

"How can you be so sure?"

"Because it has to be, doesn't it? The universe is huge. There are all sorts of things out there we haven't even started to imagine."

He smiled, pleased to hear there was someone else in the world who thought about these things. "Do you think there's life out there on other planets?"

"Definitely. Maybe on a faraway planet there's a beach. And right now there's a girl and a boy lying on the sand staring out at the sky wondering if we exist."

"That's not what they're doing." He propped himself up on his elbows.

"What are they doing then?"

"This." He leaned across and brought his lips to hers. She stirred in response to his touch and kissed him.

A storm rumbled in the distance.

Maari sat up in fright. "Another storm?"

"Why are you so scared of them?" he asked.

"Let's go for a swim. The storm can't get us under the water." She stood up, ignoring his question and peeled off her clothes. She was wearing the same black bikini she'd worn the day before.

"You're forgetting something," he said, pointing to his gills and wondering how he was supposed to be able to concentrate on breathing with a distraction like that bikini.

"You'll do it today. I know you will. That's why I brought these." She threw a pair of goggles at him and put on a pair herself.

He slid on his goggles, being careful not to tangle them in his hair, and pulled a face. "We look gorgeous."

"You actually do," she said, taking him by the hand.

Together, they waded out into the water. When it began to lap at their shoulders, she asked him if he was ready.

"Let's do it." He dove under the water without waiting for her. Soon he could see her face before him. This time she wasn't blurred. With the goggles, he could see every feature of her beautiful face.

She nodded at him and pointed to his gills.

He relaxed and visualized the water moving through them. Instead of fighting it, he embraced it, thanking the water for feeding his lungs.

The water flowed into his gills and he concentrated on accepting the gift of life it gave him.

He looked across at Maari who was smiling, raising her arms above her head in celebration.

He smiled in return. He'd made her proud. He'd made himself proud.

She pointed out to sea, asking if he was ready to explore the underwater world that had so far eluded him.

He nodded and together they swam. The world became darker, reminding him of his dream when his world went black. Then as he swam further and deeper, he saw lights.

He paused and Maari urged him forward.

Aquatica. The day had come. He'd finally see it for himself.

The lights got brighter, and the greens, blues and browns of the sea became reds, purples and yellows. An enormous archway stood before them. He looked down to notice its footings rooted deeply in the ocean floor. A neon sign lit the arch and he saw the word "Aquatica" spelled out across its curve.

He became aware of a faint buzzing sound, which he knew to be a frequency that was sent out to keep the fish away. That seemed like a shame. Although sharks were fish, he supposed. And he definitely didn't like the idea of encountering any of those today. Not that there were too many left in the ocean these days.

Maari took his hand and they swam through the arch. It was like swimming into a new world. He immediately saw what all the fuss was about. Huge sections of the ocean floor had been cleared and the sand had been colored green, creating a rolling park that stretched for miles. Bright sculptures and flowers lined winding paths that nobody would ever walk down. Instead, the people swam above. Children did somersaults and handstands while parents clapped and smiled. These children weren't trapped in their homes hiding from the sun. They were free to enjoy the world whenever they pleased.

He noticed a row of palm trees that sprouted from the

sand, and swam over to one, curious about how it was possible for a tree to grow without the sun.

One touch of the tree told him it was artificial. Yet it looked so real. Some of the magic of this new world evaporated as he was reminded of the false nature of what he saw. Maari was right. The utopic world he'd found himself in couldn't compete with the magic created by mother nature. The human attempt to create a world of beauty was a mirage.

Maari urged him on and they swam through the park. They reached the other side and he saw the airlocks he'd heard so much about. When he'd seen them lowered into the ocean, they'd looked like shipping containers, but now they were rows of inviting homes and businesses. No wonder people were choosing to move their lives down here.

He followed Maari down one of the streets and she pointed to a building that looked very much like a coffee shop. The front door was made from rubber with a slit down the middle.

Maari squeezed through and disappeared.

He followed and found himself in a small, square room filled with air. He gasped for breath as the water poured from his gills and his mouth sucked air into his lungs. Transitioning back to how he'd breathed his whole life was more difficult than he'd anticipated. How quickly his body had adjusted to being fed oxygen through his gills.

"Sorry, I should've warned you about that." Maari squeezed the water from her hair and let it drip onto the metal floor to drain away through a series of small holes.

"What did you think?" she asked, removing her goggles, her eyes brimming with excitement. "Is it as good as you thought it'd be?"

"I guess so," he said.

"You don't sound so sure about that."

"I'm not."

They laughed.

"You did so well out there. Are you proud of yourself? You did it." She hugged him. Her body felt warm from the heated water. Just another luxury for the residents of Aquatica.

"Yes, I did it." He'd beaten his fear, woken his gills and seen what all those around him took for granted. He hugged her, wishing he could stop the clock on this moment in time. The world felt so good when she was in his arms.

"Feel like a milkshake?" she asked, breaking away and reaching for a white plastic cloak that hung from a row of hooks on the wall, slipping her goggles into a pocket.

"Sure." He followed her lead and reached for a cloak of his own.

"They won't let you in wearing only swimmers," she said, putting on her cloak.

"That's a shame," he said, as her bikini-clad body disappeared in a sea of white plastic.

They squeezed through another rubber door and Nax blinked at the burst of color that surrounded him. It was a coffee shop like any normal one he'd seen, except every surface had been coated with bright colors. They dazzled like the brightest rainbow.

"What's with all the color?" he asked Maari, as they slid into a booth at the back of the shop.

"No idea. Everything's like this down here. Maybe they're trying to make up for the absence of the sun."

"Nothing can make up for that."

A waitress wearing a purple wig and orange overalls approached the table. Nax had noticed all the staff wore this ridiculous attire and wondered if they were okay with it. He was starting to appreciate the dull color of his school uniform. It'd be a relief to wear it again now he'd seen the alternative.

The waitress raised her penciled-in eyebrows at them.

"Two chocolate milkshakes please," said Maari. "Number eight, seven, zero, three."

The waitress nodded and left.

"What's with the number?" Nax asked.

"My customer number. Nobody carries real money down here."

"Of course not," he said, thinking that he should know this. He'd lived in this town his whole life. She'd been here only a number of days and already knew more about it than he did. He should be the one teaching her.

"Hello? Anybody home?" Maari was waving her hand in front of his face.

"Sorry, did you say something?"

"I said I hope you don't mind me ordering for you? I just wanted you to try the chocolate milkshakes here. They're my favorite thing about Aquatica."

"Don't tell me they have cows swimming around down here."

"Cows?"

"You know, for the milk."

She laughed. "Not yet, but I'm sure right now someone's sitting there trying to work out how to make that possible."

"How many times have you been here? I thought you said you just moved here."

"We used to come here every summer. My parents love it. That's why they jumped at the chance to move here."

"Where did you live before?"

"Inland. It was a horrible. Each year it was getting worse as people started leaving to live by the coast. It was turning into a ghost town. I give it five years and nobody will live there at all."

Nax was reminded of the image of himself being the last man standing on the land.

"Do you think you'll live down here one day?"

"Maybe. I hope not. I want to stay above the surface. It's creepy down here."

The waitress returned with their milkshakes.

"Have a nice day," she said with a scowl.

"See?" Maari said to Nax. "It's the happiest place around."

He laughed and took a sip of his milkshake. His mouth filled with sweetness that made his tongue tingle. It was different to a milkshake on the surface.

"What do you think?" she asked.

"It's amazing. What do they put in there?"

"Who knows. Mermaid tails probably."

"And you call me weird." He reached across the table and she placed her hand in his.

"I never said I wasn't weird, too."

"I'll tell you what's weird," he said. "This place. I can't believe we're sitting on the floor of the ocean drinking milkshakes."

"This is nothing. Would you like to see something really interesting?" she asked, tilting her head.

Of course, he did.

CHAPTER THREE

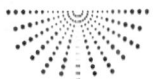

*M*aari swam ahead of Nax, leading him through the streets to the edge of Aquatica. The lights began to fade and the water cooled. They swam upwards, over a sand dune and into a gully.

He wondered where she was taking him. As they'd finished their milkshakes, she'd told him about an old woman called the Truthseeker who was said to live beyond the dune. Maari didn't know anyone who'd met her in person. Those who knew of her were afraid, speaking in hushed tones about her as if she might hear them.

Nax had asked why she'd want to meet such a woman and Maari had explained that if you asked her a question, she'd tell you the truth. It didn't matter what the question was, she'd know the answer.

At one stage, people had visited her in droves, until they came to realize that sometimes the truth was best kept hidden in the depths of the ocean.

"What do you want to know?" Nax had asked, wondering what trouble could lie behind Maari's innocent eyes.

"We all have things we want to know," she'd said.

"Then why haven't you gone before?"

"I was scared. But when you're with me, I feel strong. If you can face your fear of the water, I can face this."

He'd smiled to know he'd inspired her. Despite how pathetic he must've looked the first few times she'd seen him, he'd somehow managed to impress her.

Perhaps he could ask the Truthseeker a question himself. The only problem was knowing where to start. Would he ask about the woman in his dreams? Would he ask about his father? Would he ask about Maari? Did she really like him? His mother had told him once that if something seemed too good to be true then usually it was.

Of course, she liked him, he'd thought as she squeezed his hand. They were connected somehow. He could feel it.

Maari came to a stop and pointed. He looked into the murky depths and could just make out a dark, solid shape.

He raised his eyebrows at her. Was she sure? Did she really want to go through with this?

She nodded and they swam on.

A fish darted past and he jolted, looking about for any sign of a shark. He hoped the Truthseeker's house was warm inside. He was starting to shiver.

They approached the black, iron walls of the house. Tin cans had been tied with string to the roof and floated ominously in the depths of the water. He hesitated. There was a strange energy around them. He didn't want to be here. No wonder nobody came to see the Truthseeker.

He wanted to turn around and swim directly to the surface. But he couldn't let Maari continue on her own. She seemed determined to go in. Whatever it was that was bothering her must be serious. He knew there'd been more to her than the confident girl he'd met on the jetty.

What if something happened to her? He had to go with her. He had no choice. He followed her through the rubber slit that sealed the entrance and they found themselves cloaked in darkness.

"Are you okay?" he whispered, finding her hand.

His lungs heaved as he drew in air. The transition wasn't as bad as last time. At least he'd known what to expect.

"I'm cold," she said.

He wrapped his arms around her, not certain his frozen body would do her much good.

"Hello," she called. "Truthseeker?"

A bony hand grabbed him on the arm, and he jumped, tightening his grip on Maari.

"Do you seek the truth?" croaked the voice of an old woman.

The room filled with soft light and the Truthseeker began to take shape. She was small, maybe only five feet in height. Her back was crooked, and her gray hair was wild. She wore a black cloak that wrapped around her shoulders and draped to the floor.

"No," he said, trying to pull away. He wanted to get as far away from here as possible. But the Truthseeker's grip was firm.

"I seek the truth," said Maari, fire burning in her eyes.

The Truthseeker let go of Nax's arm and turned away, sliding herself through the interior door.

"Are you sure?" Nax whispered. Maybe the others who'd come before them were right. Sometimes the truth is better left undisturbed. "Let's get out of here."

Maari looked at him, her eyes filled with tears. She turned and slid through the door behind the Truthseeker.

He went to follow her, pulling at the rubber flaps, but they were sealed tight.

"Maari!" he cried. What was going on in there?

The room plunged into darkness and he sank to the floor, shaking with rage, fear and cold.

He hugged his knees to his chest and waited. He wouldn't leave without her. He'd die here if he had to. Was this why the woman in his dreams had warned him to stay away from her? Had she known Maari would lead him into danger? Still, he didn't care. He couldn't leave her. His spirit was bound to hers.

The seconds ticked by as minutes. The minutes passed as hours. He waited. Would he ever see Maari again?

He kept his eyes focused in the direction of the door, waiting for her to emerge. It didn't matter. His eyes may as well have been closed for all they could see.

A noise startled him, and he stood, feeling the seal of the door with his fingertips. The cold rubber became soft skin. It was Maari.

"Are you okay?" he said, pulling her into his arms. She didn't wrap herself into his embrace as he expected. She felt stiff. Uncomfortable.

"What happened?" he asked, wishing for a sliver of light so he could see her face.

"I want to go home," she said.

"Okay. Let's get you home." He could find out what happened later. Right now, home sounded like an excellent idea.

They emerged into the ocean and he flinched as the cold water filled his gills. They swam towards the dune, the light of Aquatica calling to them. The water slowly warmed and he felt the pain in his body ease.

They approached the underwater streets and he caught sight of Maari's face. She was pale and frightened. Whatever the Truthseeker had told her hadn't been good.

He reached for her hand, but she ignored the gesture and swam on. They went past the coffee shop, through the park and under the archway that'd greeted them earlier with such promise.

Nax went to swim upwards to the surface, but Maari pointed to the entrance of a glass tunnel that sat off to one side. He hadn't noticed it earlier. It was a long tube that ran along the ocean floor then curved upwards to the surface.

A sign lit up the entrance thanking them for vising Aquatica.

He'd heard about this. It was a decompression tunnel.

They swam into the entrance and sealed the door behind them. Water dripped from their bodies as they transitioned from gills to lungs.

He saw what looked like a chairlift his mother had taken him on once when they'd visited the snow, only these seats were built for one.

"Maari," he said. "What happened?"

He reached for her hand and she pulled away. He felt sick. Why had he agreed to go with her to the Truthseeker? They'd been having such a good time before then. Why hadn't he said no?

She strapped herself into a seat and began the slow ascent to the surface.

He took the seat behind her, too far away to speak to her. He'd need to wait until they got to the surface. They seemed to crawl. He was desperate to get there so he could ask her what'd happened. Had the Truthseeker told her something that made her change her mind about him? She was certainly acting like she no longer cared for him. Or was she in shock?

They reached the end of the tunnel, unstrapped themselves from their seats and swam the short distance to the surface.

His lungs sang with joy as they took in a gulp of fresh air. This air tasted so sweet, like he hadn't breathed for a hundred years.

He looked across to Maari to find her racing ahead of him to the shore.

"Maari, wait," he called, wading through the water behind her, his long legs closing the gap.

Just before they reached the shore, she came to an abrupt halt and turned to him.

"I can't see you," she said. "I'm sorry."

"No, Maari. What happened? What did she say to you?"

Ignoring him, she ran to the sand and took off down the beach in the full sun. She hadn't bothered to collect her clothes. She didn't even look like she remembered they were there.

He went and sat under the jetty. Picking up her clothes, he held them to his face. They smelled like her.

To think that only hours before she'd sat here by his side and kissed him. What had changed? The Truthseeker had told her something about him. She must have. What had she said? Had she confirmed he was a freak? Had she told her about the woman in his dreams? Was his father a mass-murderer and he'd inherited his psychopathic genes? It must've been something about him and it must've been something bad. If it were about her, she wouldn't have gone running away from him like that. She'd have run towards him instead.

Nax wished he knew where Maari lived so he could bring around her clothes as an excuse to see her. He'd have to wait to see her at school.

The weekend crawled. His mother knew something was wrong but left him alone. He hadn't told her about going to Aquatica yet. For some reason it still felt like something private between him and Maari.

He spent Monday afternoon before school sitting under

the jetty just in case Maari turned up. She didn't. He didn't swim without her. It'd be no fun.

He made sure he was at school on time and searched the grounds for her. She was nowhere to be found. It seemed it was her turn to ditch school.

By the end of the week, he started to feel like he was stuck in a continual loop of time. Each day was the same—sitting alone on the beach, searching the grounds of the school and nursing his heart as it splintered into fragments of loss. She was nowhere to be seen.

He'd asked several kids at school if they knew where she lived, but they'd looked at him like he was mad. Even if they did know, they'd never tell him.

Sleep was difficult too. The woman in his dreams had disappeared. He knew she was only doing what he'd asked her to, but it started to feel like everyone in his life was abandoning him. Would his mother be next?

No. She was the one constant in his life.

The weekend eventually crawled around. He dragged himself out of bed when he heard his mother leave for the factory. She worked too hard. One day he hoped to make it up to her and be the one to work while she stayed home in bed.

He poured himself a cup of hot tea and took it to the living room. He had a pile of homework to do, but it was unlikely he'd get very far. His brain was fixed on Maari. He missed her. The short time they'd spent together had contained the happiest moments of his life. Why had it come to an end? It didn't seem fair.

If he knew why, then perhaps he could come to terms with it. But if she wasn't talking to him, how was he supposed to ever find out? Only two people knew what had taken place in that cold, dark airlock under the sea—and he wasn't one of them.

He slammed his tea onto the table, wincing as it spilled over and burned his hand.

If Maari wouldn't tell him what happened, then there was only one other way to find out. He'd visit the Truthseeker.

It was the last place in the world he ever wanted to return, but it was the only place that could give him the answers he so desperately needed.

What had Maari asked the Truthseeker and what had she been told? It was time to find out.

He changed into his swimming shorts, grabbed a banana from the kitchen and gulped it down in three bites. He stopped himself from running to the beach. He needed to conserve his energy to fight the bitter cold he knew he'd soon encounter. Years ago, people had worn suits made from rubber to swim in the ocean, but that had become impractical since the appearance of gills. Plus, Aquatic was heated so nobody saw the need.

He walked to the end of the jetty and dove off, the moonlight bouncing off the olive skin of his back. He didn't care who saw him. He had nothing to be ashamed of now. He could do what they did.

He plunged deeper under the water, found the archway to Aquatica and swam through the park. He stopped for a moment at the village beyond.

This was his last chance to change his mind. Was he ready to find out the truth? Whatever it was, it wasn't going to be good.

Bring it on, Truthseeker! He kicked his legs, propelling himself through the water toward the sand dune.

The shock of cold didn't seem so great this time. He wasn't sure if it was due to the adrenaline that was racing through his veins or because he was expecting it. Perhaps he just didn't care. There were more important things at stake than the temperature of his body.

He reached the Truthseeker's house. If it could be called a house. It seemed more like a chamber built to torture the poor souls who dared to venture inside.

He slipped through the entrance and breathed air into his lungs. It was dark. Quiet. He waited. How long until the bony fingers would grab his arm? He'd be ready this time.

It didn't matter how ready he was, he still jumped when the old woman took hold of him.

"Do you seek the truth?" she hissed as the room filled with soft light. This time he noticed her teeth, yellow and sharp. Her nose was broad and crooked, like it'd been broken more than once. Her eyes were filled with menace and anticipation.

"Yes," he said, flinching. "I seek the truth."

She let go of his arm and disappeared through the interior door.

He followed. This time it opened for him.

The room was dark, lit by one globe that hung from the ceiling by a wire. The walls were draped in dark red velvet curtains. A mattress lay in the corner of the room next to a table of bottles and jars.

Two tattered armchairs had been placed in the center of the room to face each other.

The Truthseeker sat in one chair and motioned for Nax to sit in the other. He shivered. It was impossibly colder inside than it'd been outside. The fabric of the chair felt like ice on the back of his legs.

"Hello, Truthseeker," she said. "I see you've returned."

He frowned. "I thought you were the Truthseeker?"

She smiled. It was a smile that sent terror tearing down his spine. "We are all Truthseekers in this life, are we not?"

He nodded, not daring to disagree.

"You're ready this time to seek the truth?"

"Yes."

"Well, what truth is it you wish to seek?"

"What did you tell my friend? She'll no longer talk to me. I need to know what was said in this room." He leaned back in his chair and immediately jumped forward as the cold fabric stung his back.

She tapped her bony finger on her chin. "I cannot tell you that."

"What do you mean, you cannot tell me that? That's the truth I seek."

"But it's not *your* truth to seek. That truth belongs to the girl with the golden hair. Do you understand?"

"No, I don't understand. You said something about me. You must have. Why else would she push me away? If you spoke about me then surely that's my truth to hear."

"That's not your truth to seek," she snarled, leaning towards him.

He wanted to scream. He'd gone to all this trouble for nothing. Now he'd never know what happened. He wasn't sure he could spend his life like this.

"Why don't you ask me about the woman instead of this girl?" she said, laughing at his distress.

"What woman?" He knew what woman she spoke of. But how could she know about her?

"Do *not* play games with me." Anger chased the laughter from her face.

"Then tell me about the woman I dream of. Who is she?" He sat forward, looking her anger in the eye.

"You're an interesting soul, aren't you?" she said. "I haven't met one like you before. And you have no idea who you are."

"Who am I? What does that have to do with the woman?"

"You are Matthew. Her beloved, dear, precious Matthew."

His eyes widened. That was the name she'd called him in

his dream. Was this the truth he was meant to seek when he'd come here? And did it have anything at all to do with Maari?

"The woman you see is named Lin. She's a Soulweaver who sits beside another called Shen."

"What's a Soulweaver?" He wondered if this was supposed to make sense.

"She weaves lives for souls on a faraway planet called Earth."

So, there was life on other planets. He'd known it, although he'd never heard of anywhere called Earth. What a strange name. The only planet he knew of that had life was his planet.

Neron.

"But she looks human," he said. "She's nothing like an alien from another planet."

"Maybe it's you who's the alien," said the Truthseeker. "Did you ever think of that?"

"What are you talking about? I'm not an alien."

"We're aliens to humans on other planets, just as they're aliens to us."

"Humans? They're human?"

"Just like you. Fancy that. Did you imagine them to have green skin and three sets of eyes?"

"So why would someone from another planet care about me?"

"Because when you were Matthew you didn't live on Planet Neron. You lived on Planet Earth and Lin was your wife."

Nax stood. He'd heard enough. This woman was playing with him. No wonder Maari had fled in despair. She'd probably been convinced she was mad.

He needed to get out of the cold, out of the ocean and back to the safety of his bed where he could think.

"See you next time, Truthseeker," the woman said, sitting back in her chair and closing her eyes.

"There won't be a next time," he said, walking to the door, his legs buckling under his weight he was shaking so much.

"There's always a next time," she said in a hoarse whisper. "If not in this lifetime, the next."

He slid through the door and into the cold water that lay beyond.

The journey back to the surface felt like being rolled in broken glass. His body was in pain, his mind in agony. Was this how Maari had felt when they'd left last time?

By the time he strapped himself into the chair in the decompression tunnel, he thought he was going to pass out. He urged it to hurry as it slowly dragged him towards the surface.

He focused on the image of his bed. Nothing else. He couldn't think about what he'd been told. It was too ridiculous. It couldn't possibly be true. But she'd known things she couldn't possibly have known. She wasn't a complete fraud.

Later, as he lay in the warmth of his bed, he was unable to recall how he'd gotten there. He seemed to have traveled from the tunnel to his bed in the blink of an eye.

He pulled the blankets over his head and curled up in the dark. He'd gone to the Truthseeker with one question and returned with a hundred more. He allowed his mind to go back to the conversation they'd had so he could decide which parts of it he was prepared to believe.

The woman in his dreams was called Lin. She was some kind of special soul on a faraway planet who was in charge of everyone's lives. And he'd once been married to her when he was an alien called Matthew. Sorry, a human called Matthew who so happened to live on some strange planet called Earth.

It was absurd. The only part of it he found easy to believe was that the woman's name was Lin. The rest was crazy talk.

Although, he couldn't deny that the one time Lin had spoken to him she'd called him Matthew. That couldn't have been a coincidence.

He thought back to all the times he'd looked into the sky and wondered about life on other planets. Was it possible there was a planet out there called Earth? And was it filled with life that was human, just like life on Neron?

He'd always believed something like this was possible. Why was it now that he was given evidence to support it, he was finding it harder to believe than ever?

If what the Truthseeker said was true, then it'd explain exactly why Lin had wanted him to stay away from Maari. If she'd once been his wife then she was jealous. Did she really expect he'd walk away from the girl he loved in favor of spending time with an apparition?

He felt more determined than ever to win Maari back. Whatever the Truthseeker had told her, they could face together. They'd work this out side by side as he was sure was their destiny.

PART II

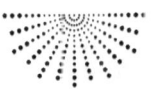

MAARI

"*A*re you ever going to get out of that bed?" Maari's mother stood in the doorway, hands on hips, glaring at her daughter.

"Leave me alone, Mom." Maari scowled and pulled the covers over her head.

"You've got to get up some time." She peeled the covers back and put her hand on her daughter's forehead. "I don't know what's wrong with you. You don't feel hot, but I wish you'd let me take you to the doctor."

"Fine, I'll get up." She swung her legs out of bed and stood. Anything to avoid going to the doctor. He'd only poke and prod her then tell her mother there was nothing wrong. The sickness she felt was in her heart, not her body. It felt like it was broken in two and the one person who was able to glue it back together was the same person she needed to avoid. It didn't seem fair.

"Is it the new school?" her mother asked, following her to the kitchen. "Did something happen?"

"The school's fine." She slumped down on a stool at the counter. The house was small. Tiny would be a better word for it. There wasn't room for a table in the kitchen, so instead they crowded around the small counter that separated it from the living space. It was all they could afford this close to the coast. She missed her old house.

"Would you like a hot chocolate?" her mother asked, tucking her short blonde hair behind her ears. She was an attractive woman. Maari knew that by the way men stared at her in the street. The number of admirers hadn't seemed to dwindle as the years had passed by. They'd just aged right alongside her. It annoyed her father, which Maari always found amusing. Did he really expect they couldn't see the same thing he had when he fell in love with her all those years ago?

"What are you thinking?"

"That you're beautiful," Maari said.

"Sure you were. So, is that a yes to a hot chocolate?"

"That'd be nice. Thanks, Mom. And I really was thinking that, you know."

Her mother smiled an unconvinced smile and poured some milk into a saucepan. "You know you can tell me anything, don't you? Is this about a boy?"

Maari paused, wondering if she should tell her. It would feel good to talk about it. But how much should she say? There were parts to the story that were certain to make her parents furious—especially the part that involved the Truthseeker.

"His name's Nax. He goes to my school." Sticking to basic facts seemed like a good idea.

"You like him?" Her mother turned from the stove as she stirred the milk.

She nodded. "A lot."

"Then what's the problem? I can't imagine him not liking you in return. Does he have a girlfriend?"

"No, he likes me. It's just complicated."

"Love is always complicated, Maari."

"Not for you and Dad."

"We weren't always an old married couple, you know. Trust me, we've had our share of complications. Everyone has." She poured the milk into a large mug, added some powdered chocolate and passed it to Maari. "What's he like?"

She took a sip from the mug and felt the sweet liquid slip down her throat. "He's a lot like this hot chocolate."

Her mother laughed. "What does that mean?"

"He makes me feel warm on the inside."

"Well, you're in big trouble then. You should know that a man can never make you as happy as chocolate."

Maari laughed. "I'm serious. He's amazing, Mom. There's something so special about him. He's so different to all the other boys. In fact, he's so different that everyone hates him."

"They hate him?" The smile on her mother's face faded. "What's wrong with him? Maybe they know him better than you. How's he different?"

"He's not different in a bad way." She jumped to his defense. She knew she should've kept her mouth shut. Only a few sentences in and she'd managed to alienate her mother from Nax. "He's just a deep thinker. He has these incredible green eyes that are filled with soul. And he treats me like I'm made from precious gold."

"You *are* precious gold."

Maari smiled. "It's like he can see deep into my heart and he loves what he sees."

"And you feel the same way about him?"

"I know it sounds crazy, but yes. I feel like there's something drawing me to him. Is that how you felt when you met Dad?"

"Not exactly, no. But that feeling certainly did grow with time. You need to be careful here, Maari. You're still young. You have your whole life ahead of you. This will probably be the first boy of many that you'll feel this way about."

Maari drew in a breath. Her mother didn't get it. She was belittling the way she felt about Nax. "You're not listening to me. I knew I shouldn't have said anything to you."

"No, I'm sorry. Please talk to me. It's just that the way you're talking is pretty intense. To be honest, it scares me."

"The way I'm feeling is pretty intense."

"I get that. I see that. But I don't understand why if you like him and he likes you, you've spent a week in bed crying."

"You really want to understand, do you? You really want me to tell you? You can handle this?" Maari's voice was tense. All the emotion she'd felt since the day she saw the Truth-seeker came to the surface.

"Maari, what's going on? Yes, I can handle it. Just talk to me." She sat next to her daughter and clutched her hands in her lap.

She looked into her mother's eyes and saw desperation and concern. What would be the worst thing to happen if she told her the truth? Would she be grounded? That would be more of a blessing than a punishment at the moment. At least if she were confined to her room, she'd be unable to go anywhere near Nax.

"I went to see the Truthseeker."

"You what? Maari, you know how dangerous that is! Don't you listen to anything your father or I tell you? Do you think we make this stuff up for fun?"

"I know. I'm sorry. I didn't want to upset you, that's why I didn't tell you."

"What could you possibly have wanted to ask her that was so important? Was it about this boy?" She was angry, but perhaps not as angry as Maari had expected.

"I've been having dreams, Mom. Terrible dreams."

"Dreams are just dreams. They're not real. There's no truth in them."

"These are different dreams. I've never dreamt like this before. It's like I'm awake while I'm asleep."

"What are they about?"

"A woman with dark hair. She visits me every night." She clutched her hands around her mug trying to disguise the way they shook.

"But she's not real. You're dreaming. We can figure this out."

"I'm not crazy, Mom. She is real and she follows me. She won't leave me alone. And wherever she is, lightning follows her. Huge flashes of it light the sky behind her head. And there've been so many storms this week, I feel like she's climbing out of my dreams and into my reality. She's coming to get me. I know it."

"That's not true. Nobody's coming to get you. Storms happen all the time."

"I was in the water the other day and heard thunder. I climbed up the ladder and only moments later it was struck by lightning. I'm telling you, Mom, she's trying to kill me. I didn't know what else to do, so I went to the Truthseeker."

"You asked her about this woman?" Her voice was a whisper, her brow furrowed in a way Maari had never seen before.

"Yes."

"And what did she tell you?"

"The woman's real and she doesn't approve of me one little bit."

"What's there not to approve of? What have you ever done to hurt anyone?"

"She wants me to stay away from Nax. And if I don't..."

"This is silly. That Truthseeker has a lot to answer for, filling your head with such rubbish. This is why we didn't want you to see her. She's never helped a person in her life. She destroys them."

"She didn't fill my head with rubbish. She just confirmed for me what was already there. I didn't have to tell her about the woman in my dreams. She already knew. I just hadn't connected her appearance to Nax. She only started visiting me when we moved here."

"Right, so let's say for a moment that what you're saying is real. Why would this woman want you to stay away from Nax? Maybe she's trying to protect you. You already said the other kids don't like him. Maybe there's something about him that everyone else can see and you can't."

"It's the other way around. I can see things about him that they can't. And I like what I see. She most definitely isn't trying to protect me. She's trying to keep me away from Nax —at any cost. I'm scared." She threw her arms around her mother and felt her warm embrace in return.

"Nobody's going to hurt you," she soothed.

Maari hoped she was right. But how was she going to live without Nax? Now that she'd found him, she didn't want to let him go. She remembered the hurt on his face when she left him standing on the beach. He must hate her almost as much as the woman in her dreams, for the way she'd treated him.

She knew that wasn't true. He didn't hate her. She could feel his love despite the distance she'd put between him. He'd be just as confused and hurt as she was.

The thought of him upset made her head spin with grief.

"Do you mind if I go back to bed for a while?"

Her mother shook her head and watched her walk the few short paces to her room.

A few moments later she heard her mother close the front door. She did it in such a way as to be quiet, but in the close confines of their home, it was a noise impossible to disguise.

Maari's heart pounded. Where was she going? Was she going to talk to her father?

She lay back down in bed and squeezed her eyelids closed. *Do not cry*, she told herself. Tears wouldn't help her. She'd cried enough of them to know that for certain.

Nax's face found its way to the surface of her mind, as it always did. She saw him smile, his perfect white teeth framed by soft lips she yearned to kiss once more. His thick curls dripped with beads of water that ran down the dark skin of his broad shoulders. She always imagined him in the water, a sea of emotions swimming across his face. He was nervous yet courageous, hardened yet tender, naïve yet wise. But most of all, he was hers. She could see it in the way he looked at her. She owned his heart and he owned hers.

Why was this woman trying to get in their way? What did she care if two teenagers fell in love? Why couldn't she just leave them alone?

She drifted off to sleep, awakening when she heard the click of the front gate. She knew it wasn't her mother. She could feel who it was. Feel the warmth of his energy as it made its way down the short length of gravel that joined the gate to the front door. Nax had found her. She shouldn't let him in. She mustn't. It would only lead to disaster. The Truthseeker had been very clear about that. She must stay away from him.

The sound of thunder rumbled in the distance. She was being warned.

He knocked on the door. It was a loud knock. Desperate.

"Maari," he called. "I know you're in there."

How had he known how to find her? She hadn't told anyone at the new school where she lived. She'd been too embarrassed. Her neighborhood wasn't exactly one where anybody aspired to live. She'd felt ashamed. Now her shame was different. She was ashamed she'd ever felt that way.

What did it matter where she lived? Did it make her a different person? She didn't care that Nax saw her house. She knew it wouldn't matter to him in the slightest.

"Maari. Open the door. Please."

She stood at the door with her forehead pressed against the thin wood panels. This piece of timber was all that stood between her and disaster. If she let Nax in, the woman in the sky would be sure to strike her down.

She pressed her hands to the door and drank in his energy. She might not be able to touch his skin, but at least she could bask in his love for a moment more.

"I went to see the Truthseeker," he said.

Her heart stopped. He'd gone back? So, he knew. Then why was he here? Why would he risk her life like that? He was supposed to love her.

"I need to talk to you, Maari. It's important. Please."

There was something in the way his voice broke with emotion that tore at the center of her soul. She couldn't leave him out there. She had to explain. Then they could go their separate ways.

The thunder came closer. The woman was getting angry.

"Just give us one last moment," she muttered to the sky, reaching for the door handle.

She flung the door open and saw the deep furrows of Nax's brow fade into ones of joy.

He stepped forward and put his arms around her. She wanted to push him away, but instead found herself slipping her arms around his slim waist and burying her face in his chest. He smelled so good. He felt so good. How could this be wrong? They belonged together.

A flash of lightning hit the road outside. The noise of the thunder that accompanied it was deafening. Nax didn't flinch. He hadn't even seemed to have heard it. She pulled him inside and closed the door.

"You shouldn't be here," she said. "How did you find me?"

"I'm not sure." He followed her into the living room, and they sat down on the sofa. She tried to put some space between them but found herself unable to.

"You're not sure how you found me?" She was puzzled.

"I knew you lived in this direction, so I took a lucky guess." He smirked.

"You expect me to believe that? Really?"

"You'll think I'm mad if I tell you. And anyway, it doesn't matter."

"Trust me. Nothing you say will make me think you're mad."

"I just walked up and down the streets until I felt you. I knew when you were near, so I concentrated on what I felt and my feet led me here. See? Crazy." He looked away, embarrassed. He really did seem to be worried she'd think he'd lost his mind.

"No, not crazy. I knew you were here before you knocked on the door. Is that crazy, too?"

He shook his head, his eyes crinkling with love.

"What's going on with us?" she said. "I don't understand. I feel like we're being both pulled together and pushed apart. Why is she doing this to us?"

He reached for her hand and held it. His skin was warm and smooth. "She?"

"Yes. She. The woman in the sky."

"You know about her? Maari, start from the beginning. Tell me what the Truthseeker said."

"That's not the beginning."

"Then what is? Please, I can't stand this. What's happening here? What did you ask her?" His eyes pleaded with her. He was just as desperate for information as she was.

"I asked her about the woman from my dreams."

"You see her, too?" He looked surprised.

"Too? You mean, she comes to your dreams as well?"

"Yes, I see her. I've seen her ever since I can remember. She's always been there. Is that what it's like for you?"

"No, I only started to see her when I met you. She's trying to kill me, Nax."

"She's not going to do that. I won't let her."

Thunder continued to rumble outside, its presence becoming harder to ignore.

"I'm not sure you can protect me," she said. "The Truthseeker said the woman wants me to keep away from you or she'll strike me down with that." She pointed to the window.

"So, that's it." He looked strangely relieved. "At first I thought you didn't like me anymore, so I went back to see the Truthseeker. I wanted to know what she told you, only she wouldn't tell me what you'd discussed. It wasn't my truth to ask, apparently. Instead, she told me about the woman from my dreams."

Maari tilted her head. "Who is she? What's going on?"

"Her name's Lin. We used to be married." He looked away as his cheeks flushed.

"Married? How's that even possible?"

"According to the Truthseeker our souls live different lives on different planets in the universe. Once upon a time, I lived on a faraway planet and Lin was my wife."

"That's ridiculous."

"I agree, but why would she tell me that if it wasn't true? I've been thinking about it and I can't work it out. She knew things she couldn't possibly have known. Did she know things about you, too?"

Maari nodded. "So, we're supposed to believe this woman, Lin, is jealous and her spirit has come to Neron to make my life miserable? That's kind of creepy."

"I agree. But I don't love Lin. I don't want her in my life. I want you. You must believe that." He looked into her eyes and she felt herself sinking into him. With just one glance he could cast a spell on her that rendered her powerless.

"I do believe it." Her voice dropped to a whisper as if Lin could hear. "How do we get rid of her? How do we make her go away?"

"I don't know. Apparently, she's some kind of powerful being. A Soulweaver. She weaves new lives for souls on her planet."

"Then why can't she leave you alone to live yours? Isn't she satisfied with the souls on her own planet? I haven't done anything to her. Why can't she just leave us alone?"

"I'm so sorry." He ran his hand through his hair and drew in a breath of frustration.

"It's not your fault."

"It is. None of this would have happened to you if you hadn't met me."

"I was always going to meet you, don't you think?" The pull of energy between them was too strong. They would've met eventually. It seemed beyond their control.

He nodded. He felt it, too.

She leaned in closer to him and swept her lips slowly across the nape of his neck. She breathed in his scent as her mouth made its way to the strong line of his jaw, trailing soft kisses across his chin as her lips found his. At that moment she didn't care if their love upset the woman in the sky. She needed to kiss him. To be kissed by him.

"Goodbye, Maari," he whispered, breaking away.

"You're leaving?" She clutched the front of his shirt.

"I need to keep you safe. I'd never forgive myself if something happened to you because of me. We can't see each other anymore. It's the only way." He stood.

"No." She rose to her feet, desperation flooding her body.

This couldn't be happening. He couldn't be leaving her. "No. We'll figure this out together. Don't go."

"Let him go, Maari."

They spun around. It was her mother, standing in the doorway, her face as white as the moon that hung high in the sky. They hadn't heard her come in over the sound of the storm. How much of their conversation had she overheard?

"No, Mom. He's not going anywhere."

"Go!" Her voice was loud. Demanding. "Go and never come back. Do you hear me? If you love my daughter then go far away. Help me keep her safe." Nax nodded.

Then he fled.

Maari tried to run after him, but her mother held her arm. She thrashed madly trying to release the grip, but it was like her mother had the strength of ten men. There was no getting away.

She knew she'd never see Nax again.

CHAPTER FIVE

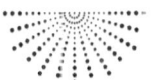

"*W*hy, Mom? Why? You don't know him." Maari begged her mother to release her. If she was fast, she still might be able to catch up to Nax.

"I know enough about him. You're not going anywhere."

"How could you do this? That was a private conversation. How dare you listen in."

"I didn't listen in."

"Then why?"

Her mother's grip tightened and Maari winced in pain. "Mom, please. You're hurting me."

Her grip loosened, but she didn't let go. "There's no point in running now. He's long gone."

"Then let go of me. I won't follow him. Please."

"Okay." She let go of her daughter, positioning herself in the path to the door.

"Where have you been?" Maari asked. Something must've happened to turn her against Nax like this. When she'd left the house, she'd seemed almost supportive of the relationship. Was it because she saw them kiss?

Then she noticed her mother's damp hair, the smell of salt staining her skin.

"You saw the Truthseeker, didn't you?" Fear clenched Maari around the chest.

"Of course, I did."

"Why would you do that? You've always said she's dangerous."

"She is dangerous. More dangerous than I ever imagined. But you know I had to go."

"Why? I told you what she told me."

"Exactly. And I wanted to give her a piece of my mind for scaring you like that. I thought if she understood what she did to you I could convince her to tell you that everything's going to be fine."

"You didn't convince her, did you? She's the one who did all of the convincing. What did she tell you?"

Her mother slumped onto the sofa and put her head in her hands.

Maari sat beside her, tentatively placing a hand on her back. She was cold and shaking, reminding her of a drowning kitten she'd rescued once.

She turned to Maari with a sudden jerk that startled her. She grabbed her hands. "You need to stay away from Nax. Promise me you'll stay away."

"I'm not promising you that. I'm sorry, but you haven't told me anything. Tell me and maybe I'll understand." She knew she'd never understand, but she had to get her mother to tell her what had happened. What had the Truthseeker told her?

"I asked her why she'd told you that story."

"And?"

"She kept saying that she only speaks the truth. She can't be responsible if we don't like what we're told."

"Why did that spook you so much?"

"She went on to tell me things about my life that nobody knows. It was like she'd been inside my head and heard every thought I've ever had. And that was when I knew what she was saying was true. She has no reason to make up lies. She's drowning in the truth."

"And that's all that happened? There must be more. You asked her something else. You must have." She looked into her mother's eyes and knew she was right. She'd been told something that'd rocked her to the core.

"Yes." She was whispering now as if the volume of her words could diminish their effect. "She wouldn't tell me about your life so instead I asked her about mine. I asked her if my life would be a happy one."

"What did she say?"

"She said no. She said I'd spend my life crying for a girl with golden hair who loved a boy made from thunder."

Maari's stomach churned. So, it was true. This woman called Lin was going to take her life. Was it too late to change her fate? Was knowing the future the key that could unlock a different outcome?

"There must be something we can do," she said. "Did you ask her how we change this?"

"Of course, I did. She said she doesn't write the future. She only sees it. Then she turned her chair and refused to say another word. Maari, you must stay away from him. You must. We'll move back inland far away from here. Once the woman in the sky sees you aren't a threat, she'll change her mind. I know she will. She'll leave you alone."

Maari nodded, desperate to reassure her mother. She'd never seen her like this, and it was frightening. She looked like a small child who was both retreating from the world and fighting it with all the power she had.

"I'll keep away from him." she said. "I promise I'll keep away. Everything's going to be fine."

She hugged her mother, stroking the damp strands of her hair as she sobbed into Maari's shoulder. She wished she believed what she'd just said. Everything was not going to be okay. There were only two possible outcomes and both of them filled her with dread.

Either she lived a life without Nax by her side or she died long before she was ready to go.

Maari didn't leave her house for two weeks. She began to feel like a bird in a cage, her wings longing to stretch themselves out so she could fly across the sky.

True to his word, Nax had disappeared. He was serious about protecting her. Her mother was serious, too. But not her father. He didn't believe a word of the story and thought his wife and daughter had gone completely mad. He refused to leave his job under the ocean and as a result a series of passionate arguments had unfolded.

Her mother told her she was making plans in secret to take her inland. She was prepared to leave her husband to protect her daughter. Maari didn't want that. She loved her father. She loved her father being married to her mother. They were a family. They needed to stick together.

The woman faded from her dreams and the thunder sat in silence. It seemed Lin was prepared to let her live if she stayed away from Nax. Or rather, if he stayed away from her.

As the days dragged by, her life being spared began to feel more like a curse than a reprieve. The pain of missing Nax gnawed at her, radiating throughout her body. Each day was worse than the one before. Was this how life would be forever?

Much to her father's horror, her mother had withdrawn her from school permanently, believing it was more important for her daughter to stay alive than to get an education. Maari had to admit she had a point. She wondered if Nax had gone back to school. She doubted it. He was probably far away by now.

"Will you check on him for me?" she asked her mother over dinner one morning.

"Who?" she replied, barely looking up from her toast.

"You know who. Please?"

"You promised to stop caring about him. Asking questions about someone is not something you do if you don't care."

"I never promised that. I promised to keep away from him. I'll never stop caring. Nobody can make me do that."

"He's gone, Maari." She dropped her toast on the plate and stared at her, trying to gauge her reaction.

"You already checked? Why didn't you tell me?" How could she keep something like this from her? It seemed almost cruel.

"He's nowhere to be found. His mother is sitting in their house like it's some kind of shrine, waiting for him to come home."

"That's terrible." Maari remembered the time she'd briefly met Lorarn. She'd been so protective of Nax. It was obvious he was her entire world. She must be heartbroken. The poor woman. "I want to see her."

Maybe there was something she could say that'd make her feel better.

"No! Are you mad? I'm pretty sure staying away from Nax includes staying away from his mother."

"I can't stay in this house forever. I'd rather be dead than live like this. It's not living. It's existing. And existing sucks."

"Maari, how could you say such a thing?"

"She's right," her father said, walking into the room. "Let

her go out. You've kept her prisoner long enough. This is ridiculous."

"She's not a prisoner. This is for her own good. I wish you'd support me."

Maari sighed. Another argument was sure to explode. "I'm going to my room."

She walked to her room, pausing at the door. Her parents' voices continued to rise as the argument heated up. She was glad her father was standing up for her. Maybe he'd get through to her mother and convince her of all the things she couldn't. Hopefully he could manage that before her mother snuck her away and broke up their family.

She crept to the front door and opened it very slowly. The sound of her parents' raised voices masked the noise of the lock sliding back into place as she closed it.

It was dark outside. She saw the old woman across the road clipping her roses. She waved at Maari and smiled, oblivious to what had been going on so close to her door.

Maari smiled back, a surge of joy filling her heart at the contact with the outside world. This was ridiculous. She couldn't stay caged up forever. What did her mother expect? Of course, she'd sneak out.

She stepped off the porch.

And she ran. Down the front path. Down the street. Down toward the beach. She turned left to Nax's house, feeling the muscles in her legs wake from their long sleep. She was free. She was taking her future in her own hands instead of waiting for it to come to her.

She pushed faster. She didn't have much time. Her mother was sure to notice her missing before too long. And she'd know exactly where she'd gone.

She tapped on the front door. The thunder came to life and began to rumble in the distance. She looked to the sky, daring the Soulweaver to strike her down. Nax wasn't home.

Was she supposed to keep away from his mother, too? Just how many people were on the Soulweaver's list?

Lorarn opened the door, her face as dark as the night's sky. Her red hair was wild as if it hadn't been brushed for days. Black rings circled her eyes and she looked so thin it seemed possible she'd break in half.

She looked at Maari and anger lit her eyes. "It's not a good time," she said, closing the door.

Maari stuck her foot in the door just in time to keep it open.

"Please. You must talk to me."

"I have nothing to say to you. Please, leave me in peace." She stomped on Maari's foot with a force that made her instinctively jump back.

The door slammed in her face and she sat on the edge of the porch nursing her injured toes.

A bolt of lightning lit the sky followed by a huge flash that struck the ground several feet away. Frustration swelled in Maari's belly, drowning out the pain in her foot. She was being harassed. No. She was being hunted and she'd had enough.

"You missed!" she shouted, walking out onto the road. "I'm right here."

She wasn't sure if it was the adrenaline that was still pulsing through her veins from running so far after being cooped up for so many weeks or if she legitimately didn't care about her life. All she was sure about was she could no longer live in fear. It was time to end this at any cost.

She stretched out her arms and closed her eyes, preparing herself for whatever came next.

A bolt of lightning hit only a few feet away, shocking her eyes open. What was she doing? Was she really ready to die? The next bolt would be sure to hit her.

The will to live forced her legs into action, but it was too late. Light filled the sky and she felt her body being thrown across the road, a huge weight crushing her chest and pinning her to the ground.

She gasped for air. She couldn't breathe. Her chest was being constricted by the weight, making it impossible to draw air into her lungs. Was she dead? Or was she dying?

More flashes lit the sky, only this time it was different. It was more like an electrical storm.

Then the sky went black and the world was quiet once more.

She pushed at the weight upon her, certain she was alive. Why had the Soulweaver gone if she'd failed to take her life? Was she only trying to scare her?

Whatever was pinning her to the ground shifted slightly. It was enough to allow air back into her lungs and she took several deep breaths. The oxygen fed her body, bringing her back to life. With each breath she regained more of her senses.

She reached her hands upward and touched flesh that was not her own. There was a person on top of her. A person who was no longer filled with life.

She wondered who it could be. Who would sacrifice their life to save her own? It wasn't Nax. She was certain of that. She'd know if it was him. She'd feel his presence like she always had. His aura would be wrapping her like a blanket and soothing her fears.

Was it her father? Had he followed her? Or was this a random act of a stranger?

She heaved her weight to one side and the body rolled off. She ached with the relief of being free of the pressing weight.

She turned to look at the body. It was a man. She scrambled to her hands and knees, her face inches away from his. She strained her eyes in the dark to see his face.

A car drove down the street, sending a brilliant path of light ahead of it.

The man's face lit, and she saw the face of her savior. Dark, curly hair, green eyes frozen in terror.

She'd been wrong.

It was Nax.

"No!" she cried, beating her hands on his chest. "No!"

She didn't hear the sound of doors opening as people stepped out of their homes to see what her screams were about.

She didn't see the woman with red hair running down her front path.

She didn't feel the woman shove her aside as she threw herself on top of her son.

But she could taste the acid that filled her mouth. It was the taste of grief. It was the taste of pain in its purest form.

Nax had given his life to save her own and she hadn't even known it was him.

She looked at his lifeless body and knew why she'd failed to recognize him. It wasn't him at all. His body was only his shell. It wasn't what made him who he was. It was his soul that she'd fallen in love with and his soul was no longer here.

If what the Truthseeker had said were true and he'd lived other lives before then surely, he'd live more lives again. They wouldn't be separated forever. She'd find him and they'd be together again. Just like they were meant to be. The woman in the sky hadn't won. She'd never win. Nobody could win against a love as great as theirs.

"I'll find you, Nax," she murmured, looking at the sky. "Wait for me."

CHAPTER SIX

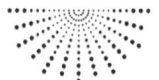

*M*aari sat on the side of the road, unable to move. The scene around her was one of chaos. She saw an ambulance, police cars and firetrucks. People were craning their necks over the safety tape that had been put up to keep them away.

A policewoman had wrapped a blanket around her shoulders and told her to stay put. It wasn't like she could run away even if she wanted to. She remained trapped in a cocoon of shock, trying to process what had just happened.

Lorarn was still sobbing over her son's body. She was doing exactly what Maari felt like doing but couldn't. She had to hold onto her tears. If she gave into them and allowed them to begin their journey down her cheeks, she'd fall into a hole so black she may never find her way out.

The sound of Lorarn's broken heart made her retreat further inside herself to a place where her ears were deaf. This was a mother who'd never be the same. This event would change her in a way that was irreversible. Maari wanted to reach out to her and tell her she felt the same but knew not to.

Lorarn would never understand how deep her feelings were. She'd also be blaming her. People always looked for someone to blame when things went wrong.

Was it her fault?

Definitely, she decided, as she wrapped the blanket tighter around her shoulders. Nax had jumped between her and a lightning bolt. He'd saved her life. If she hadn't gone to his house that evening, he'd still be alive. She wouldn't be any more responsible for his death if she'd taken his life herself.

When she'd snuck out of her house, she'd thought she was risking her own life. She didn't realize she was risking his. If she'd known that, she'd never have set foot outside.

But she had and now Nax was dead.

Gone.

And who knew how many years it would take to find him again. Would he be reborn on Neron or sent to another planet? The Truthseeker had said he'd lived on another planet before so it stood to reason, he could be sent to another one again. The world was a big place to find someone, but the universe was much, much bigger.

Her earlier confidence of finding Nax again began to wane. Then she remembered the electricity she'd felt the first time she saw him, and her heart warmed. What they had was special. They were meant to be together, if not in this lifetime then the next.

She saw the ambulance officers gently shift Nax's body onto a trolley. His beautiful face disappeared as they covered him with a sheet. She'd never look into those soulful eyes again. She'd never reach up and touch the thick crop of curls that crowned his head. Never again would she feel the smoothness of his skin or taste the sweetness of his lips.

Her legs began to run to him long before her mind realized what she was doing. She tore at the sheet, ripping it from the trolley and placed a hand on each of his cheeks. He was still warm, but there was an unnatural stillness about him. His soul may have left, but this was still the body of the boy she loved.

An ambulance officer gently but firmly grabbed her by the arms and tried to pull her away.

"Please," she begged. "Let me say goodbye."

"Get away," cried Lorarn, lunging at her. "You killed him." She began pummeling her with her fists.

She didn't feel the pain of the blows. She was too numb. Instead, she felt the pain of Lorarn's blame. It was a pain she felt she deserved.

Two police officers separated them and dragged them away, while the sheet was replaced and Nax was loaded into the back of the ambulance.

Maari felt her legs collapse and her weight being held by the strong arms of the policeman who had her in his vice-like grip. She turned her face into his starched shirt and sobbed. His grip became an awkward embrace as she lost control of who she was or where. All she knew was Nax was dead. Taken from her as suddenly as he'd appeared.

As she cried, so did the sky. Large raindrops began to fall and a strong wind stirred to life. The crowd of onlookers quickly dispersed as people dashed back to the safety of their homes. The ambulance drove away taking Nax's body with it.

The rain fell harder and the wind blew stronger. The woman in the sky was furious. She'd tried to kill Maari and had instead taken the one soul she was trying to protect.

"Are you happy now?" Maari called out, her words drowning in the roar of the storm. "See what you've done!"

The policeman bundled her into the back of his car. She cradled her face in her hands and blocked out the angry world that surrounded her. She hated the woman in the sky. What had happened to make her so evil?

Maari remembered being taken to the hospital in the same way an adult remembers their first day of school. It was a blurry memory and she looked at it almost as if it happened to someone else.

The doctors prodded both her body and her mind. She answered their questions providing as little information as she could get away with. What was she supposed to tell them? She'd upset an evil spirit, who'd tried to strike her down with lightning and somehow Nax had gotten in the way?

Even in her muddled state she knew that sounded ridiculous.

So, she told them the same thing she'd told the police. She had no idea what had happened.

It was true. She didn't really know. Well, she didn't understand it anyway.

Her parents had arrived at the scene just as she was being driven away and had met her at the hospital. She was glad to have them there. She needed someone on her side.

It wasn't until they brought her home that she noticed the change in her father. Her mother continued to wear the same worried expression she'd had since she'd visited the Truthseeker, only now her father's expression matched his wife's. He was deeply troubled.

The fighting between her parents ceased. They now walked the same path with the same purpose in mind—to protect their daughter at any cost.

They seemed to agree it was possible she was safe now that Nax was gone. There'd be little point in hurting Maari now that it was impossible for her to seek out Nax. But they didn't want to take any chances. She'd be kept safe inside their house until this whole thing blew over.

Maari sat in the living room and stared at the front door, waiting for a chance to escape. But with two wardens to guard her every moment, this proved impossible.

There were so many things she wanted to do. She wondered which she'd do first if she ever managed to get out.

She wanted to go to Nax's funeral. It didn't seem right for him to be buried without her there. She wanted to go to the beach and sit under the jetty, imagining he was by her side. She wanted to return to the place he died and pretend she could turn back time.

Most of all she wanted to visit the Truthseeker. She was the only person who seemed to know what was going on. She'd know what had happened to Nax and where he was now.

A sigh slipped through her lips. What was the point in wanting all these things if she could have none of them?

What she didn't want was to be stuck in this house. The longer she sat here the more it seemed Lin had won. Turning her into a prisoner was just another way of taking away her life. Without her freedom, she had no life. Without Nax, she had no joy.

She needed a plan. There must be a way to sneak out just for a few hours without her parents' knowledge. But how? Her father had taken time off work and her parents had been sleeping in shifts. What she needed was for them to sleep at the same time.

"I'll put the kettle on," her father said.

"No, I'll do it," said her mother getting up and heading to the kitchen.

An idea lit Maari's mind and she hurried to her room, rifling through her top draw until she found what she was looking for. The doctor had given her some pills to help her sleep. What if she were to slip some to her parents? Would that give her enough time to visit the Truthseeker and return before they woke up?

She turned the bottle around to read the label. She didn't want to hurt them. The pills would just do what the doctor had said—help them sleep.

Before she could change her mind, she tipped four tablets into the lid of the bottle and crushed them into a fine powder with the end of a pencil.

Drugging them would be so easy it seemed cruel. But it was for the best. She needed to get out of the house. They wouldn't let her because they didn't understand and there was no way she would ever make them understand. She had no choice.

She pulled her sleeve down over her hand to hide the lid of powder she clutched in her palm. Her hands were shaking. All she was doing was giving them a good sleep. No harm would be done. She could do this.

Her mother was pouring boiling water into the teapot. She set it down on the bench to let the leaves infuse.

"You look tired, Mom," said Maari.

"I am," she said, yawning.

"Why don't you go and join Dad? I'll bring your tea in to you."

"Thanks, sweetheart." She kissed Maari on the forehead. "I'm sorry."

"For what?"

"For keeping you in the house. You know it's only because we love you so much, don't you?"

"But I'm safe now, Mom. She has no reason to hurt me anymore." Maybe she wouldn't need to drug the tea. If only she could convince them to let her go.

"Plenty of people get hurt for no reason. Maybe revenge is her reason. How can we begin to guess how she thinks? It's safer you stay here for now." She turned to leave.

"Mom?"

"Yes?"

"I love you." It suddenly seemed important to tell her. She wanted to make sure she knew.

She smiled at Maari. "Thanks for understanding."

She looked at her mother with sad eyes. She didn't understand. She'd never understand. And that was why she had to do what she was about to do.

Her mother walked the few paces it took to reach the living room and sat on the sofa next to her father, their backs both facing the kitchen.

The teapot stood innocently on the bench staring at her. She gently removed the lid and tipped in the powder, swirling the liquid to help it dissolve.

She got out two mugs and added a spoon of sugar to each, hoping it would be enough to mask the taste. She added an extra quarter of a spoon just in case. She poured the tea, together with a dash of milk and carried the mugs to the living room.

"Here you go," she said, setting them on the coffee table.

"Thanks, love," said her father. "You're a good daughter."

"You're a good dad."

She rushed from the room before he saw the tears in her eyes. What she was doing was wrong. She wasn't a good daughter at all. She was the worst daughter in the world.

Now was her chance to stop this nonsense. She should rush in the room and bump the table, spilling the tea to the floor.

So, why wasn't she moving? Instead, she stood in the kitchen and waited. Her stomach churned. Would it even work?

"Go to bed, darling," she heard her father say to her mother.

"Wake me in a couple of hours," she said. "You need some sleep too."

"Okay."

Maari knew he wouldn't—even if he hadn't been drugged. He loved his wife too much to wake her when she was tired.

She heard her mother kiss her father and head to the bedroom.

"Goodnight, Maari," she called out. "Thanks for the tea."

"Goodnight," she called back.

What kind of person drugged their parents so they could sneak out of the house? A desperate person, she decided. A desperate person who needed answers.

Fifteen minutes dragged by before she heard her father snoring in the living room.

It had worked. Finally, she was free to leave.

She crept to the front door, hesitating before she opened it. There was something she needed to do first. Just in case.

She went back to the kitchen and scribbled a note to leave on the bench.

Dear Mom and Dad. I'm very sorry. Truly, I am. I need answers. I can't go on like this. Please, don't look for me. I'll be home soon. I love you both so much. Maari xx

She kissed the note she hoped they'd never see. She'd destroy it as soon as she got home.

The world called to her from beyond her door.

She went to it.

Maari sat on the edge of the jetty and let the sun warm her skin. This was the place she'd first seen Nax and this was what he'd been doing. At the time she hadn't understood why.

He didn't believe the sun would hurt him. And ultimately it hadn't. He'd been right. She didn't think it would hurt her either. And if it did... well, she didn't really care. Nothing could hurt more than the pain she already felt.

She stretched out her arms and squinted as the sun's rays reflected off her fair skin. She wondered if she stayed out here long enough if she'd turn the deep olive color of Nax. He'd had magnificent skin.

She thought about what she'd come here to do. She'd need to be brave to face the Truthseeker again. The last time she'd made this trip had been terrifying. That time she'd had Nax by her side and the world held so much promise. This time she was alone with a future that frightened her even more than the thought of not having one at all.

The water was cold as she plunged in. It was a stark contrast to the warmth of the sun. She took a moment to adjust to the temperature, knowing it would get colder. Much colder.

She propelled herself downward to Aquatica. At least she didn't need to worry about running into anyone who knew her. That was one advantage of an underwater world—small talk with strangers was impossible.

The streets of Aquatica held even less appeal for her than usual. Their gaudy colors offended her. There was no beauty here. Humans were kidding themselves if they thought this was the life they were meant to live.

She swam over the sand dune and into the gully where the Truthseeker's house sat quietly on the seabed. The first time she'd made this trip, filled with anticipation, it'd seemed so far away. Now she was filled with dread it seemed to take no time at all.

She looked at the ugly tin cans floating on their strings at the doorway. How ironic that this horrible old woman was her only link to the most beautiful love of her life.

The water was just as cold as she remembered. She shivered as she pushed her way through the Truthseeker's front door, hoping she wouldn't be left in the dark too long.

"Do you seek the truth?" the old woman snarled, clutching her on the arm almost immediately. It was like she'd been waiting for her. Expecting her.

"Yes!" Maari shouted the word like it was the last word that would leave her lips. She wouldn't be here if she didn't want the truth. This was the last place on Neron anyone would want to be if they didn't have to.

The Truthseeker slid through the interior door. Maari followed, her heart eager, her mind afraid. Would she find peace or was her world about to fall apart? It already had, she decided. Nothing worse could happen to her that hadn't already taken place.

She sat in the armchair across from the Truthseeker, flinching as the icy fabric stung the back of her legs.

"So many visitors," the Truthseeker muttered, shaking her head. Her gray hair found its way out of the bun that had been piled on her head. It fell limply around her face. She laughed. "So many visitors."

Maari waited in silence. She'd learned last time to let the Truthseeker lead the way.

"First you. Then the boy. Then your poor mother. Then the boy came back and now you. Soon it will be your mother again."

"Nax came back to you?" She wondered when. It must've been after she'd seen him. "What did he ask you?"

The Truthseeker shook her head. "That's not your truth to ask," she snarled, her mood turning sour.

"Of course not." She kept herself calm. She should've known she'd say that. Although, she'd noticed the Truthseeker often told other people's truths. She just liked to choose which truths she'd tell and which she'd keep to herself. She seemed to enjoy the power it gave her.

"The first time the boy saw me I told him he'd see me again, but he didn't believe me." She waved a bony finger in the air.

"He's dead." She looked into the Truthseeker's eyes, waiting for a reaction.

Her eyes glimmered and she nodded slowly. "I know. Stupid girl."

"Why am I stupid? Tell me. How did you know?"

"I told the boy the only way to save you from the lightning was with his

life. As soon as I saw you here, I knew he'd done it."

"It's your fault!" Maari leaped from her chair. The Truthseeker had told him she'd be struck by lightning. She'd probably even told him when and where. He'd waited for her and saved her life.

"It's his fault for loving you." The Truthseeker spat out the words like poison. Was she jealous? Had she ever loved or been loved? Or had she been born this spiteful woman filled with malice? Had she even been born at all?

"I was young once," she added, glaring at Maari. "Pretty eyes, pretty hair, just like you. You're no better than me."

"I didn't think—"

"Quiet! What truth do you seek?"

She paused and sat back down. She'd come this far. She couldn't leave now. She wanted to ask about Nax but knew she wouldn't be told. She'd need to ask about herself and hope the information she wanted came out.

"I want to know if this is personal. Was it me Lin specifi-cally disapproved of or would she have disapproved of any girl who dared to love Nax?"

"Oh, it's you." She rolled her head back and cackled. "You and only you. She'd have been happy for him to love anyone else. Anyone else at all."

So, it was true. What had she done to deserve this?

"Tell me why."

"Because Nax loving you was this Soulweaver's worst nightmare."

"But why? What did I do to her?"

"Because you were Mother before she was." Her voice was serious, her face frozen with menace.

"I'm not a mother. I don't understand."

"I said, you *were* Mother. You were the Soulweaver of planet Earth before the woman who haunts you, only you tried to destroy your planet. As punishment you were sent far away here to Neron. You might be as sweet as pie now, but I'm afraid in your past you've been a very naughty soul, my dear Mother Maari."

CHAPTER SEVEN

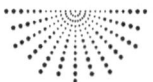

"That's a lie." Maari stood once more. The Truthseeker had taken it too far. How could she believe what she'd just been told? She'd once been a Soulweaver of a faraway planet that she'd tried to destroy. That took ridiculous to a whole new level.

"Sit," the Truthseeker barked. "It's time you understood."

She did as she was told. Her shivering worsened. The cold was becoming unbearable. How much longer could she stand it? Her teeth chattered.

The Truthseeker sighed loudly and the room filled with warmth.

Maari closed her eyes and felt herself begin to thaw.

"Happy now?" the Truthseeker snarled. "I can't have you dying on me just yet."

"Thank you." She rubbed her hands together and nodded. "What is it I need to understand?"

"You need to know who you are."

"What do you mean? I know who I am."

"You know only the life you live now. This life of yours is just a small crumb compared to the lives you've lived before."

"Did I know Nax? Did I know this woman called Lin?" She sat forward in her seat, desperate to make the connections and understand why she felt this way about Nax and why Lin seemed to dislike her so much.

"Hush." Her voice was as cold as the air she'd only just chased from the room. "Your soul sparked to life thousands of years ago on a planet named Earth."

"That's impossible."

"Nothing's impossible. In those early days you lived a tough existence. Violence and hunger ruled the short lives you lived. Each time you were reborn, things slowly improved until eventually you were rewarded for the lessons you'd learned and you were born a queen of the desert. You were a fair queen. Tough but kind. You caught the Author's attention."

"The Author?"

"The creator of the universe. It was a universe that was growing faster than he imagined. He needed help to manage the billions of souls that'd taken up life on the thousands of planets he'd spread across the sky."

"Thousands? And all human souls living on them?"

"Yes. All human just like you and me. The Author selected a Soulweaver for each planet to help him weave lives for new souls. He chose you to rule planet Earth. And rule you did for two thousand years."

This seemed even crazier than all the stories she'd heard before. She was a Soulweaver who'd been around for thousands of years. It couldn't possibly be true.

"Initially, you did a wonderful job," the Truthseeker continued. "You recognized that progress needed to be made slowly. You placed the right souls into the right lives to help nurture this progress. Things ran smoothly until one day you became aware of a hideous invention created by human hands that you yourself had crafted into life."

"What was it?" She was being sucked in now. What had been invented that held such importance?

"The atomic bomb." The Truthseeker said the words slowly as if that would bring them sense, but Maari didn't understand. Atomic bombs had not yet found their way into life on Neron.

She looked at the Truthseeker in puzzlement.

"Imagine a device that could make an explosion big enough to bring a city to the ground with a single blast."

"You mean completely topple it?" That sounded awful. What would possess someone to invent such a thing?

"That's exactly what I mean. It frightened you then as it frightens you now. It confused you, too. It turned your world upside down. How could a human invent something with the pure purpose of destroying the beautiful world you'd been striving so hard to create? A bomb that would not only crumble buildings and poison the air but would tear souls from bodies that you'd so carefully placed. You saw it as a slap in the face. It was a giant step backwards in the evolution of the human race."

She could see why. The souls on planet Earth must be a vicious race indeed to dream up such a device.

"Go on," she said, keen to hear more.

"You were convinced you'd failed at your job. Horrified that this had happened during your watch. Then your fear became anger. Why should you take such great care to weave lives for a race that seemed to have no regard for the lives of their fellow mankind? All they cared about were themselves. Eventually your anger became hatred ... you really were far more interesting in those days."

She raised her eyebrows, almost as if accusing her of a crime. When Maari didn't respond, she continued.

"You decided to let the human race destroy themselves in the hope you could start again. You'd know what to look for next time. You'd know how to stop it. This race of humans was beyond saving. They were so determined to kill each other and the planet they lived on, you decided it was time to give them their wish."

"That's terrible." She fought back tears. Was she really capable of such a thing? "I'd never do that."

"You did that." The Truthseeker leaned forward in her chair and fixed her gaze on Maari.

She squirmed as she tried to accept what she was being told.

"And let's just say that once it was brought to the Author's attention, he wasn't at all happy with you. He sent you far away to a new life here on Neron where he hoped you'd learn your lesson."

"Why didn't he just kill me? If what you're saying is true, it sounds like I deserved it."

"The Author believes in forgiveness. He thinks everyone deserves a second chance." She shrugged as if this were a concept impossible to understand.

"And Lin took over as Soulweaver?"

"That's right."

"But Lin's evil. Why would the Author make her a Soulweaver?"

"She's not evil. She just loves Nax. Surely that's something you understand? Her actions toward you came from a place of love."

"Who's been looking after Earth while she's been so focused on me and Nax?"

"Her soulmate, Shen, sits by her side. The Earth has two Soulweavers now."

"I thought you said Lin was married to Nax, not Shen." This was getting confusing. Each answer she received only seemed to raise yet another question.

"Your soulmate isn't necessarily your husband." The

Truthseeker rolled her eyes as if pained by having to explain something so elementary.

"Then why's Lin getting involved with life on Neron if she's supposed to be looking after Earth?"

"Let's just say she has a special place in her heart for Nax. He was an important soul in her journey. Lin and Shen would've liked to have kept him with them on Earth, but they knew his soulmate didn't exist there. It didn't seem fair that they had each other while he had no one. So, they asked the Author to find his soulmate and take him to her. That's where you come into it."

Maari's eyes widened. So, she *was* Nax's soulmate. She'd known it. She'd felt it in every cell of her body the moment she'd first seen him.

"It wasn't easy for the Soulweavers to let Nax go. Lin decided to keep an eye on him without Shen's knowledge. She wanted to see him experience true happiness with his soulmate. She visited him in his dreams and stayed by his side. At times she was the only friend he ever had, until you came along. She recognized your soul instantly and was filled with fear. She would never have agreed to let him go if she knew you were the one he was destined to love."

"I would never hurt Nax. I loved him. I still do."

"This is true, but you must remember that she doesn't know your soul as Maari. She knows you as Mother. And the way you ended up you were anything but the perfect catch. The thought of you being Nax's soulmate tore her apart."

"So, she decided to intervene."

"Exactly. She couldn't let you be together."

"Where's Nax now? Will he be sent back to Neron?"

"Not if Lin has anything to do with it."

"Don't we have a Soulweaver on Neron? Can't she do anything about it?"

"He," she corrected.

"Well can't he do something? Isn't he supposed to care about Nax?" She was starting to panic. If Nax wasn't sent back to life on Neron, he'd be almost impossible to track down. She had to find him again.

"I'm not sure Nax was ever his favorite?"

"Favorite? Are you serious? Soulweavers have favorites?"

"Everyone has favorites. And Nax isn't one of them."

"Doesn't anybody on this planet like him other than his mother and me? This isn't fair."

"It's not fair, but it is how it is. It *is* just you and his mother who like him. Even his father couldn't stand him. As soon as he'd been conceived, he took off. He could sense there was something not quite right about his baby from deep inside his lover's womb. Nax might be human, but he wasn't right for this planet. People can sense that, and they keep away."

"Then why didn't I sense it? I loved him the moment I first saw him."

"Because you weren't meant for this planet either."

"But people like me."

"They can sense your power. You glow with it. Just one of the perks of being an ex-Soulweaver I suppose."

"But his mother... she loved him."

"She's his mother. That's what mothers do."

"So, the Soulweaver will be happy to see the back of Nax, is that what you're saying?"

"Most definitely. In case you hadn't noticed he's been carefully crafting Neron into a world under the ocean. It's his obsession. Nax never really fitted with that plan. He was still too attached to his life on Earth. Sometimes he even seemed to remember parts of it. They're very similar planets in many ways until you take a closer look."

"Will he go back to Earth?"

"Most likely he's already there. I'm guessing Lin sent him there the moment she realized she'd taken his life instead of yours."

"Wouldn't the Author have stopped him?"

"Not if Neron's Soulweaver agreed to it, which I'm certain he would've. I doubt the Author even knew what was happening."

If the Truthseeker was right—and it seemed she was right about most things—then Maari needed to find a way to get back to Earth, too.

"How do I get there?" she asked. "If Nax is on Earth then I want to go there. Lin has her soulmate. She needs to let Nax have his, too. I need to go to him."

"That's impossible."

"I thought you said nothing's impossible."

The Truthseeker smiled. "It's time for you to leave now."

The air began to freeze around them. Each breath Maari drew in was colder than the one before. Soon her breaths were coming in short gasps that expelled clouds of fog.

The Truthseeker turned her chair and her eyes glazed over.

"Tell me how," Maari pleaded, standing in front of the old woman and bending over so their faces were only inches apart.

Her eyes remained glazed. It was like someone had flicked a switch to the off position. She didn't even seem to be breathing.

"I need to find him." Her voice broke in frustration. She knew she wouldn't be getting any further answers today.

"Please." She grabbed her on the arm, wanting to shake her into consciousness.

As soon as she made contact, the old woman's head snapped up and her eyes came into focus. Her face filled with menace and a strange noise began to escape from her lips. It was a deep, hissing noise that reminded Maari of the sound a snake makes in the moment before it attacks.

She leaped back in fear but didn't leave. She didn't have the all the answers she'd come for and she wasn't going to leave without them. She needed to know how to find Nax and this old woman was the only person who could give her that information.

The room grew colder still and Maari felt herself being drawn towards the door. A force was pulling her. She stumbled as she fought against it, but it was no use.

"Truthseeker. No!"

Her feet began to slide across the floor. She was slammed against the door and pulled through it.

She fell to the floor of the small entry room as the force let her go.

Immediately she leaped to her feet and tried to prize the door open. She remembered Nax trying to do the same the first time they'd visited the Truthseeker. He hadn't been able to and he was far stronger than she was. It seemed this door only let in people the Truthseeker was interested in talking to.

She sank to the ground, unwilling to leave. The air was even colder in here. She rubbed her upper arms with frozen hands that failed to bring her any comfort.

Every cell in her body willed her to leave. To swim far away from here where it was warm. To make her way back home to her bed, cover herself with blankets and let the soft hum of the radiator sing her to sleep.

Her brain refused to listen.

She needed to find Nax. If she left now, she might never get the chance to return. It wasn't possible to just keep drugging her parents. If they found out about this, they'd probably move her far away from here and keep her locked up forever.

Pain shot through her hands and feet as the blood in her body retreated to her vital organs in an effort to keep her alive. She began to tremble violently.

"I seek the truth," she called, desperately hoping to be let in once more. Surely the Truthseeker wouldn't let her die out here? She wasn't exactly the kind of person who exuded compassion, but to allow someone to freeze to death was pure evil.

She had no choice but to take the gamble that the Truthseeker was not as evil as she feared.

The fog that escaped her mouth with each breath she exhaled seemed somehow to enter her mind. She was finding it hard to think clearly. What was she doing here? What was it she needed to know?

Nax.

She held onto his memory, pouring his love into her heart, hoping it was enough to keep it beating.

She lay down on the icy floor. She was tired, her brain so exhausted from the effort of keeping her alive that it could no longer make the decision to leave.

"I seek the truth," she called again, forgetting she'd only just said those words.

Nax.

He came to her mind again. Only this time he was standing a few paces away, reaching out. She struggled to her hands and knees and crawled to him. Each inch she drew closer, he moved an inch away. No matter how hard she tried, she couldn't reach him.

"Nax!" That one word took all her effort to say, yet somehow it seemed to warm her. It spread from her lips, to her throat, to her chest, to the pit of her stomach.

And now she was hot. On fire.

She writhed on the ground in pain.

"Nax!" she called again, realizing he was gone. "Come back." It never occurred to her that perhaps he hadn't been there in the first place.

Her breathing began to slow as her heart struggled to continue on.

She didn't notice the fog her breath produced. If she had, she'd know it was still cold.

The heat she felt was the heat of death. It was gripping her, wrapping her, preparing to take her soul.

"I seek the truth," she whispered.

Her eyes closed and she fell asleep.

Her heart beat one last time before it fell asleep, too.

She'd lost her gamble.

And she'd paid for it with her life.

The world was black. Blacker than Maari had imagined possible.

Then suddenly it was light. So bright she thought her eyes had gone blind.

She was in a tunnel. It was warm.

The pain had lifted from her body and she felt whole once more.

The Truthseeker must've saved her.

"Maari." At the sound of her name she stepped forward. It was a step that took her closer to the source of the bright light.

"Maari." It was a man's voice calling. Not the Truthseeker. Perhaps she hadn't saved her at all? Who was that?

Was she dead? The realization hit her and panic slid over her soul.

The light shone brighter and her panic washed away.

She was safe here. All she needed was the light.

"Maari."

She walked closer to the light, wanting to be near it.

She approached and it began to spin. Bright colors sparked from its core and she stepped in without fear.

As the light swirled around her, it stole all the troubles from her mind. It tore them away, replacing them with feelings of peace, love and safety.

"Maari," the man continued to call. His voice was like warm honey.

She walked on.

A green mist appeared in front of her. She stopped, hypnotized by the beauty of the patterns that formed as it began to take shape.

Soon the mist had gone and, in its place, stood a man. He was tall, slender and wore only a pair of tightly fitted black pants. The smooth, pale skin of his chest was bare. She noticed a set of gills on his sides. They shimmered, almost as if they were drawing in the air that surrounded them. There wasn't a single hair on either his body or his head, which made his skin shine.

He reached out his hands and she saw soft folds of skin webbing his fingers. It was then she noticed his pants weren't pants at all. They were scales, lining his body from his waist down. He didn't have feet. Instead he had a wide fin on which he stood.

She'd heard of mermen. Like Nax, she feared this was what the human race was evolving into. This was the first time she'd seen the reality of what was possible. Was this the form humans on Neron were destined to take?

"Who are you?" she whispered, taking his hands. "Are you the Soulweaver?"

"Yes, I am Father."

She had forgotten what the Truthseeker had told her

about this man. No memory existed of his apparent dislike for Nax. If the Truthseeker were standing beside her, telling her this, she would never have believed it. This man had cast a spell on her. When she looked at him, she saw love.

"It's a pleasure to meet another Soulweaver," he said.

"I'm not a Soulweaver."

He smiled at her. His teeth were white. Dazzling. And sharp.

She looked closer and saw he had two rows of teeth. She jolted in shock.

"Do not fear me," he said.

A sense of calm pulsed from his fingers and into her own. It traveled up her arms and flooded her body, soothing the depths of her soul.

"Where am I?" she asked.

"You're in the Loom. It's time for the knowing." He drew her in and wrapped his arms around her.

The light from his body enveloped her and they shot into the air. They flew faster and faster until her head began to lose pace of what was happening.

Images of her past lives entered her mind. It was just as the Truthseeker had described it. Simple, humble beginnings filled with misery. Then slowly, the misery merged into a sense of hope, accomplishment and joy.

She saw herself as a queen, surrounded by souls who loved her. But never did she feel true love herself. None of the souls lit her heart on fire.

Then she saw herself as a Soulweaver. Each soul she'd woven over thousands of years rushed by in billions of long strands of white light.

As they continued to pass, their light began to dull.

Soon they were a murky, yellow color and she knew these were the souls tainted by evil. These were the souls working against the good of the planet.

She saw herself crying out in frustration, clutching her head in her hands and thrashing about in pain.

The stream of souls came to an abrupt halt and she felt herself falling. Her stomach dropped as she fell faster, spinning out of control.

Just as she thought she could no longer stand it she came to a stop and she saw herself once more. Only this time she was on Neron.

Except she wasn't Maari. She was a middle-aged woman lying in a hospital bed. Her face was lined beyond her years. She was confused. She was miserable. Nurses hovered around her bed as if in fear. This was her first life on Neron —before she was Maari. She shuddered now at the memory of the difficulties that life had come with.

Then she was gone.

Now she saw Maari. Young. Beautiful. Hopeful.

Nax appeared by her side and she saw her soul light with wonder.

Then just as quickly, her soul turned dark.

She felt herself being pulled away as she flew upwards this time. As she soared through the sky she was filled with wonder for the universe. Her soul had a place in it. She deserved to be here.

She became aware that Father was still holding her hand. As they stopped once more, he turned to her and smiled.

"The journey of your soul has been more interesting than most. Are you ready for your reflection now?"

She knew this was her opportunity to consolidate all the lessons learned in her most recent life. It was also her chance to say goodbye.

"Please, Father. I don't wish to reflect. I need to be returned to life, but not on Neron. I beg you, Father. Please send me wherever Nax has gone."

"Neron needs you," he said. "Your journey is not complete."

"I don't belong on Neron. I don't feel right in your world under the sea. Please, I belong with Nax."

He looked offended. Almost angry. She'd upset him.

"The Author sent me your soul," he said.

"Then return me to him."

As the words left her mouth, blackness engulfed her once more.

Father had not said a word in response.

Instead, he left her hanging in a world of silence.

Maari had never thought much when she'd heard people describe silence as deafening.

Until now. Until the silence was so overwhelming it robbed her of her senses, taunting her, torturing her.

It stretched on and on.

Time passed and she was greeted with more time.

When she'd failed as Soulweaver, the Author had given her a second chance to redeem her soul on Neron. Was she being punished for being ungrateful? Should she have accepted her fate and continued to live her life without Nax?

Would that be preferable to this life of silence?

No. Never.

Time went on. It exhausted her. Wore her down so slowly she didn't notice her sense of self begin to fade.

She had no idea how long she'd been there. Markings of time had long since ceased to hold any meaning. Would this ever end?

"I'm sorry!" she eventually screamed in the dark. She should never have asked to see the Author. She should've reflected on her life on Neron and continued to redeem her soul. She could find Nax later. There was so much regret in her soul.

"I'm sorry!" Her words carried no sound, yet somehow, they seemed to have been heard.

A soft blue light appeared in the darkness.

She blinked.

"Maari," the light called. Her heart began to weep at the sound of her name. The silence had been broken and it lay shattered in pieces at her feet.

The light came closer, circling her, making soft sounds of wind that rang like hurricanes in her ears. Blessed hurricanes. She didn't mind if the light extinguished her or brought her back to life. As long as it didn't leave her here floating in the nothingness.

The light took the form of a man. His dark skin was in contrast to the Soulweaver who sent her here. His eyes were the color of night and his hair had been cropped so short it seemed to be painted on. This man wasn't the Soulweaver. Who was he?

"I'm the Author," he said in answer to the question she had not yet asked. "You asked to see me."

"How long have I been here?"

"As long as you needed to."

"I don't understand."

"You were here much longer last time."

"Last time? You mean, I've been here before?"

"Before I sent you to Neron I left you with some time to think. I thought you'd learned your lesson that time, but Father decided you needed more time to think. I decided to leave you here until you were really sorry this time. I don't want to see you here again."

"Haven't I been punished enough?" Anger rose within her. "You sent me to another planet, far away from home. You gave me a life of misery in a hospital bed then you gave me another with hope and love, only to rip it right out of my hands and watch me die with grief. Then you left me in the silence for so long it made all your other punishments feel like rewards."

"I could've extinguished your soul. These punishments— as you call them—were not meant to be punishments at all. I needed to make sure you were really sorry for your actions. You had lessons to learn. If you're not really sorry, then I can leave you with more time to think." His voice was calm, his eyes were kind, but his words held a threat that scared her so deeply her head began to swim.

"No! Please. No more time to think. I'm sorry. What I did was a horrible thing. I lost faith in humankind. I took lives that shouldn't have been taken. I forgot what it was like to be human. I forgot how important it is to forgive."

"Yet forgiveness is the very thing you are asking from me now. There has never been another like you, Maari."

"I thought all souls were unique."

The Author laughed. "You're right."

"How do I get back to Nax?" She had to try again. She'd accept a life on Neron if it meant she could escape the silence she'd been floating in for so long, but if there was any way to reunite with Nax's soul, then she had to ask.

"Soulweaver Lin did wrong. She separated you from the soul your heart yearns for."

"Will she be punished?"

"Do you want her to be?"

She realized she didn't. As long as she was reunited with Nax, it didn't matter what became of Lin. She shook her head.

The Author smiled. "Lin has a difficult lesson to learn. She needs to learn forgiveness. Without it, she's failing terribly as a Soulweaver. I'm going to leave the Earth in the hands of Soulweaver Shen for now. He's strong. Fair. Wise. And he knows how to forgive."

"What will happen to her?"

"She'll live another life on Earth. A life where she can learn to forgive."

"Will Nax be sent to Earth, too?" The thought of Lin breathing the same air as Nax while she was stuck on Neron was too much. If he was even on Earth at all.

"He was already sent. Lin took his soul from Neron and birthed him into a life of privilege on Planet Earth. I would've stopped it had I known, but it's too late now."

"Then you must send me there. Please, Author. For Lin to learn forgiveness then surely you need me there, too. I'll show her how I've changed. I'll help her understand."

"So, you have forgiven her?"

Maari paused to consider the question. She knew there was no point in lying to the Author. He read her mind more clearly than he heard her words. Had she forgiven Lin?"

"I'm on my way to forgiving her, Author. I understand why she did what she did and that's the first step to forgiveness. She loves Nax. I'd do anything I could to protect him, too. If you give me a chance, I promise to find it in my heart to forgive her."

The Author nodded his head slowly.

"It makes sense for Lin's journey to return you to Earth. For Nax's, too. But what I need to consider is what's best for your journey."

"Surely returning me to the planet I tried to destroy is good for me. I'll have to live with the consequences of the decisions I made back then."

"That's true. But I cannot allow you a life of privilege, like the one given to Nax. You'll have to work for your survival. Life will not be an easy one for you. And I cannot guarantee you'll ever find Nax."

"I'll find him. I know I will."

"All right then. But are you sure? The Earth is not how you remember."

"I'm sure." She wanted to scream the words, they rang so true in her heart.

"Close your eyes," he said, placing his hand on her head. His hand was warm, his touch gentle.

"Thank you," she whispered.

"Travel well, my child."

PART III

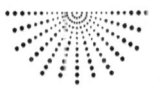

TARA

"Quickly! Over there!" Tara pointed to a piece of metal that was protruding from the mountain of rubbish she was scampering over with her sister.

She had better eyes for spotting treasures, but Aashi was smaller, which meant she was faster. They weren't the only scavengers who'd waited for the truck to dump its latest load of refuse. They had to be quick if they were to get anything useful at all.

Tara watched her sister scale the top of the mound, her small bare feet gripping the uneven surface with precision.

"I can't get it. It's stuck," she called back as she wrestled with the corner of something that looked like it could be their best find of the week—or perhaps the year.

"I'm coming." Tara cautiously picked a path through the rubble. Last year she'd cut her foot open and it'd taken months to heal. She was more careful now. She hated to think what would become of Aashi if anything were to happen to her.

"Back off. It's ours," Tara snarled at an older boy who was getting dangerously close. He wore a tattered backpack, a find from a previous day that he was now filling with anything remotely useful.

The boy looked at the sisters and shrugged, deciding whatever the treasure was it wasn't worth the trouble.

Tara knew it was. She'd known it the moment she caught sight of it, reflecting in the hot morning sun.

The two girls heaved at the object, wriggling it back and forth until it dislodged. As they slid it out, several plastic bags rolled aside, spewing out their stinking contents. A large rat scurried over to investigate.

"We did it," cried Aashi, her dark eyes smiling with pleasure as the sun glinted off her brown skin.

Tara returned the smile, except her eyes were tainted by fear at their find. How long would they be able to hold onto such a treasure?

It was a large sheet of tin. Yellow in color and jagged at the edges. The girls couldn't tell what object it had come from originally. The side of a fridge? A washing machine perhaps? Having never owned either of these things, they were far from experts in identifying such objects.

What they could identify was that it was a marvelous find —and a rare one. Metal like this was generally recycled before it hit the dumping ground.

Now they could be the ones to take it to the metal merchant. It'd be sure to fetch enough to feed them for a few days.

"Can we keep it? Please, Tara," Aashi begged. "It'll keep us dry."

Tara shook her head. "You know it'll only get stolen."

"We'll hide it," said Aashi. "We'll cover it with other things. Nobody will know it's there."

She shook her head again. She hated saying no. Monsoon season was approaching and Aashi hated being wet. The roof they used to keep them dry leaked terribly, needing to be regularly replaced with whatever they could find at the dump. There was only so much rain that cardboard and hessian could keep out.

"Please, Tara. Please. We'll never find another like it."

"Okay," she said, relenting. "Just until the rain stops, then we'll sell it."

Aashi grinned, pleased with her victory.

It was a smile that tore at Tara's heart. At thirteen years, she was five years older than Aashi enough for her innocence to have ebbed away. Her sister shouldn't have to celebrate finding a piece of tin on a pile of rubbish. A piece of tin so battered someone had decided to throw it away.

They found a torn tablecloth and wrapped it carefully around their treasure. It was a terrible disguise, but still better than none at all.

The girls made their way down the mound of rubbish, stopping briefly so Tara could scoop up an apple that had seen better days, but would provide enough sustenance to keep them alive a little longer.

"You have it," she said, taking a bite and handing it to Aashi. "You need it more than me."

Aashi accepted it without complaint, taking furious bites as they walked. She was hungry. She was always hungry. If only there was enough food to fill her tiny stomach.

Tara wondered how much longer she'd be able to keep them both alive. As a rule, she tried not to think too far ahead. Each day she could get them through was a bonus.

It was just the two of them now, but once they'd been part of a family. They'd had a mother, father and a brother. They'd never had much money, but life had never been like this.

Their father had worked in a bakery. His wages at the time had seemed meager, yet now Tara thought they were a fortune. They'd lived in one of Mumbai's largest slums, but still they'd had a house. Two small rooms with no running water or electricity and Tara remembered it as a palace.

When the accident happened, their lives had changed. Her father had gotten his arm caught in one of the bread slicing machines and bled to death on the bakery floor. She was only four years old at the time and barely remembered him now. He was more like a shadow than a real person.

Her mother took a job as a clothing machinist to keep a roof over their heads, despite the fact she was pregnant with Aashi. She was tired all the time, sleeping almost every moment she wasn't working. Her wage was even less than her husband's had been, so while she worked Tara was left in the care of her seven-year-old brother, Bakul, who'd take her to the market to scavenge for food.

"Come on, Chicken," he'd say, as he led her through the winding streets. He always called her Chicken. She had a habit of walking with her hands tucked behind her back, her eyes darting around the ground for a treasure someone may have dropped. Bakul had once said it reminded him of a chicken and the name had stuck.

Any scraps of food they could find at the market would add to the evening's meal. Sometimes it was the difference between eating or not.

A bond developed between Tara and Bakul that tugged at her heart even now. She loved her brother with his wiry black hair that seemed to grow in clumps rather than strands. His chocolate brown eyes were huge, and she'd wondered if they'd gotten that way from having to watch over her all the time. He had dark skin, as did most people in Mumbai, but she remembered him as being a shade lighter than she was. He was most definitely handsome. And he was her hero.

Despite their hardships, somehow, they managed to survive. Strangely, Tara remembered these days as happy ones. For back then, the responsibility for her life lay in someone else's hands. Like it did for Aashi now. She owed it to her little sister to give her at least a taste of what it felt like to be a child.

She remembered the day she'd sat on the dirt floor of their primitive house with Bakul waiting for their mother to come home from work. Only this day she didn't return.

As night began to fall, Bakul told her to wait while he went to look for her. The baby was late. Perhaps their mother had birthed it that day.

Although Bakul had seemed so old and wise, Tara thought of him now walking out into the night and the courage that must've taken. He was only a boy.

By the time he returned it was so late Tara had drifted off to sleep. She woke to the sound of a baby.

"We have a sister," Bakul announced, cradling a newborn awkwardly in his arms. "Mother says her name's Aashi."

"Where's Mother?" Tara asked, looking around frantically. She didn't care much for this sister who'd be just another mouth to feed. She'd only just turned five and wanted her mother for herself.

Bakul pointed to the corner of the room, where their mother lay sleeping on a mat.

Tara crawled over and snuggled into her side. Her breathing was rapid, her skin clammy.

"What's wrong with her?" she asked Bakul.

"I don't know," he replied.

Tara had looked at him clutching Aashi to his chest, his skinny arms jiggling her up and down, yet still she screamed.

"How do we stop her crying?" he asked. It was the first time she'd seen uncertainty in his face, and it frightened her. She'd never known him to not know what to do.

Once again life as Tara had known it came to an end. She

was no longer the baby of the family and now had to earn her keep.

Bakul went out alone during the day to scavenge, leaving Tara to care for her sick mother and baby sister. Times were impossibly tougher than they were when they had their mother's wage.

This continued on until the day her mother got cold. Tara heaped blankets upon her, yet her skin grew colder still. So, Tara crawled under the covers and tried to warm her with her body. When Aashi started crying, she put her under the covers, too.

That was how Bakul found them when he returned with his day's pickings.

Tara couldn't understand why he was so angry. It frightened her. Then she realized his anger was in fact grief. Their mother was dead.

It took almost a full year before the authorities caught up with them and they were taken away from the slums. The man in the suit promised to keep them together, but he lied. Bakul was taken to an orphanage for boys and Tara and Aashi were placed in another.

They'd screamed as they were separated, their small hands reaching out for each other.

"Chicken!" he'd sobbed over and over. She remembered looking into his eyes for a final moment and he fell silent. In that one look, they were forced to say all their goodbyes, for they were sure they'd never see each other again.

Tara had wept for her brother, constantly asking the nurses to bring her to him. One day a nurse snapped at her to be quiet. She said there was no use crying over a boy who was now dead. Bakul had died from diphtheria and Tara was told to get over him and stop bothering them with her problems.

She wasn't sure what diphtheria was, but it made no

difference. She'd lost the boy who was her brother, her father and her best friend wrapped up in one—and she mourned him with deep pain in her heart.

Despite living the next three years in the most cramped of conditions, surrounded by people, it was a time of great loneliness for Tara. Her only joy was the one person whose existence she'd resented at first—the person who'd taken her mother from her.

Aashi.

It wasn't that the other girls at the orphanage weren't friendly. Tara just didn't see the point in opening her heart to anyone who wasn't already in there. It hurt too much when they were taken away.

When Bakul died, she became acutely aware that her sister was the only family she had left. It was just the two of them now and she made up her mind to care for Aashi in the same way Bakul had cared for her. It seemed the only way she had left to honor his memory. Nothing would ever come between her and her sister. And the love she piled on Aashi was returned in spades by this indomitably happy girl, who knew no other life so instead embraced the one she had.

In the early days there'd been an older girl who'd paid her and Aashi a lot of attention. She was a strange girl who seemed to spend her life lost in a world that existed only in her mind. The rumor was that she had some kind of special ability. She saw things in her dreams. So disconnected from reality she was that she used to grab Tara on the arm as she walked past and hiss the word *Maari* at her. Tara corrected her a few times telling her that wasn't her name, but she eventually gave up and did what the other girls did—walk past her as if she were made of air.

When Aashi turned four, the girls were told to say goodbye to each other. Aashi had been selected for adoption and was to be sent the next day to a family far away.

Tara remembered the look of fear on Aashi's face as she'd clutched her hand and trembled. She'd never seen her sister like this. She remembered the bravery Bakul had shown the night Aashi was born. He'd been seven, two years younger than her. She could be brave, too.

When the night turned dark and the orphanage grew quiet, Tara woke Aashi from her dreams and together they crept into the yard. They slipped through a small hole in the fence and ran.

They never looked back, although now Tara wondered if perhaps they should have. Was it right for her to have made this decision for her sister? She could've had a better life. Perhaps it was only she who was destined for a life of misery. Why drag Aashi down with her?

It was too late for regrets, she thought, as they set the yellow piece of tin down in front of their home. Aashi was eight now, too old for adoption.

She looked at the collection of refuse they'd fashioned into their home. Over the years they'd added bits and pieces from the dump as they could get their hands on them. Despite it being one of the most poorly made homes in the village, the girls were proud of it. They'd made it themselves.

The village, as its residents knew it, sat to the side of the rubbish dump and was home to a collection of Mumbai's poorest citizens. Each resident had built their home with a mixture of pride and despair and they spread across the landscape like a disease.

Yet this strange place had seemed an oasis when the girls had first stumbled upon it. After running from the orphanage, they'd spent the first few nights under the stars.

They eventually found their way back to their old neighborhood, but either nobody remembered them, or they didn't care to try. The last thing anyone needed was two more stomachs to fill.

It'd been a silly idea anyway, Tara had eventually realized. That was the first place the authorities would look for them. She couldn't risk them being taken back to the orphanage for that would mean having Aashi ripped from her side.

Out of desperation they'd ended up at the rubbish dump in search of food. It was there they'd seen the village. Nobody would find them in that sea of human misery—not that she expected anyone was looking very hard.

The girls had walked through the makeshift streets, looking for an abandoned house to stay in. It wasn't as easy as that. They soon learned there was a pecking order to these things. Those at the top—the toughest and most fearsome— were given first choice at picking through the belongings of anyone who left or died.

As new arrivals, who were neither tough nor fearsome, the girls found themselves at the bottom of the pile.

A mute woman with gray hair and no teeth had eventually taken pity on them and allowed them to sleep in her home. It was no more than a large cardboard box, but the six walls of darkness offered the illusion of safety and the girls gratefully squeezed in together at night to share what was to become the last days of the old woman's life.

They woke one morning with the stench of death seeping into their cardboard walls. The woman was stiff and they'd had to drag her out of the box by her feet. A man in the village had seen them and wordlessly collected her body with a wheelbarrow and carted her away. Tara never found out where she was taken. She didn't want to know, for she realized it was likely to be a place she'd be taken herself one day. Perhaps a day not too far away.

She remembered crawling back into the box and crying so hard that Aashi began to scream. The body of the old woman had reminded Tara of her mother's death. She missed her. She missed Bakul. She missed being cared for. Loved. Wanted.

This life she'd been given seemed like a cruel joke, only she wasn't laughing. She barely remembered what it was like to laugh. All she knew was how to fight. How to survive.

Now the one person to show them kindness had died.

These were the thoughts that had blackened her mind as she wept in the safety of the putrid box. She decided she must be cursed. For all these tragedies that had befallen those around her, had one thing in common.

Her.

She'd grabbed hold of Aashi's trembling body and begged the universe to protect her little sister. If the curse were to be so cruel as to take her away then the man with the wheelbarrow may as well scoop her up right now, for that wouldn't be something she'd be able to live with.

Nobody challenged the girls for their home made from cardboard, likely due to the smell. Tara didn't mind the odor so much. She could hardly detect it over the stench of the rotting refuse at their doorstep. It was a stench so bad it overpowered any smell a human body was capable of making, dead or alive.

"We did it," said Aashi, breaking into Tara's thoughts and dragging her back to the present. "It will make the most beautiful tin roof in the world."

"We haven't done it yet," she said. "We don't know who might've seen us."

They pulled away the layers of hessian that covered the roof of their home. Together, they hoisted the piece of tin above their heads and lay it flat on the rotten timber frame they'd built from various finds.

It was still very early in the morning with not many people around. If they were lucky nobody would've noticed them. From a distance it'd be possible to mistake the tin for a large piece of cardboard.

They replaced the hessian bags—being careful to cover every inch of the tin—and went inside.

"It's beautiful," said Aashi, lying on her back and staring up at their new yellow roof. "It's just like the sunshine."

Tara was glad she'd agreed to keep it. The look of pleasure in Aashi's eyes at that moment was worth forgoing any meal they could've purchased.

She lay down next to her sister and looked at their roof made from sunshine.

"Are you happy?" she asked.

"It's the happiest day of my life," said Aashi, beaming. "I feel like a princess in a castle."

"You don't even know what a princess is."

"I do so." She crossed her arms and pouted. "One day a handsome prince will come to rescue me. You'll see."

Tara sighed. She'd never given much thought to handsome princes. Or even handsome beggars. She'd never fall in love. Falling in love meant having babies. And that could never happen.

It wasn't the thought of having extra mouths to feed that worried her. It was her fear of having to open her heart to another human being, only to have them ripped away.

Besides, this was no world to bring more humans into. She'd heard India now had two billion people living in it. She wasn't sure how many two billion was, but it sounded like an awful lot. No wonder everyone had to fight for space.

She looked around at the space she and Aashi had claimed as their own patch of dirt on the crowded planet they lived on. If she lay on the ground and reached out her arms and legs as far as they could go, she could almost touch each of the four corners, but it was plenty of space for the two of them. She loved their home.

The outside may be covered with hessian and cardboard —and now a glorious piece of tin—but the inside was a rainbow of color. The girls had collected plastic packets, bottle lids and pieces of cloth, grouping them by their colors and lined the walls with curving rows of reds, yellows and blues. It was beautiful. It was also practical, helping to block out some of the weather. Now with a roof made from sunshine, it was perfect.

The floor was lined with bamboo mats they'd collected and stitched together, and four wooden crates were piled in one corner in which they kept their possessions, including a strange jumble of kitchen utensils, a few clothes, one precious blanket, two buckets and a comb.

There was no food. There never was. The moment they came across any, they ate it. They'd learned that lesson in their early days in the village. Whenever you set foot outside, your house could be ransacked—if not by people, then by rats. If you owned anything of value, it was safest to keep it with you at all times. And the safest place for food was in your stomach.

It also made no sense to keep anything for the future, for in the village nobody knew if they'd live to see another day.

Tara turned her head at the sound of a wheelbarrow making its way past their house. It was the same wheelbarrow that had taken the old woman away all those years ago and it was the same man who wheeled it. His name was Vikram and without him, Tara knew they'd both be dead.

Aashi scrambled to her feet and poked her head out between the folds of torn fabric that served as their front door.

"Vikram!" she called, waving madly at the man she so adored.

Tara didn't need to rise to know what response Aashi

would get. Vikram would be walking on, without giving her so much as a glance.

This had been their daily ritual of the past four years. Vikram pretending not to care for the attention of his young admirer and Aashi determined to make him smile at her just one time.

It was hard to tell how old people in the village were, but Tara guessed Vikram might be twenty years of age. His face was hard with years of dirt pushed into the creases that lined his brow. His body lean yet strong from the merciless routine he put himself through each evening.

He lived next to the girls and Tara could hear him puffing and panting at night as he performed hundreds, possibly thousands, of push-ups on the floor of the small home he lived in.

When they'd first arrived in the village, Tara had lain awake at night wondering what he was doing. She'd gathered her courage one night and snuck out into the darkness to spy on him through a small gap in his door.

Her dark eyes had widened to see the determined way he'd pushed himself through his exercises.

"Why?" she'd wondered. With food so scare, who'd want to burn so much energy like this?

It didn't take long for the reason to become obvious. Two nights later she'd been woken by a commotion outside. Someone had tried to sneak into Vikram's house and steal his wheelbarrow. He'd woken and held the intruder in a headlock so tight it was a miracle the man's head didn't come flying off.

Just before the man was about to draw what he believed would be his last breath, Vikram had thrown him to the ground and watched him crawl away. The man never bothered him again. Or anyone else in the village. In that one night, he'd crawled from the bottom of the pile to the top.

Strength was an important device in the toolbox of survival. Tara had taken in this lesson and wondered how she could keep Aashi safe. She could do a million push-ups and she'd still be a scrawny girl, looking after a sister who was both younger and weaker than herself.

The next day, Tara had presented Vikram with an orange Aashi had found at the dump. It was a perfect orange—a shining jewel of deliciousness. Aashi had cried when she'd ripped it from her hands, looking at Tara with confusion and hatred.

Vikram had taken it from her outstretched hands and nodded. Without a single word spoken he'd understood the deal she was offering him. He needed food, as did everyone in the village. Tara and Aashi needed protection.

Aashi's tantrum at losing her prized piece of fruit had continued into the night.

"Shhh!" Tara had hissed, not wanting Vikram to hear. "That orange has saved our lives."

"But I'm hungry," Aashi wailed, beating her little hands on the walls of the cardboard box.

"I know," Tara said, stroking her hair. "I'm hungry, too."

Aashi's cries stilted in her throat as the entrance to the box was torn open. In the moonlight they saw a pair of dark hands and Tara had shrunk back in fear, pushing her sister behind her.

"Vikram," she called out, hoping he could hear her from his bed and that the orange had been enough. She hadn't expected to need his help so soon.

The man leaned into the box and she saw it was Vikram himself. This did little to quell her fear. Had he misunderstood the deal? Had he thought her gift was a sign of affection? She knew some men were like that. Bakul had warned her about them more than once. It was for this reason that she was glad for her plain looks. She hadn't needed a mirror to know her face was not the sort to attract interest from the opposite sex. Aashi on the other hand ... her face frightened Tara with its raw beauty. She saw the way men looked at her despite her tender years.

"Please don't hurt us," she pleaded, pushing Aashi further behind her.

He reached out a hand. She fought the urge to scream. Then she noticed him rolling something along the floor of their box. It landed at her knees. It was Aashi's orange.

She picked it up, confused. Was the deal off? Was he refusing to protect them?

"Eat," he said. "I'll watch out for you."

He looked at her and for a moment his eyes held hers. This was the moment she'd remember all her life as the happiest she'd ever been. It was the first real victory in life that she'd created for herself.

Vikram had pulled his head from the box and secured the folds of cardboard so they closed once more.

Tara held out the orange to her sister and together they ate. It was the sweetest taste the world had to offer, for it tasted of kindness as much as it did the fruit itself.

She savored this moment, tucking its memory into her heart and the girls had often whispered about it at night, retelling it, each time making Vikram slightly more heroic, more handsome, more wonderful, until he'd become the hero to Aashi that Bakul had been to her.

Instead of leaving him food, they now left him presents they made from scraps. They were mostly useless trinkets but Tara thought it important to remind him of his promise and Aashi saw it as a vital part of her plan to make him smile. As much as they felt Vikram's protection they never felt his friendship. He kept himself distant from all in the village without exception.

They were never sure what he did with all the gifts, but

he never returned them, so they continued to hand them over. Once they'd seen him wearing a necklace they'd made him as he walked through the village. Aashi had clapped her hands and squealed as she rushed up to him. He'd looked at her with a stony face and continued on his way.

"He's not your prince," Tara said, as Aashi returned to her place on the floor to admire her sunshine once more.

"I know that. He's yours."

"Don't be crazy! Is your head made from noodles?"

Aashi giggled.

"Why are you laughing?"

"I'm just imagining my head made from noodles and you slurping me up as I sleep."

"I wouldn't get the chance. You'd have slurped yourself up before I got close."

"I'm hungry, Tara."

"I know. Me, too."

"Can we go back to the dump?"

"There'll be nothing left by now. This roof was our breakfast. And the apple."

"But I'm hungry." She rubbed her stomach.

"Let's get some water." She picked up their buckets. "That'll fill you up."

"All right," said Aashi, getting to her feet. She wasn't convinced. She'd had water for breakfast many times and knew it would do nothing to satisfy the monster that growled in her belly.

They began their walk across the village, weaving their way between the homes of their neighbors. Nobody stopped to smile or wave at Tara. They knew she liked to keep to herself and they were happy to let her.

Aashi walked ahead, swinging her bucket and taking small skips as she went. She waved at each person she passed, not concerned whether she received a response or not.

The crowd around the water tap was relatively small, with only a few people queued up before them. The authorities had installed this tap with a grand show, pretending that they cared. Tara knew the truth, as did everyone else. It'd been installed to keep them hidden in their village instead of upsetting the other residents of Mumbai when they'd had to venture outside for one of life's most basic necessities.

They'd installed three lavatories, too. Not proper ones connected to pipes. Just large holes in the ground that'd filled to the brim so quickly that nobody ever went near them—except the rats.

Instead the villagers were forced to relieve themselves anywhere they could find, which was often in the middle of the street. This of course led to disease outbreak and a death toll in the village that served to keep the population under control. New residents departed as quickly as they arrived.

Three times a day Tara would take Aashi to a quiet spot behind the huge pile of rubbish to take care of their toileting. She refused to let go what little dignity she had left. She would *not* empty her bowels in the streets she walked in, nor would she allow Aashi to.

Twice a week they'd carry their buckets of water to wash themselves, then use the water to wash their clothes. Yet still they wore a layer of dirt like a second skin. That was part of life in the village.

Their turn came for the water tap and they filled their buckets.

"Can we wash today?" asked Aashi.

"Tomorrow," said Tara.

"But I'm hot. The water will cool me down."

Tara frowned. It wasn't a hot day by Mumbai's standards. She put a hand on her sister's forehead. She was burning up.

"Drink," she said, forcing a bucket to Aashi's lips. Please

let this just be exhaustion from carrying the piece of tin. Don't let her be sick. Please.

She wasn't sure who she was begging but beg she did. There were no doctors in the village. No medicine. Getting sick was serious.

"Tara, why are you scared?" asked Aashi, blinking at her with innocent eyes.

"I'm not scared. Let's go home and rest. Here, give me your bucket. I'll carry them both."

They walked home, the trip taking twice as long as it had before. The buckets were heavy and Aashi's pace was slow.

"My head hurts," Aashi complained.

Tara noticed her shivering. "Are you still hot?" she asked.

"No, I'm cold now."

"We're nearly there," said Tara, her concern growing. Aashi wasn't normally one to complain. Now that she thought of it, her morning had been full of complaints. "You can lie under your sunshine. It'll take your headache away."

Their little house came into view and Tara came to a stop, her heart breaking into tiny pieces.

The sunshine wouldn't be taking Aashi's headache away.

Their sunshine was gone.

CHAPTER NINE

*W*hen Aashi saw the roof missing from their home, she went quiet. She didn't cry. She didn't shout out. Instead she stood very still and let her eyes do all her talking.

Whoever had taken that roof had taken her innocence and crushed her happy spirit. Aashi's belief that life could be beautiful in the ugliest of situations had vanished and Tara saw her age years in only the moments it took for her to understand what'd happened.

"Go and lie down," Tara said, looking at the pile of hessian that lay on the ground. "I'll fix it up."

Aashi went inside without a word. Tara decided her silence was justified. No words could bring back what had been stolen from them.

She repaired the roof as best she could, restoring it to the form it had held only hours before. Only now that form looked wrong. Hideous.

Vikram walked past as he headed to his home. For a rare moment he caught her eye, understanding what'd happened while he'd been away.

"It's not your fault," Tara said. He couldn't watch over them every moment of the day.

He tilted his head and stepped into his home.

She went inside and lay down next to Aashi, staring up at a muddy brown sky that'd once been Aashi's sun. She hated it. She hated whoever had done this to her sister.

In a rare moment of weakness she found herself holding back tears. She hadn't cried since the day the old woman in the box had died. There was no point. Nobody ever heard and it only left her feeling worse.

She wouldn't cry now. Instead she touched Aashi's burning forehead again. Sleep had claimed her quickly. Her skin was clammy, her breathing labored. She was sick. Very sick. And Tara was scared.

"Please, tell me how to make you better," she begged.

Her world spun as a sick feeling took hold. The curse was taking Aashi from her. It'd been waiting all these years. Waiting for her to love her sister so much she'd rather die than live without her. Life had been cruel to her, but it appeared the torture was only just beginning.

She had to fight. She had to find a way to save her.

She kissed Aashi on the cheek and went to Vikram's door.

"Please, Vikram," she called. "I need help."

"I didn't take it," he said. "Leave."

"I know you didn't. That's not why I'm here."

He came to the door looking puzzled. It was unusual for anyone in the village to disturb him.

"Aashi's sick. I need to get her to the hospital."

His face filled with concern. Was it possible he cared for them despite the distance he'd always placed between them?

"She looked fine this morning."

"I know, but she went downhill very quickly. She needs a doctor. I can't carry her." She looked at his wheelbarrow. "Can I borrow this please?"

"I'll help you," he said.

"Hurry," she said, grateful for his offer.

He followed her inside her home, his eyes darting around at the shock of color that greeted him. It was the first time he'd stepped through the door despite living a mere number of feet away.

Once his eyes found Aashi, they held still.

He lifted her small frame from the floor and carried her outside. She looked tiny in his arms and Tara was reminded of Bakul cradling her as a baby the night she was born. She bitterly regretted taking her from the orphanage. If she'd allowed her to be adopted, she'd be a thriving, healthy girl now.

"We have to save her," she said, holding the door open.

He carried Aashi outside and lowered her into the wheelbarrow.

She stirred, gripping her arms tightly around his neck and nestling her face into his shoulder.

He hesitated and stood up, still holding her in his arms. Without a word he walked in the direction of the hospital.

Tara didn't show her surprise. Instead she walked by his side, pouring all the love she had in her heart into both Aashi and this strange man she'd known so long yet barely knew at all.

They left the village and with each step they took, the landscape began to change, until it became unrecognizable from the place she knew as home. People often said the village was stuck in a time warp, but the reality of this never struck her until she stepped foot outside it.

She felt like she was on another planet. The streets were sealed with bitumen, which felt rough under her bare feet. The buildings were made from concrete, designed to last many lifetimes not just the life of its current inhabitants. Electricity shone from shop windows and the cool breath of air conditioners filtered out onto the street. She could hear music and people chattering in languages she didn't recognize.

Passersby stopped to stare at the three beggars from the village. The looks on their faces ground hopelessness into Tara's soul. Would she ever break free from the cycle of poverty she was born into?

She wanted to stare at them in return. To tell them how ridiculous they looked as they walked along talking to themselves. They were talking on their phones, of course—phones that were tucked away safely in their bags transmitting sound directly into their ears and somehow able to pick up what they were saying in return—but they looked like they were talking to themselves. And this made them look like fools.

Tara had found many phones at the dump, but they were useless to her without any money to connect to a network. Not that she had anyone she needed to contact. For her, a phone was just another piece of junk with which she could line her walls to keep out the rain.

Silent cars made from lightweight plastic raced past them at high speed. Bakul had told her that once cars had been made from heavy steel, not even fitted with crash sensors to stop them from running into each other. Car accidents had taken many lives in those days. It seemed hard to believe. Why would anyone have taken a ride in one of those death traps?

A man in a gray uniform greeted them at the door to the hospital. He pointed to the left, which Tara knew to be the section of the hospital dedicated to treating the poor—those who had no identification or money to pay their way. The guard didn't even ask them any questions. He just pointed. It was obvious which section of the hospital they belonged in.

Tara glanced to the right and glimpsed a waiting room. It

looked like a room from a king's castle, all bright and shiny. She wished she could take Aashi there. Perhaps that's where her prince was waiting for her, ready to rescue her from the grip of illness and this life of misfortune. If only Aashi could live long enough to find him.

She'd never believed Aashi's stories of the prince who'd come to rescue her, but now it seemed vital to cling onto her dream—for she had so few of them to cling to.

She looked at Vikram. Had he been the prince under Aashi's nose this whole time? Maybe when she got well and grew into a woman, Vikram would save her from the horrible life Tara had trapped her in. Then Tara would be free to sink into the refuse and give in to her struggles.

It seemed unlikely. Vikram was no more able to rescue Aashi than he was able to save himself. And strangely Aashi had always insisted that Vikram belonged to Tara.

They entered a dimly lit room, filled with others of their kind—dirty feet, tangled hair, blistered hands and hardened hearts.

A nurse approached and handed them some medical masks. This was the hospital's attempt to contain the disease that festered in the room. There was also a filter attached to the wall, designed to attract and kill germs. It was humming and spluttering, unable to keep up.

It was for this reason that only the desperate came here. Often people would leave sicker than when they'd arrived.

"Please. My sister needs help," Tara said.

"All these people need help," the nurse replied. "She'll need to wait her turn."

"She can't wait. She's very sick." She looked into the nurse's eyes, begging for her understanding.

"I'm sorry." The nurse rushed away toward a new group.

Tara pulled her mask over her face then gently affixed Aashi's.

"Bend forward," she said to Vikram. He complied and she stretched a mask across the bottom half of his face, noticing for the first time what beauty lay in his dark eyes.

There were no available seats, so instead they remained standing.

"Are you all right to hold her?" she asked Vikram, concerned he might drop Aashi after carrying her for so long.

He nodded. She looked as light as a kitten in his arms.

Please let her be seen soon. Tara was sure she didn't have much time. Her forehead felt like it was on fire and her shivering had gotten worse. Tara didn't need a thermometer to know her fever was rising. It had all happened so quickly. To think that just this morning they were pulling the piece of tin from a pile of rubbish. The tin they no longer had.

Volunteers ran this section of the hospital. Some were from India, but most were from abroad. Tara wasn't sure what would drive anyone to work in a place of misery like this. Perhaps it was because they knew they could leave at any moment. It was much easier to be a tourist in hell than to be chained to its walls with a lock that had no key.

Patients frequently died in this room and Tara could feel their spirits lurking, leering, wishing her harm. The hospital didn't seem to mind how many people died. It was fewer patients to treat. Less money to spend on them. Their lives were worth little. India had two billion other lives to worry about.

Bakul had said it was like this all over the world. It started with the curing of cancer and was quickly followed by the elimination of heart disease and lives lost on the road. The population all over the globe had exploded and the world was struggling to cope.

Two women were called into the treatment room next

and Tara and Vikram took their chairs. It was a relief to sit down.

Tara glued her eyes to the door the women had walked through and begged it to open for Aashi next. She was getting even worse.

She saw Vikram glance down at the trembling girl in his arms. Terror filled his eyes. He saw it, too. She didn't have much time.

He got to his feet and carried Aashi to the nurse, his intention to plead with her clear to all who watched.

"We were here first," complained an old man.

"My son is sick, too. See him next," called out a woman, whose son looked perfectly well.

"Sit down," called another man. "We're all waiting."

Vikram turned to face the room. He cleared his throat, his eyes filling with tears as he shuffled Aashi in his arms and pulled the mask from his face.

"She's only a little girl," he said, holding Aashi out to them. Her eyes were closed, her chest rising in increasingly slow breaths. "She hasn't even had a chance. If only you knew what her life has been like, you'd want to help her, too. She's a good person. The kind who'd let all of you go before her if only she could wake up and talk. She has no mother to speak for her. No father. Just that brave girl over there who's raised her despite still being a child herself. I know you're all sick, but none of you will die if you don't see a doctor in the next few minutes. She will. Give her a chance. *Please.* Nobody else has. Not ever."

It was more words than Tara had heard him speak in the whole time she'd known him. And they were the most beautiful words she'd ever heard. To think that this man who'd kept himself so distant from them for so many years, felt like that. She walked to his side and touched him tenderly on the arm.

A doctor came to the door to call his next patient.

"See her next," said the mother who only moments earlier had asked for her own son to be seen.

The crowd of people in the room pushed them forward in a rare sea of compassion.

The doctor stood, frozen. Puzzled. This had never happened before.

Then he looked at Aashi and burst into a flurry of action. Within moments she'd been swept into the treatment room, torn from Vikram's arms and laid on a bed, a team of medical staff surrounding her.

Tara and Vikram were pushed back, a nurse asking them to stand to one side as they worked furiously to save the life of the girl who'd never been given a chance. Until now.

"Thank you," said Tara, looking up at Vikram.

He looked at her for a moment. Then without a word he left.

Tara was running. She wasn't running anywhere in particular. That wasn't the point of it. She needed to get as far away from the hospital as possible.

After Vikram left she'd stood there watching the medical team work on Aashi. The concern on their faces punched dread into her gut. It was all her fault. She knew it. It was the curse. Maybe if she went far away the curse would forget about Aashi and leave her alone.

She fled the hospital and wove her way through Mumbai's streets. Her feet led her to places she'd never been before. That seemed like a good thing.

She passed supermarkets, hostels and clothing stores. Not that she saw any of them. Their bright lights and bold signs were a blur of color, not so much from her speed, but from the tears that burned her eyes.

The further she ran, the cleaner the streets became, the more expensive the clothing on the people who stopped to stare at her. Hostels became hotels. Supermarkets became convenience stores. Clothing stores became boutiques. It was as if she'd crossed an invisible border and left the India she knew far behind.

Her legs came to a halt as she became aware of a group of teenage boys blocking the pavement in front of her. A teacher was standing with them, preoccupied with a map instead of attempting to usher them off the path.

The boys turned to stare, their mouths agape at the sight of Tara.

She stared back at them, mirroring their look of confusion. She'd seen pale faces before, but never so many of them at the same time. They must be on some kind of school trip. Each boy had skin in different shades of pink. The same color as a pig she'd once seen at a market. They looked eerie. Ghost like. Was this a sign that Aashi had been taken to the heavens?

A boy from the back of the crowd stepped forward and she saw he had a face as dark as her own. But that was where their similarities ended. Everything about him was different, from the clothes that hung to his body to the aura that hung from his soul.

The boys said something to her in a language she didn't understand but recognized as English. She made no effort to reply. Instead she allowed the tears that stung her eyes to slide down her cheeks as she stared at the boys, wondering what their presence meant. It somehow seemed significant, only she couldn't work out how.

These faces were so different to the ones she was accustomed to looking at. They may as well be the faces of aliens.

She looked at the strange colors of their hair. White, yellow, brown, black and…was that orange?

She stepped toward the boy with the hair made from the color of fire, feeling drawn to him. She reached out her hand wanting to touch his hair. It was beautiful. Instead of backing away, as the other boys had begun to, he bent forward, allowing her to place her hand on the soft crown of his head.

The moment they made contact, she leaped back, shocked into the reality of what she'd just done. Why was she touching this stranger? Had she lost her mind?

The boy with hair of fire said something to her. It sounded reassuring. She didn't think he wanted to hurt her.

He held out his hand and she saw he held a small black device the size of his thumb. It was a camera.

He said something again.

He was asking if he could take her photo.

How odd. Her whole life people had just taken from her without asking. Nobody had asked her if they could take the roof off her house. What made this boy feel he needed her permission for anything?

He held up his hand and she looked at the small dark circle in the device that pointed at her. She could see the shimmer of the hologram her image was projecting.

Nobody had ever taken her photo before. Nobody had cared enough to want to remember her face in any moment of the future. How sad that her face should mean more to this strange boy from the other side of the world than it had ever meant to anyone from her own land.

Except Aashi. Aashi would want Tara's photo.

The thought of her sister sent tears of fear rolling down her cheeks once more. She couldn't lose her. She couldn't leave her. She had to get back to the hospital. What if she woke up and she wasn't there? She'd think she didn't care. What if it was too late and she was gone?

She drew her eyes from the camera back to the pale blue irises of the boy with hair of fire.

He reached into his pocket and drew out two notes. It was more money than she'd seen at any one time in her life. Was he giving it to her? Had he thought she was begging?

She wanted to be the sort of person who could turn away and leave him standing there with his money in his hand. Money that clearly wouldn't change his life yet could change hers in ways she couldn't imagine. To think that all those soul-destroying times she'd begged people for money, they'd given her nothing. Now that she hadn't asked, she was being handed a small fortune.

He nodded at her, his eyes filling with unmistakable kindness. It reminded her of the way Vikram had looked at her the night he'd returned Aashi's orange.

She didn't need to speak the same language as this boy to know he was a good person. Was that why he affected her so?

He reached out and took her hand in his, tucking the notes into her palm. She stared at wonder at the contrast of his pale skin against her own dark hands. He was the complete opposite to her in every way, yet somehow they seemed the same. Their hearts beat to the same rhythm, their dreams flew on the same path.

The other boys called out to him. She knew what they said wasn't kind. Were they chiding him for caring?

She turned to them and felt the coldness of their hearts.

The teacher looked up from his map, noticing her presence and yelled something at her, which she was sure was meant to scare her away.

It did.

She ran once more.

She heard the boy with hair of fire call out to her, but knew he'd never find her in the crowded streets that lay before her. Not that she was sure he'd even tried to follow.

Finding her way back through Mumbai's labyrinthine streets was impossible. If only she'd paid more attention earlier. She had no idea where to turn.

She hadn't learned to read. She'd never had the opportunity. Perhaps if she had, that might've helped. Or perhaps not, she decided.

She tried asking a few people for directions, but they ignored her, thinking she was asking for money.

That wasn't what she needed. She had money. Enough for her and Aashi to feast like princesses. Finally, she'd be able to fill her sister's stomach with the food she so craved. Was this what Aashi had foreseen when she'd spoken of the prince who'd come to save her? Was this boy with the hair of fire Aashi's prince?

She sat on the curb of the road to catch her breath and try to figure out her next move. The folded notes were still in her hand. She had no pockets. She had no bag. Just the pink dress she'd found at the dump last year. If she looked closely, she could see the faded rows of butterflies that'd once decorated the fabric. It was a dress made for a younger girl than Tara, but years of malnutrition meant it fit her perfectly. Soon she'd have to find something else and pass this one to Aashi.

Aashi. Sweet, beautiful, Aashi. What was happening with her? Had the doctors helped her or had...

She couldn't think about that.

A taxi pulled to the curb and a man in a suit emerged.

She leaped to her feet and slid into the back seat. The only other time she'd been in a car was when the authorities had pulled her from the slums and taken her to the orphanage. She ran her hand across the smooth surface of the plastic seat.

"Where to?" the driver asked, turning to look at her. His eyes widened.

"Out!" he screamed. "Out!"

"I have money," she protested. "Look. Here." She waved one of the notes at him.

"Then buy yourself some shoes," he said, still pointing to the door.

"Please. My sister is sick. She's in the hospital. I have to get to her. I don't know how to find it on my own."

He paused then snatched the note from her hand, holding it to the light to check its authenticity.

Satisfied it was real, he began to drive. He didn't ask which hospital. He knew. There was only one hospital that would treat the sister of someone who looked like Tara.

She sat quietly in her seat, watching the world outside. She liked being in this plastic bubble. It was safe. She wondered if this was what being dead felt like—seeing the world, but not being able to reach out and touch it.

The driver glanced at her in his mirror. She didn't take the time to wonder what he was thinking. He'd surely be glad to drop her off, take her money and never see her again.

She looked at the back of his neatly combed head and drew in the scent of soap from his shower. He had a photo stuck to his dashboard of two young girls, perched on their mother's lap. No doubt his wife and daughters.

She leaned forward and tried to peer into the face of his older daughter. To catch her eye, if only in a photo. What was it like to be this girl? To have a mother with a lap to sit on, a sister who wasn't your responsibility, a father to bring you food? Yet still somehow this girl didn't look happy. Her eyes brimmed with sorrow.

It was a look that filled Tara with anger. How dare this girl be unhappy. What could possibly have happened to make her sad? Did she spill a drink on her party dress? Was her favorite television show cancelled? It made her feel sick. This girl had no right to be sad. She should try smelling the death of all who surrounded her. Or waking every morning wondering if this would be the day she'd get to eat something.

If she were this girl in the photo, she'd spend her life smiling—like Aashi did despite the horrors of her life.

She knew she was being unfair. It wasn't the girl's fault she'd been handed a better life than Tara. Happiness was a complicated business.

She dropped her gaze from the photo to the small tin of mints that was sitting on the dash. She knew what mints were. She knew their smell from tins she'd found at the dump, but she didn't know their taste. The tins she'd found were empty. Maybe she'd buy Aashi a box with the other note she still had tucked in her hand and they could try them together.

The driver noticed her gaze. He reached for the tin. For a moment she thought he was going to give it to her. Instead, he threw it into a compartment in his door.

She heard the mints rattle. Of course, he wasn't going to give them to her. He was probably saving them for his daughters. They'd know what mints tasted like.

They arrived at the hospital and the driver pulled into the taxi rank.

All thoughts of mints and frowning girls left her mind. For somewhere behind these walls was Aashi. A girl who knew how to smile.

She slid out of the taxi. Aashi needed her.

"Girl," the driver called through his open window.

"Yes?" she asked, worried she hadn't paid him his full fare. She didn't want to part with the remaining fortune she clutched in her hand.

He held his hand out to her.

"Here," he said, waving her money.

She took it. Not slowly and graciously like she knew she should. Not hesitantly like she had with the boy with fire hair. She snatched it from his hand before he changed his mind. That was what survival instinct did.

He reached down and again his hand appeared with a gift. The mints.

She took them. This time her hand was slow and gracious. The money had been hers. These mints had not. It was the first gift she'd received since her parents had died. She'd had more kindness bestowed upon her in this day than she had in the last six years.

Her brain wanted to say thank you, but instead her mouth said sorry.

The driver's eyebrows crossed in confusion and he drove away.

She stood and watched him. She *was* sorry. Her mouth hadn't lied. She was sorry for misjudging him. She was sorry for being angry with his sad daughter. She was sorry for taking his fare. She was sorry she still existed when her brother did not. Most of all, she was sorry for leaving Aashi when she needed her most. That wouldn't happen again.

Please let her be alive, she whispered to the sky. *Let her be alive and I'll never leave her side again. I'll give my life to protect her, just please keep her safe.*

She wondered who she was talking to. There was no man in the sky to hear her pleas. If there were, he'd have helped her years ago instead of throwing her crumbs of kindness on the darkest day of her life. All the money in the world wouldn't make up for her sister's life being snatched away.

As she wandered through the corridors of the hospital, her fear grew. She pushed back thoughts of what she'd do without Aashi. It was too frightening. The thought of it was knocking the air from her lungs. The reality of it would knock the life from her soul.

She turned the corner to Aashi's room. The curtain had been drawn around her bed. Was that a good sign or bad?

She approached and prepared to pull the curtain back. What was behind there?

Her eyes closed and she took a moment to focus on Aashi. Could she feel her? Was her energy pulsing from the bed beyond the curtain?

Yes. She was still there. She was certain of it.

She pulled back the curtain and saw her beautiful little sister sleeping. Color had returned to her cheeks and a long tube was attached to her arm. Someone had bathed her, brushed her hair and dressed her in a clean, white hospital gown. A crisp sheet tucked her tightly into the bed and her head lay resting on a pillow. It was the only pillow her head had touched, the only bed on which she'd ever lain.

Aashi could be anyone lying there like that. Rich or poor. It tugged at Tara's heart to see her sister sleeping as any child in the world should be allowed to sleep. How would she be able to take her from this and return her to a mat on a dirty floor with rats that ran across her face as she slept?

She reached for Aashi's hand and took it in her own, feeling dirty next to her neatly scrubbed sister. She'd only been gone for a few hours, but what a difference those hours had made. Whatever medicine the doctors had given her, had cured her. Brought her back from the brink. She was going to be okay.

"I'm here," she said, her voice echoing around the quiet hospital room.

Aashi's eyes fluttered open. She smiled and fell immediately back to sleep.

It was many hours before she stirred again. Tara remained by her bed, as if she could guard her from harm. If she poured enough love and energy into Aashi's soul then maybe she could keep her safe.

"Tara," said Aashi, sitting up and wrapping her arms around her neck. "Where did you go?"

"I've been sitting here the whole time."

"No, you haven't. You went away."

"I meant I've been sitting here since the last time you woke. Don't you remember?"

She shook her head.

"I brought you something," she said, holding up the tin of mints.

"No way! You found a tin with some still in them?"

"Yes." She didn't want to explain the strange events of the afternoon. She tipped two mints onto Aashi's lap and they each picked one up.

"One, two, th—"

It was too late. Aashi had already put the mint into her mouth.

Tara slipped the mint between her lips and together the girls let out a squeal of delight. For a split second they were just two little girls enjoying a treat.

"It's even better than I imagined," Tara said, swirling her tongue around her mouth as she tried to get used to the strange sensation. It felt like it was burning her, yet with no pain. Sugar and heat combined, making her eyes water.

"This is what heaven tastes like," said Aashi, her face brimming with delight.

Tara reached for Aashi's hand and tipped the contents of the tin into it. There was no discussion about whether or not they'd eat them all now. It was understood they would. When you lived in the village, pleasures were to be seized the moment they were unearthed.

Aashi began to divide the mints into two piles.

"No. You have them all," Tara said. "They'll make you strong."

Aashi's eyes flashed with delight then quickly faded. "No. We'll share them. That's the way we do things."

"I already had some while you slept," Tara lied. "This is your half." She couldn't take a piece of heaven from this innocent girl, no matter how small it was.

Aashi shoved the entire handful into her mouth at once and grinned with bulging cheeks.

Tara could hear her grinding them with her teeth then giggling madly when they started to burn her mouth. She closed her eyes and tried to store the sound into the deepest part of her memory. It was the sound of joy. The fact that it was her sister's joy and she'd been the one to give it to her made it one of her proudest moments.

Soon the mints were gone and all that was left was the lingering joy they'd brought with them.

"Why are you crying?" Aashi asked, looking concerned.

"They're happy tears."

"I've never seen you cry happy tears."

"I suppose I've never been happy like this."

"Tell me why you're happy?" Aashi leaned forward, as if waiting for a story.

"I'm just happy that you're better." She patted her on the knee. "That's all I needed to make me happy."

"I saw you in my dream," Aashi said, leaning back on her pillow.

"What was I doing? Riding a horse? Flying to the moon?"

"You were talking to a prince." Her face was serious. It made Tara smile.

"Really? Was he wearing a crown made from gold?"

"No. No crown on his head. Just fire."

"Fire?" Tara's heart leaped.

"Yes. His hair was made from fire."

CHAPTER TEN

"Tell me about your dream," said Tara, anxious to hear more. Was it possible Aashi had seen her talking to the boy with hair of fire? It couldn't be. But how had she known otherwise?

"I told you about it already," said Aashi, shrinking back into her bed.

"No, you didn't. You told me nothing. I want to know every detail." Her tone was harsh despite the effort she was putting into sounding calm.

"Please don't be cross with me, Tara," she said, seeming to be trying to work out how she'd managed to upset her sister.

"I'm not cross. I promise. You just surprised me, that's all." She tried to coat her words with enough sugar to make them convincing. If Aashi got scared she'd tell her nothing and she really needed to hear about the dream. "I think your dream might be important. Would you tell me about it?"

She nodded. "First, I saw you running. You looked so beautiful, but you looked sad, too. You scared me. I wanted to help you, but I couldn't. I wasn't there, you see. I was just watching. Then I saw the prince. I saw him see you.

You looked at each other and I was screaming out in my dream for him to help you. I was begging him. Then he gave you something. Money, I think. And I was calling out to you to stay with him, but you didn't. You started running again."

"Then what? What did the boy do?" She was still wondering if he'd chased after her or stood and watched her leave.

"I don't know. I must've woken up."

Tara sat on the edge of the bed and tried to take in what she'd just been told. Aashi had been there. She'd seen her. What did that make her? Some kind of witch? A fortuneteller?

"Have you had dreams like this before?" she asked.

Aashi nodded.

"I need you to listen to me. It's very important. Don't tell anyone about these dreams. Only me. Do you understand? I don't want anyone taking you away from me."

"Why would they take me away?" The fear in her eyes intensified.

"Because your kind of dreaming is special dreaming. People won't understand. They'll want to ask you lots of questions if they find out." She knew she was being paranoid, but there was no way she was going to risk Aashi being taken away from her for one of those medical studies she'd heard rumors about. This secret of Aashi's was best kept exactly that—a secret.

"Why's my dreaming special?"

Tara held out her hand and showed Aashi the folded notes. "You dream was real. You did see me. I *was* running. The boy *did* give me money. I don't know how, but you saw it all."

Aashi smiled. "We're rich," she whispered. "I knew he'd save us."

"He hasn't saved us. He's helped us, but this money won't last forever. It's enough to feed us for a while, that's all."

Her eyes lit up at the mention of food.

"I'm so sorry, Aashi."

"Why?" She reached for Tara's hand. "You don't need to be sorry."

"I do. I'm sorry for giving you a life where you're hungry all the time."

"You didn't give me this life. It's not your fault."

"It *is* my fault. If only I'd let that family adopt you, then things would be different for you."

"No!" She was angry. "You couldn't let them take me. Not without you. You're my sister. I don't want to live with anyone else."

She squeezed her hand. "Will you forgive me then?"

"There's nothing to forgive. I love you, Tara."

Tears filled her eyes once more. She couldn't remember Aashi ever saying these words. Her actions had always spoken of love, but these words were new.

"I love you, too." She leaned forward and kissed her sister's hand.

Aashi grew strong in the hospital. The nurses quickly became smitten by the girl with the fighting spirit and smiling eyes. They convinced the doctors to keep her there longer than was strictly necessary. In that time, they attended to her every need. Her hair was washed and trimmed, her nails clipped and painted, her teeth cleaned and flossed. She was put on an intravenous drip that poured vitamins into her body and given trays of meals that filled her tiny stomach.

Tara was starting to see a new girl emerge from under the filth of the village. She was healthy, she was clean, and she was happy. Her hair gleamed, her eyes shone, and her skin felt like silk.

The nurses would sneak Tara into the bathroom with Aashi whenever they could and allow her to scrub herself clean under the shower. She hadn't known warm water flowed from taps. It felt so good to stand there and watch the dirt run down the drain. She could never get herself this clean with the water they collected in their buckets no matter how hard or often she scrubbed.

She spent every morning sitting by Aashi's side. In the afternoon she'd return to the village, fearing if she didn't their small home would be taken over by a new arrival. She needed to make it clear their house was very much still spoken for.

It felt strange in there alone. Sleep didn't come easily without the soft sounds of her sister dreaming. It was incredibly lonely lying there in the dark. She listened for the sounds of Vikram exercising or snoring, catching the slightest sound he made and clutching it to her heart. She loved this man, for this was the man who saved her sister. A sister who was so much more to her than that—she was her sole companion in life.

Although Vikram had begun to speak to her on occasion, she wouldn't yet count him as a companion. Their conversations were short and a means for him to establish the status of Aashi's health. He was so formal, and she began to wonder if she'd imagined that heartfelt speech he'd given in the hospital. It seemed like those words had come from a different mouth to the one that grunted at her as he passed her in the street.

She hadn't spent the money yet. It seemed wrong to do that without Aashi. It was something she was looking forward to doing together when she came home. She'd put it into a discarded chocolate wrapper and buried it under one of the bamboo mats on the floor. It frightened her to leave it there unattended all day, but she felt she didn't have a choice. It was more frightening to walk around with it.

Eventually the nurses' pleas with the doctors to keep Aashi in the hospital began to fall on deaf ears. There was a shortage of beds. She was well. It was time for her to go home.

On her last day they brought her gifts of clothing, toiletries and sweets, wrapping their offerings in kisses, hugs and tears. They knew she'd soon return to being the skinny girl covered in filth who'd come to them in such poor health, just as Tara knew these kind nurses would soon forget her sister as they began fussing over someone else. If they really cared then why had none of them offered to take Aashi in? Were their own homes too good for the likes of a girl from the village?

Aashi had accepted their gifts just as she'd accepted their other kindnesses. She didn't question them, and she didn't ask for more. That was one of the joys of childhood Aashi still had—the ability to be happy with what she had. It seemed to Tara that as people got older their expectations of life grew. The more they had, the more they wanted.

Aashi's company on the walk home from the hospital felt like the first break of sunshine after a monsoon. Tara wore one of Aashi's new dresses that was too large for her, accessorizing it with an enormous smile. She'd missed her sister more than she could've imagined. People weren't meant to walk the earth alone. Except Vikram perhaps.

"Why are you so happy?" Aashi asked.

"I missed you. It was lonely all by myself."

"You had Vikram."

"Of course. And you know what excellent company he is."

They laughed.

"How come he never came to visit me?"

Tara had told Aashi the story of how she'd arrived at the hospital and the part Vikram had played in saving her life. She'd smiled to know she'd finally gotten him to show her that he cared. It was one of the first victories of Aashi's life.

"He asked about you every day," Tara said, feeling the need to defend him.

"But he never came."

"He was leaving you alone to get better. You know how he is, Aashi."

"Why's he like that?"

"I don't know, but I'm sure there's a reason. Maybe someone hurt him."

"But we've never hurt him. We like him. Maybe we can teach him to like us."

"He already likes us. He just shows it differently to how we do."

Tara could see her thinking about this, trying to decide if she agreed. She hadn't heard his speech in the hospital. It was harder for her to believe that he cared.

They approached their house and Tara held the door open, bowing theatrically.

"Welcome home, Princess Aashi."

Aashi curtseyed and squealed with delight as she saw the ceiling of their home. While she'd been in hospital, Tara had trawled the dump for anything yellow and carefully stitched her findings together before securing them to the ceiling.

Aashi ran her hands over the golden pieces of cloth, plastic and mesh that formed her new roof of sunshine.

"It's even nicer than the last one," she said, wrapping her arms around Tara. "Thank you."

"Nobody can take your sunshine away."

"I'm the sunniest person in India." She spun around in a circle, laughing.

Tara had known the hours it'd taken her to cover the

ceiling would be worth it. With each stitch she'd placed, each join she'd made, she'd been piecing together Aashi's innocence. Watching her twirling and laughing was proof she'd succeeded.

For all the hardship Tara had been given in life, she'd also been given the world's most precious gift—a sister whose soul had been woven from a fabric of precious gold.

When you live in the village, the years don't roll by. Instead they crawl, making their presence known.

By the time Tara was a woman of twenty-three years of age, she felt as if she'd lived a complete lifetime. She'd seen great joy and experienced acute pain. She'd laughed, she'd cried, she'd fought, and she'd foraged. But most of all, she'd survived.

She knew no matter how many years she lived, she'd never forget the day that started with finding a piece of tin and ended with her sister in a hospital bed telling her she loved her. It was the most important day of her life and was as clear now as it had been when she was living the memory itself.

That day had changed everything.

It was the day she'd learned humans could be as kind as they could be cruel. It was also the day she'd learned of Aashi's gift of second sight.

As she'd watched Aashi grow from a girl into a young woman, she'd tried to learn more about her gift. Aashi, who was so open about every other aspect of her life, clammed up whenever the topic was raised. This wasn't something she was willing to discuss, and Tara wondered if it was due to her panicked reaction when she'd first discovered it.

She was desperate to know if the boy with hair of fire had

appeared again in her dreams. She wondered if he was thinking of her, for she was often thinking of him. She'd lain awake each night remembering their strange encounter on the street. She wondered if he still had the photo he'd taken of her. She hadn't needed a photo to remember him. She could still see every detail of his beautiful face. His eyes of sky, his skin of snow, his hair of fire.

She knew she'd never see him again, except behind her closed eyelids. If only the world weren't so big and crowded, she'd seek him out. Find him and thank him for what he'd done for her.

Spending the money had been a joy. She and Aashi had decided to spend it slowly, using it to buy themselves an enormous meal every Friday. They'd go to the market and walk up and down the aisles, knowing they had money in their pockets and any food they saw could soon be in their groaning bellies. Aashi normally bought the first appetizing meal she saw and gobbled it down, but Tara liked to string out the joy. She'd do laps of the market weighing up the pros and cons of each dish, eventually deciding on one and eating it slowly, savoring each bite. It was the difference between sucking on a sweet or crushing it between your teeth.

The temptation was to spend all of the money quickly, as was their way with any fortune they'd come across before. But their yellow piece of tin had taught them a lesson. Sometimes it was better to spread out your joy than to have it taken in one hit when your back was turned.

As they left the market each week, they'd purchase a samosa wrapped in brown paper and deliver it to Vikram. He'd look at them with curiosity in his sad eyes and accept their gift. He never asked them where they got it and they never told him.

The money lasted almost three years. The final meal they bought with it was sad beyond measure. Tara had looked at her sister and wondered if she'd have grown into such a beautiful teenager without her weekly opportunity to scare the hunger from the pit of her stomach. She feared how they'd survive without it.

But they had survived. They'd gone to the market the following Friday. They'd thought they could find a grain of fun in pretending they'd get a meal. Maybe they could trick their minds into thinking they'd been fed. The man at the samosa stall had waved them over ready to give them their weekly order. They'd shaken their heads and explained they no longer had any money. So, he'd given them a job. If they washed his dishes and cleared his tables during the lunchtime rush, he'd feed them both and send them home with a samosa wrapped in brown paper. It was a deal they couldn't refuse.

People didn't normally employ anyone from the village, but this man had trusted them because he'd known them as loyal customers. This had only happened because of the money they'd been given. Soon they were working several days a week and hunger became a problem of their past.

It was in this way that the boy with hair of fire had changed their lives. His kindness had not only helped Tara get back to the hospital when Aashi had needed her most, but it'd given them a chance at surviving long into the future.

He was a hero and placed on the same pedestal as Bakul and Vikram. They spoke of him in hushed tones with the reverence they felt he deserved.

As Tara had become a woman, her thoughts of the boy began to change. He'd be a man now. A handsome man, no doubt. Was he married? She didn't like this thought. It interfered with her fantasy of him coming back to India to find her. For some reason, every time she thought of him, strange pains would leap through her body. Her stomach would twist, her heart would ache, and sparks would light her darkest places.

Each time a tourist made their way through the marketplace, Tara would glance up from her dishes and check their face. They never wore the face she sought. It was like the boy with the hair of fire had turned to ash.

Having a job quickened the pace of life for the girls. This made Tara both happy and sad. There was little point in drawing out the hardship that accompanied each day in the village, yet to think that one day her life would be done with so little to show for it was unthinkable. She'd survived, but that hardly seemed like an achievement to brag about.

She longed for another day like the one that had changed their lives all those years ago. Did the universe grant more than one of these miracles in life?

The girls returned to the village late one afternoon to find the air filled with excitement.

"She's here," a young boy squealed as they wove their way through the tangled maze of streets, heading towards their home.

"Shhh," the boy's mother hissed.

They continued to walk, noticing that as they passed other villagers, they'd stop what they were doing to stare and whisper.

Aashi glanced at Tara nervously.

"What's going on?" Tara said, coming to a halt and turning to her sister.

"I don't know," she said, a frightened look plastered to her face.

"You do know. What's going on?"

"I don't know. I swear I don't. I just had a feeling about today, that's all."

"What kind of feeling? Please tell me it's a good feeling."

She felt weak. When you lived in the village, generally change wasn't a good thing.

"It's the boy you ask about...I've been dreaming of him a lot lately. It's like he's getting closer. I think he's coming for you, Tara."

"And you're telling me this now? You've had all day to tell me this." Anger rose in the pit of her stomach, quickly replaced by a feeling of raw excitement. Could it be true? Was it happening at last? Would she finally get to see her prince again?

She turned sharply to face two teenage girls who'd stopped to stare. "What are you staring at? What's happening?"

The girls looked to the ground, kicking imaginary stones with their bare feet.

"Tell. Me. Now," she roared with an intensity that almost frightened herself. She grabbed one of the girls by the shoulders and shook her.

"There's a man in the village," she spat out. "He was looking for you. He paid a man money and he took him to your neighbor. He's waiting for you now."

"What kind of man is he?"

"A rich man. Now let go of me."

Tara released her hands and felt her legs begin to run. The boy with hair of fire had come for her. He'd done the impossible and found her. She had to get to him.

"Wait, Tara," Aashi called, as she tried to keep up.

She didn't wait. She turned the final corner and saw a crowd gathered outside her house. They clapped their hands and cheered at her arrival.

"Where is he?" she said tugging at her clothes nervously, as if she could erase the creases and stains with her hands. There was little point. She'd looked a mess when first she'd seen him, and she looked a mess now. If he'd felt enough of a connection all those years ago, it wouldn't matter what she looked like now.

"He's in there," a man said pointing to Vikram's house.

Tara stepped forward and tapped on his door.

It opened a crack and she saw the flicker of the white of Vikram's eyes. He swung the door open and pulled her inside.

She'd never been in his house before, although her surroundings held no interest for her now. She blinked in the gloominess as her eyes struggled to adjust to the absence of sunlight. Where was her prince?

A man stood, his silhouette looming before her like a mountain.

She stepped towards him ready to greet him once more— the boy who'd saved her life. The boy who was now quite literally the man of her dreams.

"I've found you at last," he said.

Something wasn't right. That wasn't the voice of her hero. His accent was foreign but sitting beneath his words was the unmistakable intonation of someone who was raised in India. This was *not* the boy with hair of fire.

Then why was he so familiar?

He reached for her and gently took her hands in his. She blinked as his face became clear in the dim light.

"Hello, Chicken," he said.

It wasn't possible. This couldn't be happening.

"Bakul," she gasped, freeing her hands so she could wrap them around his middle and draw him close. "My brother."

CHAPTER ELEVEN

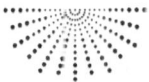

"*T*hey told me you were dead," said Tara, burying her face in the chest of this man who was both a stranger and her best friend.

"I was," he said.

She pulled back and looked at him in bewilderment.

"Not literally," he laughed. "When they separated me from you, I felt like I was dead. Parts of me died that will never come back. But then I was adopted and taken to London. My new parents brought me back to life."

"You were adopted?"

"I was lucky. I always hoped that you were lucky, too. Aashi was so young. I was certain she'd have been chosen."

Tara smiled meekly not wanting to tell him the truth. There was plenty of time for that later.

"Where is she? I was told you're never apart."

A loud banging came at the door as if in answer to his question.

Vikram opened it and Aashi burst through almost knocking him over.

She stood in the dull light, blinking.

HEIDI CATHERINE

"Tara?" she said. "Are you okay?"

"I'm wonderful."

"Who's this? It's not—"

"Aashi, this is our brother. Bakul has returned to us."

"Bakul?" she gasped. She'd been too young when they'd been separated to have her own memories of him, but Tara had told her many stories about their courageous brother who'd kept them alive when their father had died.

He stepped toward her and Aashi threw her arms around him, taking him by surprise.

"Bakul is alive! Bakul is alive!" she laughed. "Vikram, open the door and let in some light so I can see my brother."

Vikram raised his eyebrows at his bossy neighbor and opened the door. Light flooded in.

"There's nothing to see here," he growled at the crowd on his doorstep. "Be off with you."

Tara heard footsteps retreating. Vikram remained outside, giving them both privacy and protection from any chance of the crowd returning.

She looked at Bakul, noticing how handsome he'd become. He was tall and lean. His dark skin looked polished, almost shiny. His hair that had never sat quite right had been cropped short and he smelled so good. Like soap and shampoo and flowers and spice. He wore dark pants and a crisp, white polo shirt with the collar standing high around his neck. It was no wonder he'd attracted such a crowd in the village. People without money could always smell it on someone else.

He didn't look like the brother she remembered. The only thing familiar to her were his eyes. She'd know those dark eyes anywhere. Eyes that seemed almost too large for his face. They were eyes that'd seen grief and pain. The happiness that filled his life now hadn't managed to push that away.

158

"You're so beautiful, Aashi," he said, smiling at his sister. "And you too, Chicken," he added, a few seconds too late for it to be convincing. Tara didn't mind. There were days she longed to be beautiful like her sister, but mostly it didn't bother her at all. That was one advantage of living a life without mirrors adorning her walls. She didn't need to give her appearance much thought.

"How did you find us?" she asked. There were no records of their birth or their place of residence. Finding them here amongst India's billions was like finding a grain of sand on the ocean floor.

Bakul reached for a backpack that was sitting in a corner of the room. He opened it and withdrew a book.

"I can't read," she said.

"This isn't a book for reading," he said.

She looked at him, puzzled. Wasn't that what books were for?

"It has photos in it," he added. "Photos of India. My mother gave it to me. She's always encouraged me to maintain my connection to this country. To be honest, I didn't even look at the book for several months after receiving it." He opened the book at a place he had marked.

Tara wondered what all of this had to do with her. How had this strange book led her brother back to her side?

"When I eventually looked at it, I saw this." He turned the book around for his sisters to see.

The girls leaned forward to study the page.

"Tara, that's you," gasped Aashi.

It was.

Contained within the pages of the book was a photo of her. It was a younger her. A her with wild hair and dirty skin. Tears ran down her face, staining her cheeks with jagged lines and her eyes shone with agony. She wore a pink dress that was as filthy as the rest of her and it clung to her body revealing sharp edges of bones that protruded from under her skin.

This was the photo taken by the boy with hair of fire. It was the only photo ever taken of her and it'd captured the darkest moment of her existence—the moment in time when she'd feared Aashi was lost to her. Looking at it now brought back the horror of that moment. It was terror in its purest form. The terror of living life without anyone to love and without anyone to love her in return.

"Tara." Aashi reached for her.

The contact broke her from her thoughts, and she realized she was trembling.

"My poor sisters," said Bakul, wrapping his arms around them both. "I'm so sorry. I'm so sorry you had to have this life."

"It isn't your fault," said Aashi firmly, reminding Tara of the time in hospital when Aashi had rebuked her apology for the meager life she'd been able to provide her. She knew now it wasn't her fault—just as the sea of misfortunes that had befallen them wasn't Bakul's fault. She'd always felt like her life had been cursed. She was being punished for something she'd once done and could no longer remember.

"How did this photo get into this book?" she asked, breaking away. "I don't understand."

"Do you remember it being taken?" he asked.

She nodded. "Aashi was sick. I thought she was going to die. I ran from the hospital into the street and came across a group of foreign schoolboys. One of them gave me money. He also took my photo."

"Well, the boy who took your photo became a photographer. A very successful photographer. This is a book he put together of some of the photos he took when he was younger."

"What do these words say?" she asked, noticing some print on the page.

"The photo is called *"Hell through the eyes of an angel."*

Tara raised her eyebrows in surprise. She certainly felt like she'd seen hell that day—perhaps she was even living in it now—however she'd never really believed in the existence of a heaven and a hell. Life wasn't so black and white that souls could be divided into one category or another. She imagined a place beyond this life filled with souls of every tone and shade.

"What else does it say?" asked Aashi, always curious to hear more. "Are there more words?"

He shook his head. "But I did meet with the photographer to ask about you."

"You met him?" Tara asked. She couldn't believe it. Bakul had met him. That meant he knew where to find him. Perhaps she'd lay eyes on him once more before her days were done. "What's his name?"

"Finton Mercer."

"Finton," she said, turning the name over with her tongue. After all these years he had a name. A strong name. A name befitting of the prince she'd built him up to be in her mind.

"He asked me to call him Finn."

She nodded. Somehow that suited him even better.

Bakul turned to the front section of the book and held it open for her. It was a photo of a man. A man with the grown face of the boy who'd haunted her mind since the day she'd met him. His hair was still orange, his eyes still blue, his skin still white, yet adulthood had added angles to his face that she couldn't have imagined. His jawline was square and covered in stubble, the corners of his eyes were lined with evidence of a life lived outdoors and he had a tiny chip in one of his front teeth. He smiled at her from the book. It was the smile of a stranger. She realized that she didn't know this man. She never had. All she'd done was take an incident that had probably meant nothing to him and built it up in her mind to the point where she'd convinced herself that they were long lost soulmates.

"He remembered you well," said Bakul. "You made a big impression on him."

She listened with caution, wishing she could tie down her heart to stop it from leaping into the back of her throat.

"He said he's thought of you every day and wished he'd done more for you. He was worried that by including you in this book he was exploiting you. But he said it was too powerful an image to keep from the world."

"Powerful? How can an image of a skinny girl covered in dirt be powerful? It's miserable."

"Absolutely it's powerful. Look at you. You're the face of hidden India. And it's not just India. You're the face of all the people struggling in this world, with governments who'd rather hide you away than take care of you."

"There's too many of us to take care of," said Aashi. This was something Tara had told her years ago to try and take the sting out of their abandonment.

"Maybe there is," he said. "But just because a problem seems too big to solve does that mean we shouldn't even try?"

"Is that what the world sees us as? A problem?" asked Aashi.

"Let's not talk about the world's problems," he said. "I want to talk about you two. We have so much to catch up on. So many questions to ask each other."

"Would you like to see our house?" asked Aashi, her eyes brimming with excitement and pride.

Tara sighed. Did she not realize what a man with Bakul's means would think of their house? Aashi was eighteen and wise beyond her years, yet sometimes she behaved as if she were a child.

"I'd love to see it," he said politely.

As they went to exit Vikram's house Tara drew in a breath of surprise.

"Look Aashi," she said, pointing.

A plank of wood had been nailed to the wall above the door. On it sat all the gifts they'd made for Vikram over the years. They crowded the shelf, lovingly placed so each could be seen. There were dolls made from string sitting next to rocks with faces crudely scratched into them and flowers torn from the pages of books. Vikram had nailed in pegs above the shelf, from which hung mobiles and necklaces and strings with beads.

"He did love our gifts after all," whispered Aashi, her face beaming with delight.

"I think you just got the smile you've been chasing all these years," said Tara.

"What do you mean?" she asked.

"Well, if that shelf there isn't a smile, then I don't know what is."

"I like that. He's smiling at us. Just not with his mouth."

They stepped out into the sunshine.

"Thank you for letting us use your house," said Tara.

Vikram nodded at her in return. "Is everything alright?" he asked.

"It's better than alright."

"I'll wait until your brother is ready to leave," he said, looking up and down the street for any sign of trouble.

"Why don't you join us?"

He looked at her for a moment, his eyes filling with emotion she couldn't read. His feet remained firmly planted on the ground. She knew he'd be staying outside.

Aashi had already pulled back the curtain that formed their front door. Bakul stooped and stepped into their home.

Tara followed, anxious to see Bakul's face, willing it to be absent of the repulsion she feared it would contain. Instead, she saw him smile.

He lay down on the bamboo mat next to Aashi to stare at their house made from rainbows and sunshine and Tara watched them with so much love in her heart she felt it was possible she might fall down next to them and die.

"Do you like it?" asked Aashi.

"I love it. I'm so proud of you both. I'm so happy you're alive."

"Of course, we're alive," said Aashi.

He sat up on the mat and patted the space beside him for Tara to sit. His face turned serious.

"When I saw that photo, I was sure you'd be dead. I thought I'd lost my chance to find you. You were so...frail."

"The photo lies," said Aashi. "Tara is anything but frail. She's like a bull."

"A bull?" cried Tara, offended. "First I'm a chicken and now I'm a bull."

"A beautiful bull," she added. "You're strong and don't let anything get in your way. You charge ahead no matter what."

"I still don't know how you found us with only that photo as a clue," said Tara, diverting the subject away from farm animals. "Did Finn know where to find us?" She didn't like this thought. If he knew where to find them then why hadn't he come himself years ago?

"I took copies of the photo," he said, reaching for his backpack and pulling out a wad of paper. "I offered money to whoever could lead me to you. I started near the house we used to live in as children, but that got me nowhere. A few people suggested you looked more like the kind of girl who'd live in the village. So, I came here. I eventually found a man who led me to Vikram. I thought he was going to tell me either that you were dead or that you were his wife."

"His wife?" laughed Tara.

"Why not?" asked Bakul. "He's not so much older than you."

She shrugged. She'd never thought of him in that way. Her head had been so full of Finn for all these years that she'd never considered the possibility of giving her heart to anyone else.

"He's our protector," said Aashi.

Tara nodded. "Without him we'd never have survived. We owe him our lives."

"He did what I couldn't," said Bakul. "I'll take care of him."

"Are you going to take care of us?" asked Aashi, wide-eyed with expectation.

"Aashi!" hissed Tara. "Don't be rude."

"She's not rude," he said. "Of course, I'm going to take care of you. I didn't come here to find you only to leave you here. I want to take you back to London with me."

Saying goodbye to the village was more difficult than Tara had imagined. When she'd dreamed of packing her meager belongings and turning her back on it, she'd thought she'd be happy. Elated even. But she wasn't. She felt ill.

This village had been her home for twelve years. She'd spent more of her life here than anywhere else. She and Aashi had worked hard to build what they had. If only she could lift their house of sunshine from the ground and carry it on her back to London.

Bakul had seen no point in wasting time, telling them he'd organize a room for them at his hotel. He wanted to take them with him that afternoon. He didn't want to risk losing them again.

The two sisters packed up their house and ran their fingertips across the walls, burning its memory into their brains. They never wanted to forget it. No matter who they became or how much money they had, this house represented their essence—two girls who proved it was possible to make a rainbow out of a pile of trash.

Leaving their house was easy compared to leaving Vikram.

When they stepped outside their door and he saw them clutching their buckets filled with their belongings he knew they were going.

For a long time, they stood in silence.

"Thank—"

"Hush," he said, cutting Tara off. "No words. Please."

He placed a hand on each of her shoulders and brought his forehead down to press against her own. They spoke a thousand words in the silence. They were words of love and gratitude and overwhelming sadness. They were words that said goodbye.

He let go of her slowly and Aashi stepped toward him. Instead of the embrace Tara expected to see, she saw a smile.

Vikram was giving Aashi the widest smile in India. It was the smile she'd waited her whole life to receive. His crooked teeth flashed at her and his eyes sparkled with adoration.

Aashi beamed back at him.

"You have a lovely smile, Vikram," she said. "You really should use it more often."

"Don't expect it to happen again," he said.

"I love you." She threw her arms around his waist, tears pouring down her face. He returned her affection awkwardly, although Tara could tell he was pleased.

"I can't thank you enough," said Bakul, as Aashi broke away. He tucked a large wad of money into Vikram's hand.

"That's not necessary," said Vikram. "I didn't watch over them for money."

"Please, take it."

Vikram nodded and the two men shook hands.

Tara watched them quietly. Two men who knew what it was like to live in poverty. One of them plucked out by chance and given a new life. The other spending his life in a dump. This wasn't fair. Life was more complicated than any person could ever understand.

"If I can take you to London with me, I will," said Bakul. "But it'll be hard enough for me to get my sisters there. I'll get more money to you, I promise. You'll live comfortably in India. I'll never forget you and what you have done for us."

Bakul had been the best boy in the world and he'd grown to be the best man. Tara loved him fiercely. He'd look after Vikram. There was a chance yet for him to live an easier life. That thought softened her heart enough for her to take the steps she needed to walk away from Vikram, her house and the village itself.

Her new life was beginning. Perhaps the universe had forgiven her at last?

PART IV

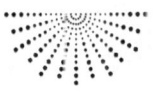

AASHI

CHAPTER TWELVE

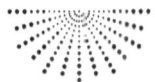

*a*shi was a fraud. She knew the world saw her as sunny and carefree, but deep inside her heart lurked a beast. She hated the beast and wanted to rip it from her chest and throw it in the fire.

The beast was what Tara referred to as her gift. It was a gift she didn't want. It haunted her dreams, pushed its way into her mind when she was awake and nibbled away at her happiness whenever it had the chance.

It wasn't always like this. When she was young the beast was her friend. In times of despair it would whisper in her ear telling her not to worry. Things would be okay. A prince was on his way to save her.

The beast gave her hope when everything else that surrounded her pointed to a life filled with misery. This hope kept her alive.

Tara did, too. Without her sister, she'd surely be dead. She'd protected her, fought for her and sheltered her since her earliest days. It was particularly honorable she did all this for someone who'd murdered their mother and left them orphans.

This was a weight Aashi carried with her. She'd killed their mother. Tara had said it wasn't her fault, but she knew it was. Their mother had been healthy until she'd fallen pregnant with her. She'd died so Aashi could be born, leaving Tara to spend her life as the carer rather than the one being cared for.

Yet still Tara loved her. And Aashi was grateful for her love, returning it with yet a deeper love. Her sister was her everything.

It was this love that caused her to turn on the beast. It happened the day she'd been rushed to hospital as a child. She'd been sick and Tara and Vikram had saved her life yet again. Her raging fever had caused her to see visions even more vivid than usual.

She'd seen Tara with her prince. Not Tara's prince. Aashi's prince. Her prince with hair of fire she'd dreamed of long before that day. He was the one the beast had whispered of in her ear. He was the one bound to her soul and she'd yearned for him since the day she'd been born, perhaps even in the days before she was born. He was her destiny— and it was a destiny that broke her heart.

For Tara believed he belonged to her and Aashi couldn't bear to tell her the hurtful truth. Instead, she tried to believe in a new destiny—one where her sister took her place at Finn's side. If she willed it to be true with every ounce of her being, then perhaps it was possible she could make it become real. After everything her sister had given her, she'd finally found a way to repay her.

Nothing would make her happier than seeing Tara in love —even if that meant sacrificing love for herself. She knew she'd never love another. Her soul had been woven together with Finn's and she felt the threads stretching between them now, strangely tightening the closer she drew to him.

Soon, they'd be in the same city. Soon, she'd be pushing

Tara into his arms when all she wanted to do was crawl into them herself.

She wriggled uncomfortably in her seat. The plane would be landing shortly. She was glad. It made her feel sick to be so far above the ground. How could something so heavy fly through the air?

Bakul had booked them onto a jet that was taking them from Mumbai to London in just under two hours. As the world's population had increased so had the need to reduce flight times in order to cater for the demand being placed on airlines. Less than a century ago, this flight would've taken almost nine hours. Meals would've been served as passengers and crew roamed about the cabin. As nice as that sounded, Aashi decided she'd prefer to be strapped into her seat, as she was now, if that meant getting out of this gravity defying contraption sooner.

The plane jolted violently, and she clutched Bakul's arm. He smiled at her.

"It's okay," he said. "Just a little turbulence."

"What's turbulence?" asked Tara, who sat on his other side.

"I don't actually know," he laughed. "But it makes the plane bump around. Don't be worried, Chicken."

She saw her sister relax. She trusted Bakul. If he told her it was okay, she believed it. Perhaps she was just happy to have someone else take charge for a change.

Aashi, on the other hand, wasn't sure she believed it. Surely, it wasn't normal for a plane to move so violently. It wasn't as if there were any potholes in the sky.

Still, it was nice to be moving away from their miserable life to one that would be happier.

They'd spent two months living in a hotel room and she'd loved it. She loved the clean sheets and soft pillows that made her feel like she was sleeping on a cloud. She loved the big bath that she filled with bubbles and soaked in until her fingers had turned to wrinkles, giving her a fright. She'd thought she was seriously ill and ran to Bakul's room wrapped in a towel, only for him to laugh and tell her not to worry. She loved the small fridge filled with temptations that Bakul had asked them not to touch. So, instead, she'd sat in front of it and stared into it until she could no longer resist and she'd sneak something out and gobble it up, certain the guilt made it taste even more delicious.

Bakul would bring them bags of food and the three of them would sit on the bed and eat until they felt their stomachs groan. Then he'd check the small fridge and shake his head at Aashi.

"Sorry," she'd say and he'd soften, knowing that she'd tried.

Most of all, she loved the changes she'd observed in Tara. Her sister slept deeply, no longer listening for noises in the night. Her eyes stopped darting around without the need to search for something of value to brighten their lives. Her bones stopped protruding from under her skin, replaced by soft curves that made her look like the young woman she was. And she smiled more often, which lit up her face making her look even more beautiful.

Aashi knew her sister wasn't what most people considered to be attractive. But to her, she was the most beautiful woman she'd ever seen. When she looked at Tara, she saw strength and love and kindness. There could be no more attractive features than those.

The girls had combed out each other's long hair and it now hung around their shoulders in waves the color of night. They found themselves constantly trailing their fingers through it enjoying the silky feel and delicate fragrance. The stench of the village seemed far behind them. Aashi wondered how her nose would react if she were to return to it now.

"What do you think Vikram's doing?" she'd ask Tara every night as they lay in their bed made from clouds.

"I expect he's eating samosas and wishing he smiled at you years ago."

Aashi liked this thought. She'd squeeze her eyes shut and beg the beast to tell her if it was true. The beast never replied. It didn't work like that. It only told her what it thought she should hear, not what she wanted to.

To pass the time, Bakul had brought them a small colorful box. He called it a web key. If they spoke into it, images would appear before them. It provided them with hours of fun. If they said the word "dog", thousands of pictures of dogs of all shapes and sizes would hover before them. If they reached out and touched one of the images, it would come to life and they'd sit there and laugh as they watched dogs jump through hoops, rollerblade down ramps or dance to songs they'd never heard.

They could use it to watch a never-ending stream of documentaries, movies and video clips. Aashi had seen television before through the windows of shops, but never in such an intimate setting. She found it unnerving at first. The people in the movies they watched seemed to be standing in the room with them. She had to resist the urge to reach out and touch them. She'd tried it and her hand had passed right though them.

Early on, Tara had held the web key to her lips asking it to teach them to speak English and they'd been presented with a series of lessons. Tara concentrated with impressive intensity, determined to learn the language of the man she loved.

Together, the girls repeated what they learned, trying out

new phrases on Bakul whenever he came to their room. He'd laugh, clap his hands and teach them yet another phrase.

Tara had surprised both her siblings with how quickly she began to pick up the language. Aashi wasn't sure if it was her determination alone or if she had some kind of special knack for languages. She spoke English almost like she'd spoken it before.

It came harder to Aashi. She felt like she was walking with bricks tied to her feet, while Tara was gliding on ice.

Their routine of sleeping, bathing, eating and learning English slowly grew tiresome. They were used to spending their days foraging, fetching water and more recently working at the samosa stall. In comparison this new life was too sedentary. Life felt too easy with the challenge for their survival taken out of their hands. They began to wish for the day Bakul would burst through the door waving their travel papers.

Eventually that day came and now Aashi found herself on this plane feeling less like herself than she ever had before.

For a start, she was clean. There wasn't a speck of dirt to be found on her body. And she was wearing clothes that fit her—clothes that had never been worn by anybody else. She doubted Bakul realized when he presented them to her exactly how much they meant. They were so fresh and soft. He'd even bought her underpants. Underpants! How good they felt. Her shoes on the other hand were going to take some getting used to. Her feet felt like they were being suffo-cated. She didn't trust the ground without being able to feel it beneath the bare soles of her feet.

It was more than just how she looked that made her feel different. She felt different on the inside. She was a person with a future to dream of and a family that extended beyond the skinny girl who was her sister, mother and best friend.

Bakul was also taking some getting used to. He was so

different to anyone she'd ever met. It wasn't easy to open her heart to anyone beyond Tara. Except Vikram, but he'd snuck his way in there so slowly she hadn't had time to notice. If only they could've brought him with them.

She glanced across at her sister. Her eyes were closed, a soft smile lay upon her lips. Aashi knew she was thinking of Finn. Imagining, perhaps, what it would be like to stand before him once more after all these years.

Please let him love her, Aashi begged the universe. *Please* let him see in her what she sees in him. She deserved to be happy.

Tara had asked Bakul if he knew if Finn was married. He'd looked at her, his eyebrows knitting together for the briefest of seconds. It was enough to reveal he understood she harbored hopes for him.

"Be careful," he'd said to her. "You don't know him. Don't make him into someone he may not be."

"So, is he married?" Tara had asked again, wanting to know the answer more than she cared about being judged for asking it.

Bakul had shaken his head. "No."

Aashi had already known that. She'd seen him so often in her dreams, lying alone in his bed. His heart was as free as it could be when it was tied to someone he had not yet met.

Which is why Aashi knew she needed to stay away from him. If he met her before he met Tara then her plan would fall apart. She had no doubt he'd feel the same connection as she did. It was too strong to be felt from only one side.

Finn would need to fall in love with Tara before she went near him. Maybe then his heart would be so distracted it would fail to notice her.

She knew her plan was weak, but she had to try. The thought of breaking Tara's heart by taking Finn for herself wasn't up for consideration. That was why she'd hung back when she thought Finn had come for them in the village, letting Tara get to him first. She'd pretended not to be able to keep up, begging Tara to wait, all the time slowing her pace. Tara knew Aashi was faster yet was so distracted she hadn't thought it strange she'd beaten her to Vikram's house by such a distance.

It wasn't until Aashi had known for certain the man inside Vikram's house wasn't Finn that she'd dared to enter.

She pushed him to the back of her mind and tried to focus on the life that lay ahead of her. What would it be like?

The web key had allowed them to tour London's streets, walking through them as if they were really there, yet still she found herself unable to imagine herself in this strange city of golden buildings and fields of grass.

Bakul's parents would be eagerly awaiting their arrival. Although Bakul had made their images appear before them during internet calls, it was always different meeting someone in person. The thought made her nervous. What would they think of her?

During their calls they'd smiled kindly at Aashi and Tara and spoken to them in their language. Bakul had taught them the dialect of Hindi that he'd spoken as a boy. It was almost as if he'd known they'd need to use it one day.

When their eyes had turned to Bakul they'd filled with such love and concern that it had made Aashi's heart bleed for reasons she didn't fully understand. It was clear they loved their son. She too could have had parents to love her like this, if Tara hadn't taken her away.

She didn't blame Tara. It was what she'd wanted, but now as an almost grown woman she wondered if it was fair for Tara to have allowed a four-year-old to make such a life changing choice. She wasn't sure she'd make the same decision again.

She looked across at her sister and felt ashamed to have

had such a thought. She knew things had turned out as they were meant to. She belonged by Tara's side. If she'd been taken to another family, she'd only have spent her life trying to find her way back— just like Bakul.

Her life hadn't been that bad, she told herself, knowing this was a lie. Her life had been a struggle since the day she'd been born. Except she'd chosen to live this struggle with a smile on her face, which often meant people failed to recognize she was struggling at all.

She'd lived a life without privacy. Not a door to close when she washed the dirt from her body, not a room of her own in which to change her clothes. Surrounded by people and vermin, stray cats and lice. Eyes on her when she ate, eyes on her when she slept, eyes on her when she emptied her bowels. Eyes. Everywhere eyes.

The only place they couldn't see was inside her mind. No-one knew what she was thinking, no-one knew what she was dreaming. Her smile was her disguise. A disguise so finely tuned that even Tara had failed to see when it was false. Her smile was the only way she knew to keep her thoughts private.

The only one who knew her thoughts was the beast. Did that count? Was the beast even real? Or was it just a clever invention of her mind so she could avoid having to accept that her gift was part of her? She liked to think of it as a separate being, but perhaps this was another lie she'd woven into her life.

"You have a beautiful gift," said Bakul. She jolted, her heart hammering. Had she spoken aloud? She turned to see he was talking to Tara, who'd taken out the sketchpad he'd given her when he'd discovered she liked to draw. Tara hadn't even known herself, having never owned a pencil or sheet of blank paper.

She'd found some in the hotel room and had immediately

picked them up. Aashi had giggled at the sight of her sister with a pencil in her hand.

"You can't write," she'd told her.

"I'm not writing," said Tara, who ran the pencil across the page in fine lines that soon began to take the shape of a face. Aashi knew whose face it was the moment she drew the square line of his jaw.

"How are you doing that?" asked Aashi in amazement.

Tara hadn't answered. It was like she was in a trance. That was the first of many drawings she sketched in the hotel room. Bakul had seen them and immediately bought the sketchpad for her.

Soon it was filled with faces. Mostly of Finn, but also of Bakul and Vikram and Aashi herself. Tara drew their mother and father and Aashi saw for the first time what they'd looked like. She wished she could remember them for herself the way Tara did.

"You know there's someone missing, don't you?" Aashi had said while flicking through the sketchpad one day.

"Who?" asked Tara.

"You!"

"Oh," she'd said, turning away. "I know what I look like."

"I don't think you do," said Aashi, taking her by the hand and leading her to the bathroom.

Tara pulled a face in the mirror. "I wish I looked like you."

"Like me?" said Aashi, astonished. "Why would you want to look like me?"

"Can't you see what I see?" said Tara, running her hand down her sister's hair. "People turn their heads to look at you in the street. You're beautiful."

"That's only because they want to feed me. Look how skinny I am! And short. My skin's too dark, my nose is too long and look at how big my eyes are. They look like two saucers balancing on my nose. You're the one who's beautiful."

Tara looked at herself for a moment, considering what Aashi had said. "I think your view of me is just as skewed as your view of yourself."

She shook her head. "Finn will agree with me," she said, her voice dropping to a hush as she tried to allay the fears she knew her sister had. "He'll see what I see. I know he will."

"I hope so." She'd turned away from the mirror and returned to her sketchpad, still refusing to draw her own face, almost as if putting it down on paper would be her acceptance of it.

As Bakul flicked through Tara's sketches now, Aashi wondered if he might ask her the same question. Why didn't she draw her own face?

The captain's voice floated through the speakers, informing them that they'd begun their descent into London.

Aashi tightened her already tight seatbelt, making sure the shoulder straps were pinning her torso to the back of the seat. If landing was half as frightening as take off had been then she was going to have to disappear deep inside herself in order to cope.

She closed her eyes only to find the beast waiting for her inside her mind.

"Soon," it whispered, the sound of its voice sweeping from one side of her brain to the other. "Soon."

She knew what the beast spoke of. Soon her path would cross with Finn's. Soon she'd meet him. Soon her eyes would look into his own as their souls connected.

"No!" she cried, her eyes springing open. Her soul wouldn't be connected to Finn's. Tara's would.

"Aashi. Are you all right?" Tara asked, leaning over Bakul, her face full of concern.

"Sorry. Yes, I'm fine," she said. "I fell asleep for a moment and forgot where I was, that's all." She pasted a smile to her face, making sure it reached her eyes.

Tara returned the smile and looked away. It was as easy as that. A simple rearrangement of the muscles in her face and her fears became invisible.

The plane lurched causing a similar reaction in Aashi's stomach. This time she didn't close her eyes. She stared at the back of the seat in front of her, knowing it would seem she was studying the image of a map that floated in the air. In truth, she saw nothing. The images were blurred to her unfocussed eyes. Instead of a map, she saw colors, dancing and swirling before her.

She was heading to her new life. It would be a life without Finn's love, but still she was determined it'd be a happy one. She'd have love of a different kind. She'd always have Tara's love. And Bakul's.

It was clear he had more affection for Tara than he did for her, but that was only because he'd known her better before they were separated. In time, he'd know her just as well. And Vikram. Would she be able to feel his love all the way from London? Of course, she would. After all, she'd been able to feel Finn's love from the same distance…

"Stop it," she said between gritted teeth. She couldn't think like that. These thoughts were dangerous. Why then, did they wash over her like a tsunami the moment she let her guard down?

"Are you sure you're all right?" asked Bakul, studying her face.

"Of course, I'm sure." She smiled at him like she had at Tara. "I'm just a nervous flyer."

He held her gaze for a few moments, his eyes filling with sadness. He didn't know her as well as Tara did, yet he wasn't buying her act. Shouldn't it be easier to fool a stranger?

"Aashi," he said, his voice low so Tara wouldn't hear over

the noise of the engine as the plane began to slow. "You must know I'm here for you. You're my sister, too. I wish you'd talk to me."

"Thanks. I'm fine, though. Really, I am." She smiled again, concentrating all her energy into making it convincing.

His face remained solemn. He reached for her hand and squeezed it gently.

"Tara sees in you what she needs to in order to survive," he said. "I see past that. I see you."

Aashi looked away, feeling this moment was too intense. Was that what it was? Was Tara unable to see her inner torment, as that would be enough to tip her over the edge? Had she needed to see her as happy so she could continue on each day with the strength to fight for their survival?

She glanced back at Bakul who was still staring at her with sadness in his eyes. He'd unmasked her. He'd been able to look past her smile and right into her soul.

She felt her world as she knew it begin to slip away. Images swirled inside her mind and her stomach clenched into a painful fist. She grabbed for the bag she'd spotted earlier in the seat pocket and heaved.

How would she live without the disguise that had kept her alive all these years? If Bakul had seen through it, then who else had? Could Vikram see the dark thoughts she harbored? Would Finn see them, too?

"We'll be on the ground soon," Tara said. "It's okay. Just hold on a little bit longer."

Aashi nodded. Still Tara was blind to what was happening. Was it fair of her to have fooled her like this for all these years after everything she'd done for her?

Bakul pressed a button in front of them and a bottle of water came rushing down a chute. He handed it to her and placed a comforting hand on her arm. She gulped down the water, washing away the acidic taste that burned the back of her throat, but unable to wash away the feeling that'd made her sick in the first place.

The plane touched down on the runway and the engines roared in protest, the sound rattling the scattered thoughts in Aashi's mind. It was time to put on her smile and greet Bakul's parents.

How could she wear her smile now knowing it was transparent? There were holes in its delicate fabric that others could see straight through.

They stood and waited for what felt like a lifetime for the passengers in front of them to begin to move.

"Feeling better?" Tara asked.

"A little. Yes."

"Can you believe we're in London?" She was glowing, obviously excited at the prospect of breathing the same air as the man she loved.

Aashi smiled at Tara then caught Bakul's gaze and gave him a look, urging him to keep her secret. Tara must never know that she'd had anything but a happy childhood. She couldn't have her feel she'd failed her when her life had been dedicated to seeing her thrive.

Bakul seemed to understand. He could've told her long before now. There was no reason for her to panic.

"Come on," Bakul said, as they followed him down the aisle and headed out to the jet bridge that connected the plane to the airport terminal.

Aashi watched her feet as she walked. Bakul had found her a pair of black ballet slippers that were so soft it almost felt as if her feet were bare. Almost.

She took a photograph in her mind of her feet stepping off the plane. She was on English soil now. India was far behind her. Her life in the village was starting to seem like a dream.

Or a nightmare.

They collected their bags and passed through a DNA scanner. Aashi gave a sigh of relief when the light flashed green, approving her entry.

They walked out to find Bakul's parents.

Aashi recognized them immediately. They were jumping up and down, waving their arms. The joy on their faces was overwhelming.

His father, Gerard, looked exactly like any other stereotypical middle-aged British man, with dark hair that was graying around his temples, a slim build hidden under his expensive jacket and some wire-framed glasses perched on top of his nose. Aashi hadn't seen anyone of Gerard's means wearing glasses before. They'd have a simple surgery to correct it. She wondered why he'd chosen not to.

Bakul's mother, Nikii, broke the mold of how a British woman was supposed to look. She was more like an Aryan gypsy, if such a thing existed. She had blonde hair that floated around her shoulders, pale blue eyes and wore a green skirt that hung from her slender hips, cascading to the floor like some kind of shimmering waterfall. Aashi was surprised at how beautiful she was. Her image transmitted via the internet hadn't done her justice.

That was the problem with technology. It did so much to make it feel like someone was standing before you, but unless you were actually in the same room it was impossible to feel their aura. That was what made Nikii so beautiful. It wasn't her sparkling eyes or the softness of her hair. It was her soul.

Nikii threw her arms around Bakul then pulled back, placing her hands on each of his cheeks, her pale skin contrasting with his dark face.

"Welcome home," she said, kissing him once on each cheek.

Gerard, was next, stiffly embracing Bakul and patting him roughly on the back. "Good to see you, son."

They then turned their attention on the girls. Tara was smiling warmly. Aashi twisted her mouth into the smile that had once taken her no effort at all to produce.

Nikii grabbed Tara first and hugged her tightly. Gerard extended his hand to Aashi and she shook it, thinking for a moment he was going to crush her fingers. He was like a giant next to her, yet his eyes were kind and she felt safe with him.

She opened her mouth to say something, only to find Nikii pulling her into her arms. She returned the embrace formally at first until the love and warmth radiating from this kind woman's soul penetrated the armor she'd built and she found herself burying her face in her shoulder and weeping.

"Hush," said Nikii, not letting her out of her arms. "You're safe now. No need to cry."

This only made her cry more and she hung onto Nikii like her existence depended on it. Other than the affection her mother had surely given her as a baby, this was the first time she'd found herself in a mother's arms. Tara had tried to be a mother to her, but she was still a child herself.

Could she dare to believe this woman who'd mothered her brother could also become a mother to her? And would she be able to return the warmth she was already pouring over her with warmth of her own?

Nikii loosened the embrace and cupped Aashi's face in her hands, as she'd done to Bakul. She looked deep into her eyes and words were spoken between them in a silent language of their souls.

Aashi had found the mother she'd been longing for all her life. Nikii had found her daughter.

The mask that Bakul had ripped from her face and thrown to the ground was no longer required. She knew with Nikii she could be her true self. There was no need for false smiles or the pushing back of tears. It was an enormous relief.

Did Tara feel it, too? She looked across at her sister to find her staring at her with an expression that looked strangely like jealousy. She let go of Nikii and reached for her sister.

"We made it," she said, her face as solemn as her heart.

"We made it," repeated Tara, curling her lips into a smile that had no hope of reaching her eyes.

It was as if they'd traded places. Aashi wondered if this was how it was to be from now on—Tara wrapping herself in false sunshine and Aashi fighting a hurricane that threatened to sweep her into the sky.

CHAPTER THIRTEEN

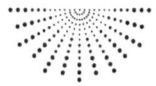

*A*ashi slept. Then she slept some more. She slept so much she lost track of days. Then the weeks began to slip through her fingers like sand. The more she tried to grab hold of time, the more it scattered around her. She had no idea how long she'd been in London.

Nikii and Gerard had set up their spare bedroom for her and Tara. Two single beds with pretty, white side tables had been placed on either side of the room. The ceiling had been painted bright yellow, raining down on them like sunshine. Yet this wasn't what drew the girls' attention. They stood in silence and stared at the wall behind their beds. A large rainbow stretched its length, painted in the same colors they'd used back in their home in the village.

"Bakul sent us a photo of your house," Nikii said when they first saw it. She was watching them anxiously to see if they liked it. "I thought this might make you feel more at home. Do you like it? We can always paint over it."

"It's wonderful," said Tara, stepping forward and running her fingers across the wall.

"What about you, Aashi? Do you like it?"

"No," she said. *Like* was not an adequate word for how the wall made her feel. "I love it."

"You scared me," Nikii laughed. "Don't do that."

"Who painted it?" asked Tara.

"I know you don't know us very well yet, but can you imagine my husband with a paintbrush in his hand?" Her eyes twinkled with mischief.

"You did this?" said Tara.

Nikii nodded. "I was so touched by the photos Bakul sent us. The inside of your house was like a pearl hidden inside an oyster. It moved me. I think that was the moment I knew I wanted you to live here as my daughters. Anybody capable of creating such beauty in a sea of hardship is a kindred spirit of mine."

"Thank you," said Tara hugging Nikii.

Aashi watched quietly, too afraid to step near Nikii in case she upset Tara. She felt overwhelmingly tired.

"Now, make yourselves at home," said Nikii. "This is your room. You live here now."

That was when Aashi had crawled between the soft sheets of her bed and she'd barely gotten up since. If it weren't for the need to eat or use the bathroom, she may never have gotten up again.

Each night she'd drag herself down the rickety staircase to the dinner table and sit politely listening to the chatter that filled the air. She answered questions when they were asked of her, but never asked a question herself, instead counting the minutes until she could return to the safety of her bed.

She knew everyone was worried about her. She'd wake up in the night to find Tara sitting on the edge of her bed staring at her. And in the day, it was Nikii or Bakul who'd find excuses to come and sit by her side. Only Gerard left her alone. She supposed he had no idea what to say to the strange Indian girl who'd appeared in his life. The language barrier didn't help either. Aashi's English was improving every day but was still fairly basic and Gerard didn't speak Hindi nearly as fluently as his wife.

The house wasn't large by British standards, but to Aashi it was a mansion. She found herself overwhelmed by the size of it. There were three bedrooms upstairs. Three whole bedrooms for one family. There was a bathroom between Bakul's room and theirs, and another inside Nikii and Gerard's bedroom. She never knew people had bathrooms inside their bedrooms. It was like living in a hotel.

Downstairs there was a kitchen, living room and what Bakul had referred to as a tiny backyard. Still, it was big enough to fit in at least a dozen houses like the one she'd grown up in.

As the population had boomed, London's property prices had soared. A house like this was worth a small fortune. Gerard was a successful stockbroker and could likely have afforded something even more extravagant, but Bakul had said his parents liked to live simply, getting more enjoyment from using their money to help others.

Aashi had heard Tara ask Bakul why he still lived at home now that he was a grown man and he'd said the thought to leave had never occurred to him. He'd already missed spending the first eight years of his life with his parents and he didn't intend to miss any more.

Aashi suspected there was more to it than that, having overheard him discussing his financial situation with his father. It seemed he'd spent his life savings looking after them in India and then getting them to London. He couldn't afford to move out of home. She added this to the growing list of sacrifices he'd made for his family. She owed him so much.

Before coming to look for them in India, Bakul had been

a teacher. He'd taken a year off without pay. Aashi felt guilty for keeping him from his students. They must be missing their teacher who was able to teach them so much more about life than how to read and write.

It took her some time to notice there was someone missing in her life. Someone who'd been with her always. Once she noticed, she was astounded it'd taken her so long.

The beast had gone.

Why now? Surely, more than ever now was the time for it to be hissing in her ear, telling her that Finn was close. Or was that the reason for its disappearance? Perhaps she didn't need her beast anymore.

In any case, she was too tired to figure it out. It was far easier to spend her days with her eyes closed than to lie awake trying to work out how to climb the mountain that seemed to have been placed in front of her.

One day when the house was quiet and she thought she was alone, Nikii came into her room.

"Shuffle over," she said, lying down next to her on the narrow bed.

Aashi was surprised but did as she was told.

"I'm worried about you. We all are," she said in Hindi. "Will you let me take you to a doctor?"

"Please, no. I'm fine, really I am. I just need some time to adjust."

"I think this is a little more than just some time to adjust. The girl I'm looking at now is not the girl Bakul described to me. Tara's sick with worry."

"I'm sorry," said Aashi.

"Why? Why would you be sorry?"

"For not being the girl you were expecting."

"Listen here, Aashi. You may not be the girl I was expecting, but you're still the girl I want. At first, we all thought you were just tired, but it's been two weeks now and you've barely said a word. You haven't even left the house. Bakul's been taking Tara all over London. Won't you let him take you, too?"

"Two weeks? Is that all?" She was sure it'd been longer. Could it really only have been two weeks? She'd lost her grip on the time.

"Yes, two weeks. What's going on in there?" She tapped Aashi gently on the forehead.

Aashi turned her head to look at Nikii. Could she trust her? Would speaking her thoughts aloud help to sort them out?

"I'm scared," she said.

"Oh, sweetheart." Nikii turned to her side and placed an arm over Aashi's waist. "I won't let anyone hurt you."

"You can't stop this hurt. It's a hurt that's already there." A wave of clarity washed over her. That was it. She was in mourning. Mourning a relationship that'd never had a chance to begin, let alone end. Her heart bled for Finn. Now that he was so close the ache was getting worse.

"Did someone hurt you in India?" Nikii asked.

"No, nothing like that. Vikram made sure we were safe."

"Are you missing him? Is that it? We're still trying to organize some papers to get him here. Bakul said he's no longer in the village. He bought himself a small apartment on the edge of the city. You can talk to him if you like?"

She nodded. "I do miss him."

"But that's not what's hurting you, is it?"

She shook her head, fighting back tears. "Can I ask you something, Nikii?"

"Anything."

"Why did you adopt Bakul? What made you choose him? I mean, do you think you could've loved another boy if you'd chosen him instead?"

If Nikii was surprised at her question, she didn't show it.

Aashi waited for her response. This was something she'd been wondering about. Maybe if she could begin to understand what it was that drew people together, then she'd have a small hope of figuring out how to be drawn to someone else.

"To be honest," said Nikii, "we went to the orphanage with the hopes of adopting a baby girl. I never imagined we'd walk out of there with an eight-year-old boy. But the moment I saw Bakul I knew I'd found my son. I can't explain it any better than that. He was sitting on a mat surrounded by other children, yet my eyes only saw him. He looked up at me and I just knew. It's exactly the way I felt at the airport when I saw you and Tara."

"So, you think it's possible when you meet someone who's destined to be important to you that you see that connection immediately?"

"I do. But I don't think everyone has that gift. It's only the people who know how to quieten their mind so they can listen to their heart. You have that ability. I saw it in you the first time you looked into my eyes."

"What about Gerard? When you were at the orphanage, did he see the same thing in Bakul as you?"

Nikii laughed. "Gosh no. He doesn't have a spiritual bone in his body. But he knows better than to argue with me when I have my heart set on something. He could see how I felt about Bakul and that was enough for him."

"What drew you to Gerard, if you're so different?" They seemed such an odd match.

"His arms."

"His arms?" Aashi smiled her first genuine smile since she'd arrived in London.

"I know it's hard to believe, but he had the most wonderful, strong arms when he was younger. I used to imagine myself being wrapped up in them and how safe that would make me feel. As I got to know him, I saw past the arms to his heart. He's a very kind and generous man."

"You didn't know straight away he was meant for you?"

"No, my mind was far too distracted by his biceps, I'm afraid. It took my heart a little while to catch up. Look, I know we're very different and people are curious about our relationship, but to me it's very simple. We complement each other. And although he doesn't understand my spiritual side, he doesn't mock me for it. Just as I don't mock him for spending half his life studying the stock market—or his fear of going blind if he lets a doctor touch his eyes."

"You're two imperfect halves to a perfect whole."

"Exactly. Finally, someone gets it."

They lay in silence for a few moments.

"Has someone stolen your heart, Aashi? Did you leave him behind in India?"

Aashi hesitated. All she had to do was nod her head and Nikii would stop probing for a reason behind her depression. This was a simple explanation that would excuse all her strange behavior. But it was also a lie.

"Yes and no," she said, unwilling to forge a relationship with Nikii built on deceit. "It's very complicated. It does have a lot to do with my heart, but there's more to it. I feel like I've been a liar my whole life."

"How so?"

"The girl that Bakul described to you isn't me. *This* is me. I've spent my whole life with a smile on my face that wasn't real. Tara worked so hard to keep me alive that it felt ungrateful to show her how I really felt. It was exhausting, but if Tara knew how unhappy I was, she'd have fallen apart. Then we'd both have been ruined. When I met you all of that changed."

"Me?" She seemed surprised.

"Yes, you. I've never had a mother and even though I'm

probably too old to have one now, it feels so good. Like I don't have to pretend anymore. And now Tara has people around her who love her, I'm not her whole world anymore. Finally, I feel like I'm allowed to fall apart without taking her down with me. I can't explain it any better than that."

"Oh, Aashi. I can't even begin to imagine what you've been through, but you have it wrong. You *are* Tara's whole world. Why do you think Bakul's been dragging her all over town? He's trying to cheer her up. She's worried about you. You must get out of this bed and try again. If not for you, then for her."

A sick feeling lodged in Aashi's stomach. She'd been so wrapped up in her own feelings, she really hadn't given Tara's much thought. Nikii was right. She had to get on with life.

"Has she met Finn yet?" Aashi asked.

"Not yet. She wants to wait until you're well enough to go with her."

"But why? That's ridiculous. She's waited so long already. She doesn't need me there with her."

"Try telling her that. I guess she's so used to having you by her side she can't imagine doing something so important without you."

Aashi sat up in bed. This was a disaster. Tara had to meet Finn without her. It wasn't possible for her to go with her.

"Nikii, I need you to do something for me. *Please.* And you can't tell Tara."

"What is it?"

"Take Tara to Finn and find an excuse for me not to go. Please. Make sure she meets him. She loves him. He must love her. Do it as soon as possible, I beg you. If you do this for me, then I promise to get out of this bed and try, just like you asked me to."

"You don't want to meet Finn yourself?"

Aashi shook her head. The tears that'd been threatening to spill down her cheeks earlier, made their escape. "I can't," she said.

"Why can't you? Come now, I'm sure you'll like him."

She almost laughed. Not liking him was never going to be her issue.

"Please, Nikii. Don't make me say it. She must meet him without me. They must fall in love. Keep me away from him."

Nikii sat up beside her and pulled her into her arms.

"I understand," she whispered. "My poor darling girl, I understand."

When Tara and Bakul returned to the house, Aashi was sitting with Nikii in the living room sipping a cup of tea.

Tara's face brightened immediately to see her out of bed.

"Are you feeling better?" she asked.

"A lot better." She did. The chat with Nikii had been like a tonic.

"She's really turned a corner," said Nikii patting her on the knee.

"Welcome back, little sister," said Bakul, stooping to kiss her on the forehead. "We missed you, didn't we, Chicken?" He turned to look at Tara, who was nodding in agreement.

"You take my place here, Bakul," said Nikii. "Tara and I have some secret women's business to attend to."

"Really?" said Tara, looking surprised.

Nikii took her by the hand and led her upstairs.

"Thanks for looking after Tara," Aashi said to Bakul as he sat beside her on the sofa.

"Always. I'd like to look after you, too, if you'd let me."

"I'm sorry for the way I've been behaving."

"You don't need to apologize. Apparently when I first

arrived in London, I didn't talk for a month. It's not easy what you've gone through. Sometimes things can catch up with you when you least expect it."

She nodded. He was partly right. There was no need to fill him in on the rest.

"How did you learn to speak English so well?" she asked. She'd heard him talking to his parents and had become fascinated with how easily the words rolled off his tongue.

"The same way they learnt to speak Hindi. Practice. We had a rule here when I was young. On weekdays we all spoke English and on the weekends we spoke Hindi. Although, as you've noticed, my mother speaks it a lot better than my father."

"I'm surprised they wanted to learn your language."

"You're surprised? Really? Have you met my mother? She'd learn to sleep standing on her head if she thought it'd help someone."

Aashi laughed at this image.

"Mum and Dad have always encouraged me to celebrate where I came from. They believe it's an important part of my journey. I'm very lucky. Some adoptive parents try to make their children's former lives disappear."

"Well, I'm very glad you taught them Hindi. It's certainly made it easier for us."

"Have you heard Tara speak English lately?" he asked. "She's amazing. I think she knows words I don't even know."

"Really?" She was surprised.

"Well, no. I was exaggerating. But really, she's very good. I'm impressed. We have to teach you next."

"I'll get there." She knew she would. The jumble of words was already starting to make sense. She wasn't able to understand every detail of conversations she'd listened to between Bakul and his parents, but she could understand enough to gather what topic they were discussing.

Nikii and Tara came back down the stairs. Bakul whistled at them. Nikii had combed Tara's hair and added a touch of gloss to her lips. She was wearing jeans and a pretty, pink shirt. It was the perfect color for her.

"Are you two right here for a little while?" asked Nikii. "I'm taking Tara out."

"Where to?" asked Bakul.

"She won't tell me," said Tara, grinning.

Aashi knew where and her heart sang with gratitude for Nikii. Perhaps once Finn belonged to Tara, she'd be able to push him from her every thought.As Nikii ushered Tara out the front door she turned to look at Aashi, raising her eyebrows for a moment. This was her chance to change her mind. To stop her sister from meeting the man they both dreamed of. To stand up and fight for him before it was too late.

"Thank you," mouthed Aashi.

He was Tara's now. The huge debt she owed her sister felt square for the first time in her life.

Nikii closed the front door behind them and they were gone.

"What was that all about?" asked Bakul. "And don't tell me you don't know."

"Love. It was about love."

And that was all she'd say, no matter how hard Bakul pressed.

An hour later, Nikii returned.

Aashi was sitting at the kitchen table watching Bakul prepare dinner. Gerard had returned home from work and was upstairs taking a shower.

Bakul opened the fridge and stood there for a moment, his eyes searching for something.

It didn't matter how many times Aashi looked in the fridge or the pantry, each time she stood frozen in fascination. There was so much food. Enough to have something to eat every single time you felt hungry.

Bakul had told her how this life of privilege had come with a high cost for first world countries. People were literally eating themselves into the grave. Obesity had become so epidemic that governments were forced to pour money into finding a cure, eventually stumbling across a rare herb that when taken in high enough doses would strip the fat from your bones. The herb had quickly become anything but rare and was now found growing in pots in almost every kitchen across the world.

Obesity became a thing of the past, but this opened up a new and more serious problem. Malnutrition. Now that people didn't need to worry about what foods they ate, they were far more likely to reach for a tub of ice-cream than a bowl of spinach. Multi-vitamin tablet sales had soared.

Aashi had listened to this story with horror. To think that while so many people in the world were starving, there were others whose biggest problem was that they had too much food to eat.

She'd noticed her waistline expanding since coming to England. How long would it be before she found herself growing strange herbs in pots? Never, she hoped.

"Where did you take Tara?" asked Bakul as Nikii threw her handbag on the floor and sat at the table next to Aashi.

"To see Finn."

They spoke in Hindi for Aashi's benefit.

"Finn?"

For a moment Aashi thought Bakul was going to drop the block of butter he was holding.

"It was about time she met him."

"But I was going to take her. When Aashi—"

"How long did you expect her to wait, Bakul?"

"I don't know. I just though … "

"What happened?" asked Aashi. This conversation was going in circles. She needed Nikii to get to the point.

"Well, he was pretty shocked at first. He opened his front door and looked at me, no doubt wondering who I was. Then his eyes shifted to Tara and the recognition slid across his face like a sunrise."

Aashi pushed down the sick feeling in her stomach. This is what she'd wanted. Why then was hearing it so difficult?

"And then?" said Bakul.

Nikii glanced at Aashi before continuing. "He threw his arms around her and they stood there like that for what felt like a week. It was very emotional. Aashi, are you okay?"

Aashi blinked and realized her face was betraying her feelings.

"I'm great," said Aashi. "That's terrific. Tara must be so happy."

"Where is she now?" asked Bakul glancing at the front door.

"I left her there."

"You left her? What do you mean, you left her?" Bakul looked furious. "How will she get home?"

"Calm down, Bakul. You're talking about a grown woman who raised herself from the age of nine—and her sister. I think she can find her own way a few miles from home. They didn't need me there. They didn't *want* me there."

Bakul put the butter on the table and took a seat.

"Do you think he loves her?" he asked.

"He just met her," said Nikii.

"No, he didn't. He met her a long time ago. I'm not sure

what exactly happened, but I know how much it affected Tara. She loves him. I see it in her eyes when she speaks of him. Do you think he feels the same?"

Nikii glanced at Aashi again, seeming reluctant to express her true feelings.

"It's okay," said Aashi. "This is what I want. Tara deserves to be loved."

"*Everyone* deserves to be loved," said Nikii, looking her directly in the eye.

Bakul seemed oblivious to the conversation that was happening underneath the one he thought was going on.

"If he hurts her, I'll kill him," he said.

"Bakul! Don't talk like that. Just because…"

"Just because what, Mum?"

"Nothing."

"Just because I've never been in love, is that it? Maybe I have been in love and you just didn't see it."

"I'm sorry, Bakul. Don't be upset with me."

He shrugged. "I'm worried about her, that's all. It's taken me so long to find her. I can't lose her again."

"Finn's a good man. You won't lose her again. Now, can you do me a favor and go upstairs to tell your father dinner will be ready in half an hour?"

"But I'm cooking dinner."

"No, you're not. Aashi's cooking tonight."

"Me?" she said, astonished. She'd never cooked a meal in her life.

"Yes, you. It'll distract you while you wait for Tara."

Bakul smiled. "I'll leave you to it."

"What did he look like?" Aashi asked when Bakul had gone.

"He looks like his photo," said Nikii. "Now, get up, you lazy lump. I'm teaching you how to make risotto."

Aashi stood. It was going to take a lot more than risotto to make her forget about Tara and Finn and what was possibly happening between them right now.

CHAPTER FOURTEEN

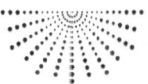

*B*y the time Tara got home it was late. Gerard had convinced Nikii and Bakul not to wait up. He didn't bother to try to convince Aashi. It was obvious to everyone she wouldn't be getting any sleep until she laid eyes on her sister.

She sat on the sofa with a blanket tucked over her and waited. It was cold in London—colder than she'd ever experienced. It would be very difficult to survive in a home made from cardboard in these conditions, yet she'd seen people doing just that as they'd driven from the airport to the house.

She heard a key in the front door and Tara's silhouette filled the doorframe.

Aashi switched on the table lamp causing Tara to jump.

"What are you doing up?" she asked.

"I wanted to hear how you went. Besides, I've had enough sleep lately to last me for a while."

Tara came and sat by her. Even in the dim light, there was no mistaking the expression on her face. She was glowing. Aashi thought she could probably turn the lamp off and Tara would light the room all by herself.

"You look happy," said Aashi, trying her best to look pleased.

She nodded. "I am. Oh, Aashi, he's wonderful. Even kinder and more handsome than I remembered."

"Nikii said he recognized you straight away."

"Yes. He said it was my eyes. He'd looked into them in my photo so many times he'd know me anywhere."

"What did you do? Did he take you out?"

"No, we sat in his living room and talked."

"In English?"

"Of course."

"So, he felt the connection, too?"

"Yes. He said he's been unable to figure out why I had such a big impact on him. There was just something about me. He felt like he'd met me before, even though that's impossible."

"Tara. That's wonderful." Was it? Was it really wonderful? Of course, it was. The fact that it was making her stomach lurch with envy was irrelevant. This was exactly what she'd been hoping for. Tara had made a real connection with Finn.

"I told him I'd bring you with me tomorrow to meet him," said Tara.

"No!" She practically shouted the word.

"Why? You don't want to meet him?"

"I do. It's just … it's just that … I'm still not feeling up to it. I only just got out of bed. Please, don't rush me. Give me a little more time before pushing me out the door."

"Come on. Please. For me? I really want you to meet him. Maybe I can ask him to come here? I'm sure Gerard and Nikii won't mind."

"Please, Tara. No. I'm not up to seeing anyone. Really, not yet."

Tara looked at her, puzzled. "Okay. He'll be disappointed though."

"He will not. You're the one he wants to see, not me. He's probably already forgotten you said you'd bring me." This wasn't true and she knew it. Finn may not know why he was drawn to Tara yet, but she was certain it was because the universe was leading him to her. She needed to give Tara more time with him. It was the only chance she had for him to fall in love with Tara instead of her.

"Did you kiss him?" she asked, feeling sick at the possible answer, but not able to help herself.

"Aashi! No, of course not. We only just met again. There's no rush."

"There is a rush! You've wasted enough time already. Don't waste any more. Find the right moment tomorrow and kiss him. Don't wait."

"Are you feeling all right? This doesn't sound like you. What's going on?"

"Nothing's going on. I just want to see you happy. You deserve it."

Tara didn't look convinced.

Aashi faked a yawn. "Maybe sleep's a good idea after all. I'm heading upstairs. You coming?"

"Sure."

"I know you'll be having sweet dreams tonight." She also knew she'd be having nightmares. Her plan of ensuring Tara and Finn fell in love had seemed like such a good one when she'd first thought of it. The reality of it was something quite different. She was going to need all her strength to follow through with this.

The pull she was feeling towards Finn was growing stronger each day.

"I love you," she whispered, just before she fell asleep.

"I love you, too," said Tara, unaware that Aashi hadn't been talking to her.

Aashi woke the next morning to the sound of laughter floating up the stairs. She heard Tara's voice and was disappointed. She was hoping she'd have left for Finn's house by now. It would've been nice to avoid seeing her this morning. She didn't like the idea of having to wave her goodbye as she set off to visit the man that she herself had dreamed of all night.

Maybe she could pretend to stay asleep? No. She'd promised Nikii she was going to try. Nikii had upheld her side of the bargain, she couldn't let her down.

She got up and went to the bathroom to splash some water on her face. She was about to head downstairs in her pajamas but hesitated when she heard Gerard's voice. She still felt shy around him.

The jeans and tee-shirt she'd worn the day before were lying folded on the foot of her bed, so she quickly changed into them and went downstairs.

"Good afternoon," said Gerard as she entered the kitchen.

"Is it that late?" she said. "I thought—"

Her heart skipped a beat. There was someone else at the table. Someone who wasn't supposed to be here.

He stood and turned to face her, running a hand nervously through his red hair.

"Aashi, this is Finn," said Tara, standing beside him as she placed a hand on his arm.

Aashi remained frozen, not in terror like she'd expected she would, but in awe of the waves of love that washed over her soul. He locked his eyes on her and she knew the game was over. Tara had no chance of winning this man's heart.

It beat only for her.

He reached out his hand for her to shake. She slipped her hand in his and immediately the world turned black.

She was unaware of collapsing to the kitchen floor. She was unaware of Finn lifting her gently in his arms and carrying her to the sofa. She was unaware of Tara running from the room to expel the contents of her stomach.

But she *was* aware of her soul pulsing from her body as it wrapped itself around Finn's in a slow dance that would last until the end of time.

When Aashi woke it was to the sound of tension. She'd never known tension to have a sound before, but there it was swirling in the air like a storm.

Nikii was beside her, gently rubbing her back. Tara was sitting in a chair with her arms wrapped around herself, staring at the floor. Bakul and Gerard seemed to have disappeared.

Finn had also vanished. The room felt empty without him.

"Aashi, are you okay?" said Nikii, placing her hand on her forehead. "I was about to call an ambulance."

"I'm fine. Sorry. I don't know..." She did know, of course. She knew exactly what happened. The emotion of meeting Finn had been too much.

"Well, don't stand up for a few moments," said Nikii. "Just in case."

"Tara, are you all right?" asked Aashi, trying to get her to look her in the eyes. Her gaze remained glued to the carpet.

"Tara? Please look at me. Are you all right?"

"What do you care?" she hissed, bringing her eyes to meet Aashi's.

"Don't be like that," said Nikii. "It's not her fault."

"Everything's her fault. Don't you get it? My whole life's been her fault. From the day she was born my life's been a misery. First she killed our mother and now she's killing me." Every detail in her face burned with hatred.

Aashi shrank back into the sofa. *This* was what she hadn't wanted. *This* was what she'd been trying to avoid. Tara had only ever looked upon her with love. Her world would fall apart if this was how she chose to look upon her now.

She got up from the sofa and crouched on the floor in front of Tara.

"Please, Tara. I didn't know he was here. I haven't done anything. I'll stay away from him. He's yours. He's yours."

"He's not mine. I was just a conduit to bring him to you. And isn't that every girl's dream—to be a conduit. How could you do this to me?"

"Tara," said Nikii. "Be fair. She tried to keep away. She wanted him to fall in love with you. That's how much she loves you. Don't punish her for that."

"That's right," said Tara. "Take her side. Everyone else always does."

"That's not true," said Aashi, feeling the need to defend herself. The force of Tara's venom was too harsh. She'd tried her best to protect her. All her actions had been for Tara's benefit.

"Of course, it's true. Everyone loves you more," said Tara.

"That's not true. Look at Vikram. I may as well have been made from glass when I stood by your side. And Bakul. I don't even come close to being as connected to him as you are. Same with Gerard. He's barely said two words to me, and I hear you two talking like old friends all the time."

"I notice you didn't mention Nikii in that list."

"Tara, enough," said Nikii. "Don't bring me into this. I think you girls need some time to think before you talk about this. You're getting nowhere right now."

"Good idea," said Tara, standing up and walking out the front door.

"Bakul," called Nikii.

He appeared moments later, having clearly been hovering nearby.

"Follow her. Don't let her be by herself."

Bakul nodded and disappeared out the door.

"Nikii, what just happened? I feel like I closed my eyes for a moment and when I opened them again my whole world had changed."

"Oh, my sweet girl. Your whole world did change. Every one of us in the room could feel what passed between you and Finn when you stood before each other. Even Gerard noticed it and that's saying something."

"Where did he go?"

"After you blacked out Tara got very upset. She was inconsolable. And Finn was sitting beside you on the sofa holding onto your hand like he was afraid you were going to run from the house and never come back. The sight of you two on the sofa like that was tearing Tara apart, so I asked Gerard to walk Finn home. I wanted to give you girls a chance to talk—without the man you both love standing before you. Gerard had to practically drag him from the house."

"What am I going to do, Nikii? Maybe I should run away and never come back."

"Don't talk rubbish."

"It's not rubbish. Tara hates me. You saw the way she was looking at me. You heard what she said. She's never treated me like that. I want to go back to India. It's the only choice I have."

"You can't go back to India. That's nonsense, Aashi."

"I can live with Vikram. He'll take care of me. I know he will. Then I never have to see Tara look at me like that ever again."

"I think it's about time you met a friend of mine," said

Nikii. "If you're determined to go away, then please go and see my friend."

"Thank you, but I don't want to be with a friend of yours. I want to be with the only friend I've ever had besides Tara. I want to be with Vikram."

"And how will you get back there? I won't give you the money for the flight. I will, however, give you the money for a train that will take you to my friend."

Aashi scowled. Nikii was backing her into a corner. Who was this friend she was so determined she should meet? Whoever she was, she didn't seem to have much choice. If she had any hope for Tara to love her again then she had to get away. Far away.

"Does she speak Hindi?"

"She speaks every language in the world."

Aashi looked at her, puzzled. Nobody could speak every language in the world.

"Do you trust me, Aashi?"

"Of course."

"Then go to her. It's the right thing to do. I can feel it. If it's meant to be with Finn then he'll be here when you return."

"Okay," she said. It wasn't Finn she was worried about. She knew he'd be there. He'd *always* be here waiting for her. It was Tara she was worried about. "But I leave now."

"Now?" Nikii seemed surprised.

"Now."

It was a quiet walk to the train station. Not the streets they passed through—they were as frantic and crowded as always —but a quiet hung in the air around them.

Aashi was too afraid to speak in case Nikii asked her

more about Finn. Nikii seemed reluctant to speak in case Aashi asked again about this mysterious friend of hers.

"Things will work out," Nikii eventually said. "Things always have a way of working themselves out."

"Always?" Aashi thought of people aboard planes that'd fallen from the sky or those who'd been swept up in tsunamis. Had things worked themselves out for them?

"Always," said Nikii. "If not in this lifetime, then in the next."

"Do you believe that?" She wasn't sure how she felt about that. On one hand she liked to think that she'd have another chance at being born into a happier life, but it also made her wonder about what evil she must've done in her previous life to have been given the one she was currently living.

They walked up to a machine and Nikii pressed some buttons. A ticket popped out of a small slot and she handed it to Aashi.

"Aren't you coming with me?" said Aashi, her pulse rising. How would an illiterate girl from India find her way across this city?

"Take a look at the ticket," said Nikii.

Aashi looked down. On the ticket was a map of the train network, each station labelled with its name. It looked more like a bird's nest. Just a bunch of scribbly dots and lines crossing over each other in a tangled mess. Once again, she wished she could read.

"Do you see that flashing yellow dot?" asked Nikii.

Aashi nodded. "Yes."

"That's where you are now. And do you see that green dot?

She looked for a moment and nodded.

"Great. That's where you're going. Just stay on the train until the yellow dot reaches the green dot."

"Then what do I do?"

"You get off the train, of course."

"I mean after that. How will I find your friend?"

"You'll find her. Don't worry. Either that or she'll find you."

"Is she expecting me?"

Nikii laughed. "Nothing happens that she doesn't expect. Don't worry so much."

"And you'll look after Tara?" If it weren't for Tara, she'd be begging Nikii to get on the train with her. But then again, if it weren't for Tara, she wouldn't need to get on the train at all.

"Tara will be fine. She just needs a little time."

Aashi clutched the bag she'd quickly packed with her belongings. It was a small bag, yet still twice as big as the one she'd carried with her from India. Nikii had made sure she had everything she might need.

"How will I find my way back?" she asked.

"That's the easy part. It's always easy to find your way home."

Aashi scowled. Nikii was being very frustrating with these vague answers.

"My friend knows how to contact me," said Nikii, noticing her concern. "I wouldn't leave you stranded. Now, you'd better get going."

Nikii pulled her into a hug, kissing her on the top of her head.

"Good luck."

"Thanks," said Aashi, feeling she was going to need all the luck the world had to offer.

Nikii guided her to the correct platform, squeezed her on the arm and walked away. Aashi was a little surprised. She thought she'd have waited with her. She seemed to have more confidence in Aashi's abilities than she did herself.

The crowd on the platform began to build and soon she

realized why Nikii hadn't waited. It would be impossible to walk against the flow of all these people once they started to make their way onto the train.

She felt wind on her face and a train came rushing down the tunnel, arriving smoothly at the platform. The doors on the other side of the train opened and a stream of people exited onto another platform. The crowd she stood in moved and she was swept onto the carriage.

No sooner as the doors had closed behind them, the train took off at a speed so great, she thought she'd fall over. The only thing holding her up was the crowd of people she was jammed in. Was this how London was coping with its population boom? Super-fast trains zooming the population all over the city in record times?

Get them in. Move them on. Get them out. Next please!

It was mind-boggling.

Aashi wriggled in her spot, wanting to bring her hand closer to her face so she could see the ticket Nikii had given her. The man next to her shot her a nasty look.

She ignored him and twisted to the right, opening up an empty pocket of air in which she could draw her hand upwards. Her fingers shook, so great was her fear of dropping the ticket. Nikii's directions had already been so confusing. If she lost this ticket, she'd need a miracle to find her way.

She saw the yellow dot and sighed to notice it was moving at an impossibly slow pace in its quest towards the mysterious green dot. At this rate she was going to be jammed on this train for hours.

They arrived at the next station and Aashi had to fight against the crowd as they pushed towards the exit doors. This struggle was only the first of dozens she had to make before the carriage eventually started to empty out.

The stop she wanted was close to the end of the train line

and by the time the green dot began to draw close, there were only a handful of people left. Finally, she felt like she could breathe.

This brought about a new problem. Once she'd stopped fighting for her personal space, her mind was left open for thoughts to start slipping in. Thoughts about Tara. Thoughts about Finn. Thoughts about not finding Nikii's friend and having to live her life on the cold streets of London.

What was Finn doing now? Had Tara returned to the house? Perhaps she'd gone to talk to him and he'd apologized for his actions after he'd realized he did in fact love her. What he'd felt for Aashi had just been a passing whim.

It was no passing whim and she knew it. He loved her and it'd filled him with confusion. He'd looked into her eyes and known he'd never love another, just as she had when she'd first seen him in her dreams.

What was it between them that caused such a reaction? Wasn't love meant to grow like a flower being nurtured in the soil? Wasn't that how Nikii had described her feelings for Gerard? It was a love that had grown over time. He hadn't knocked her over the moment he first looked in her eyes, and they were happy together.

She didn't understand it. It was like the love between her and Finn had blossomed in a time long before she could remember. Was this possible? Perhaps past lives were a more real possibility than she'd considered.

Her head began to ache from the weight of the implications of her love for Finn. It was a love that was going to cost her the close relationship she had with Tara. Of all the things to come between them, she'd never imagined it'd be love that would tear them apart.

She decided she preferred the train when it was full and her mind was distracted. Thinking didn't do her any good.

The yellow dot finally slid beneath the green one and flashed red. The train doors opened and she quickly stepped out onto the platform, afraid she'd miss her chance and never find her way back.

It was getting dark and a cold breeze was sweeping its way down the platform, scattering leaves and rubbish in its path.

She pulled her coat around her. Nikii had placed it around her shoulders before she'd left her. It'd been hot and bothersome during the journey, but she was grateful for it now. Who knew how long she'd be out there in the cold before she found the woman she was looking for. She didn't even know her name to ask a passerby.

She left the platform and found herself walking through a dimly lit tunnel. She clutched her bag tightly, fearing who else might be in the tunnel. If this were India, she'd be robbed in seconds. Or worse.

She glanced up at the security cameras. Were they protection enough? Would they stop her being mugged or murdered, or simply help the police to catch her attacker? It didn't seem much of a consolation to know her attacker would be caught. She'd rather not be attacked at all.

A dark figure appeared at the end of the tunnel. She hesitated. Should she walk on or turn back? Were all dark figures ominous? Surely, some dark figures were made from innocent civilians making their way home. She walked on.

As she drew closer, she saw it was a woman wrapped in a long cloak. Her dark hair was wild, flying around her face in such a manner it appeared to be creating the wind and not merely being disturbed by it.

She wasn't young, yet she was far from old, her skin still taut, despite the creases that lined the corners of her eyes.

Aashi knew she shouldn't stare, but her eyes were drawn

to this woman. And she was scrutinizing Aashi with the same fascinated look dancing in her eyes.

Years of having to protect herself from danger drove her feet forward. She went to pass the woman, dropping her gaze to the ground.

"Do you seek the truth?" the woman said as she passed.

The fact she'd spoken to her in Hindi had gone unnoticed, so distracted was Aashi by her fear.

She pressed on, breathing a heavy sigh when she passed safely.

Pain shot down her arm as a set of bony fingers took hold of her.

"Vikram!" she screamed, out of habit. This was the name she'd called all her life when she was in danger—only he wasn't here to help her now. Nobody was here. Was this her punishment for what she'd done to Tara? Was this how the universe had decided to deal with her?

"Do you seek the truth?" the woman said smiling, still holding firm to her arm. Her voice was kind. It had a smile in it. It didn't seem the voice of anyone who meant her harm. Yet the grip on her arm was anything but friendly.

"Please let go of me," she begged.

"Then you'll run away."

Aashi shook her head, knowing the minute she was released, she'd run.

"Nikii sent you," said the woman.

"*You* are her friend?" Aashi was astonished. This strange woman couldn't possibly be Nikii's friend. Nikii wouldn't send her to stay with someone like this, would she? It didn't make sense.

The woman withdrew her hand, sensing she'd no longer run.

Aashi rubbed her arm. It was going to bruise, yet that was the least of her concerns.

"Everyone is my friend," said the woman. "You included. Now, it's time for introductions. You are Aashi, yes?"

Aashi nodded. "Who are you?"

"I am the Truthseeker."

"The Truthseeker?"

"Come," she said. "We have so much to talk about."

CHAPTER FIFTEEN

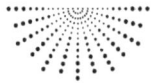

*A*ashi was relieved to discover that despite the Truthseeker's most unusual greeting, her house was relatively ordinary. It was a cream brick bungalow with a small front garden of tangled vines and weeds. Gardening was clearly not her forte.

The Truthseeker held the front door open and she reluctantly stepped inside. She reminded herself that she had nothing to lose. She'd already lost everything. There was nothing else this woman could take from her—other than her life and what value did that have without Tara or Finn in it?

The house was too dimly lit for her to get a good sense of its layout. So far it appeared to look as ordinary on the inside as it did on the outside.

"Do you mind if I call Nikii to let her know I'm okay?" asked Aashi, desperate to talk to her so she could ask why she'd sent her to such a strange woman's house.

"I don't have a phone. Or the internet." She closed the front door and indicated towards a room on Aashi's left.

"Then how did Nikii get in touch with you?"

She ignored this question, instead ushering her into the room she'd been pointing at.

Aashi blinked in surprise when she stepped inside. It was a small room, lit by dozens of candles that had been placed in a circle around two worn armchairs that sat facing each other. There was no other furniture in the room and the walls were bare.

The sight of this strange room made her hesitate. It looked like the Truthseeker was about to conduct some kind of strange ritual.

What kind of a name was *Truthseeker* anyway? It seemed fairly odd to refer to yourself by a title rather than a name. At least it was a positive title and not *Deathbringer* or *Miseryreaper*. It could be worse. Besides, Nikii trusted her and she trusted Nikii so it would all be all right.

"Take a seat," said the Truthseeker.

She put her bag down by the door and carefully stepped over the candles so as not to catch fire.

It was cold. Colder inside than it had been outside. She wrapped her coat around herself a little more tightly and sat. The chair was softer than it looked and she wondered how many other people had sat there before her and what it was that had led them to seek counsel from a woman like this.

The Truthseeker sat opposite her and closed her eyes.

Aashi wondered if she was meant to do the same but decided against it. Instead, she took the opportunity to freely stare at this woman.

She was older than she'd first thought. Fifty maybe? It was hard to tell. Her cape hid her body, but by the sharp angles of her face, Aashi assumed she was extremely thin. She was drumming her long fingers on the arms of the chair and her eyes darted around behind her closed eyelids.

She was altogether quite an unattractive woman, Aashi decided, feeling guilty immediately for such an ugly thought.

"I'm not here for my beauty," the Truthseeker said, opening her eyes.

Aashi flushed with embarrassment. This woman could read her thoughts. She felt the last walls of privacy crumble around her. There was no safe place to hide now.

"Don't look so startled," she said. "I've been called much worse. Now, what truth do you seek?"

"I didn't come here seeking truth," said Aashi. "I came here to escape the truth."

"Interesting, but we all seek truth of some kind. There's a reason you're here." She closed her eyes once more and fell silent.

Seconds stretched into minutes and Aashi began to wonder how long they'd sit here like this. Did she need to ask a question for this ordeal to be over? It seemed like it.

"Who's the beast?" she asked, not feeling the need to explain herself further. From what she'd witnessed so far, it was barely necessary to even ask this question out loud.

The Truthseeker smiled, her eyes springing open.

"*You* are the beast."

Aashi withdrew into her chair. This wasn't the answer she was expecting.

"You're special, Aashi. Not because you have a beast inside—we all have that—but because you can hear it."

"I don't understand."

"Some people call the beast their intuition. When their beast talks to them, they write it off as just a feeling they've had about something. But your beast is louder than most. It's so finely tuned that you can hear it speak to you in words. You can use these words to guide you on your path."

Could this be true? This was something she'd wondered about before. " You're telling me I see the future?"

"Mostly you see the past."

"That's not true. I've never seen my past. I only ever see the path ahead."

"Listen to me," said the Truthseeker, her eyes drilling into Aashi's soul. "I speak the truth. Do *not* accuse me of lying. When you see the man with hair of fire and feel like you are dying from love, it's because you are seeing him in your past."

"What past? I'd never met him before."

"Your life before this one, of course. Do you think your life began when you entered the body you inhabit now?"

Had she known this all along? What the Truthseeker was saying fit perfectly with some of the thoughts she'd been having. Her love for Finn was too deep to have come from this lifetime alone.

"It's not often I have a soul like you visit me," said the Truthseeker. "I've been waiting for you for a long time."

"A soul like me? Who am I?" A thousand questions poured into her mind. To think only moments ago she'd thought she had nothing to ask. She *did* seek the truth. This woman *was* the person she needed to see. Nikii had been right to send her here.

"You're a lot of people, but you're only one soul. You began your journey thousands of years ago. You've lived many lives, but in your most recent one you were a girl named Maari."

"Maari?" That name sounded familiar only she couldn't remember why.

"You know this name, yes?"

"I'm not sure where from."

"You heard it many times in the orphanage when you were very little. There was a girl there with a beast shouting in her ear even louder than yours. She recognized you and tried to warn Tara of your presence. But no matter how many times she hissed your name, Tara didn't understand."

"Why would Tara need to be warned about me? I'd never hurt her."

"Isn't she lying in pain at this very moment because of you?"

Aashi fell silent. It was true. She *had* hurt Tara, even if she'd never meant to. How she could ever have hurt Tara to the extent that anyone felt they needed to warn her of her presence? She felt terrible.

"Don't feel too bad. Tara has hurt you just as badly."

"Tara would never hurt me."

"True, but she most definitely hurt Maari."

"I don't understand. Are you saying that when we die, we're reborn as different people?"

"That's exactly what I'm saying."

"And Tara hurt me in my last life when I was Maari?"

"Yes, back when her name was Lin."

"Lin?" It was hard to think of Tara with any other name.

"Correct. You see, you both loved the same man, just as you do now. His name was Nax and he was deeply in love with you. This angered Lin greatly. Not much has changed really. It's even the same man you're fighting over."

"So Nax is Finn?"

"Correct again."

"But this time we're not fighting over him. She can have him. I'm staying away."

The Truthseeker let out a loud sigh, almost as if this comment pained her.

"I *am* staying away," Aashi protested, unsure as to who she was trying to convince.

"Aashi, Finn loves you because you're his soulmate. Just as he loved you when he was Nax. You're destined to be together. There's no point denying this or trying to force him to love your sister. It's you that he loves. It's always been you."

"Then why does Tara believe it's her?"

"Because they loved each other in another lifetime long ago. They had a child together. He's a very important part of her journey."

Aashi tried to push down a feeling of jealousy that built within her.

"So, she remembers that they were soulmates."

"They weren't soulmates. A soulmate can be by your side in many ways other than by being your partner. Tara had a very close relationship with the child she had with Finn. That child was her soulmate."

"And, where was I?"

"You weren't there." Her tone was blunt, like she was hiding something.

"I was just floating around up in the sky or something?"

"Something like that."

"There's more to this, isn't there?"

"All in good time, Aashi. You need to trust me on this. I'm telling you what you need to hear for the moment. You'll visit me many times over the years. Eventually you'll come to understand the full story."

She couldn't imagine ever coming back to see the Truth-seeker. So far once was proving to be painful enough.

"Okay." She felt she had no choice but to agree. "So, you're telling me that the reason we both love Finn is because we've both loved him in lives gone by, but as he's my soulmate he will always have a closer connection to me."

"It's not just a connection. His soul yearns to be close to yours."

"Will Tara find her soulmate? Where's he? Is he floating around in the sky, too?"

"He is actually. She won't find him in this lifetime, although it's still possible for her to find deep happiness."

"Will you tell me how we wronged each other?" She still

couldn't imagine having ever done anything to hurt her sister.

"You stood in each other's way. You tore her from Finn's soul just as she tore him from yours. You both took lives that should never have been taken. This angered the Author."

"The Author?"

"Our supreme being. The soul responsible for the creation of human life. He changed the course of your journeys as he tried to redeem your souls. You've traveled well and pleased the Author. Tara hasn't."

"But she's a wonderful person. How can you say that? She's cared for me her whole life. She's sacrificed and suffered so much. How can that not be enough?"

"True. But still she hasn't learned one important lesson. One of the most important lessons of all."

"What?"

"Forgiveness. She's never learned to forgive."

"Why is forgiveness so important?"

"Because it's the key to happiness. People will always wrong you in this life—either accidentally or on purpose. It's how you choose to respond to that wrongdoing that will define how it affects you. You can either hang onto it or you can release it."

Aashi nodded. That made a lot of sense.

"Before her life as Tara the Author talked to her and she promised to let it go. She swore to forgive you. So, he decided to test her."

"How?"

"By putting your soul in the path of Finn's, when you were Maari and he was Nax. If she could accept his love for you then the Author would know she'd learned forgiveness."

"And did she?"

"Oh, my word, no, she did not. She tried. She did. But she failed so miserably. She tried to take your life just as you'd once tried to take hers and instead she took Nax's. You were heartbroken and in your quest to seek the truth your own life ebbed away."

How could this be true? Her beloved sister had tried to take her life just as she'd taken hers. It didn't seem possible. They protected each other, cared for each other. They weren't enemies. They loved each other.

"The Author was furious and considered extinguishing her soul. She begged for forgiveness. Ironic, really. The Author decided to give her one final test. He not only gave her the most difficult of lives, but he placed her enemy by her side. You. Then he watched her love her enemy and it seemed forgiveness was possible. But this test was not great enough so he placed Finn between you once more to see if this soul who you'd fought over in lifetimes before would come between you again."

"But doesn't someone have to say sorry to be forgiven?" She tried to keep the panic out of her voice. "I've never apologized to Tara for all the things you say I've done to her. I didn't even know I'd done them."

"Forgiveness is a choice. It doesn't matter if the person who's wronged you is sorry or not. How many times do we choose not to forgive someone who *is* truly sorry? Why can't it work the other way around and we forgive someone who isn't sorry at all?"

"And if she can't forgive me?" She kneaded her hands together in her lap. The Truthseeker had said the Author would extinguish Tara's soul if she were unable to forgive her. So far, she didn't seem to be passing her test.

"Have you forgiven her?"

"I have nothing to forgive her for."

"I just told you that she tried to kill you when you were Maari. Is that not a crime needing forgiveness?"

"I must have deserved what she did to me. She wouldn't

do anything like that without good reason. I must've done something terrible to her. I hold no grudge."

"That's exactly what I'm talking about. You have chosen to forgive her. And that's why the Author is testing her and not you."

"Will she forgive me? She must."

"That's up to her. Not you. The future isn't set in stone like you believe it to be. It's our past that holds firm. The future is soft and malleable. It can change at any moment." The Truthseeker nodded at her knowingly. The expression on her face seemed familiar and the feeling of déjà vu returned.

"Have I met you before? I mean, before I was Aashi?" It seemed she'd met everyone before. Why not this woman, too?

"Not me, no. But you've met another like me. There was a Truthseeker you spoke to as Maari. There are Truthseekers all over the universe. You'd make a fine one if you honed your talents."

Aashi shook her head. She had no desire to delve into other people's lives like this. It was hard enough trying to digest all that had gone on in her own life.

"I'm afraid my talents have gone," said Aashi. "I haven't heard my beast since I arrived in London."

"Your talents haven't gone." She laughed. "You just learned to hear the beast's voice as your own. It had to happen eventually."

"Really?" Was that possible? She was sure the beast had gone. But now it seemed it had never really been there in the first place.

"Yes, really. Why do you think you've been so tired? Big changes have been happening to you."

It was strange, this woman knowing all these things about her. How had Nikii known she'd have all these answers to questions she hadn't even known she'd needed to ask? Had the Truthseeker given Nikii answers like this, too?

"Come now, you have a lot to take in. You need some rest before you return home."

"Return? No. I can't return. Not yet."

"You must. But now is the time to rest. Come. I've made up a bed for you. The last train has already gone and you have nowhere else to go."

She was right. Aashi stood and followed her to the adjacent room. There was a bed as she'd promised and a nightstand with a plate of cookies and a mug of steaming hot milk. How had she kept it warm so long?

"Goodnight." The Truthseeker closed the door and left her alone. Only she didn't feel alone. Her mind was swirling with lives gone by and the souls who were wrapped up with her on the journey she'd only just discovered she'd been on.

For the first time she began to miss the beast. Life was far easier when she'd thought she was a simple girl with a voice that whispered in her ear than to realize that she herself was a beast—an awful beast at that.

Finn was too good for her. She had to find a way to make him love Tara.

CHAPTER SIXTEEN

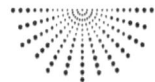

*I*t wasn't until Aashi had downed the last drop of milk the Truthseeker had left out for her that she realized she'd been drugged.

She fell onto the bed, her last thoughts ones of gratitude rather than anger. The Truthseeker hadn't needed to conceal the drugs in her milk. She'd have willingly taken them as a way to turn off her mind.

Dreams didn't take over as when she normally slept. Instead, it was a true lapse of time. She opened her eyes what seemed like moments later yet must surely have been days.

Her weary body felt refreshed. Her dark thoughts seemed a little less gray. An overwhelming sense that everything would be okay tingled down her spine.

She sat up, wincing at a sudden pain in her stomach. It was her bladder—her very full bladder screaming at her for relief.

She scuttled from the room and down the hall, opening doors until she found the bathroom. She sighed with pleasure at making it in time.

It was a small bathroom with tiles falling off the wall and

a musty smell. Still, it was luxurious by the standards she'd grown up with in India.

She stood and washed her hands, looking at herself in the mirror as she did so. The whites of her eyes had a pink tinge to them. Other than that, she looked well rested.

The shower beckoned her. She longed to stand under some warm water and refresh herself, but it felt wrong without permission. There'd be time for that later. Instead she splashed cold water on her face and combed her hair down with her fingers.

A noise coming from the other end of the house startled her. The Truthseeker was home. Was she waiting for her?

When she opened the bathroom door, she was hit with the smell of butter frying in a pan. It made her stomach groan. How long had it been since she'd eaten?

She followed the hallway down to the very end to find the Truthseeker bent over a stove frying an egg. She wasn't wearing her cape and its absence made her look like a different person—an ordinary person wearing black pants and a gray pullover. Her hair had been scooped back into a ponytail that made her face look even more severe.

"Take a seat," she said, pointing to a small table. There was only one chair. Aashi supposed only one was usually needed in this kitchen. Days like today, with a visitor to feed, must be rare.

Aashi sat, desperately hoping the egg was for her.

The Truthseeker reached for a plate and began buttering some toast.

"You must be hungry," she said, scooping the egg onto the toast and placing it in front of her.

"Thank you, Truthseeker," Aashi said between mouthfuls as she shoveled the food into her mouth.

"I'll make you another, shall I?" The Truthseeker laughed,

returning to the stove. "And you may call me by my earth name if you like. Skylar."

"Your earth name?" asked Aashi, gulping down some orange juice.

"I might be a Truthseeker," she said. "But I'm still a person."

"Of course. Sorry, Skylar." It felt wrong to call her this. "You're so...different today. It's like you're another person."

"Don't worry. It's me." She turned and looked Aashi in the eye, piercing through her with the intensity of her gaze. Yes, this was definitely the same woman she'd spoken with the night before. Or however long ago it was.

"Three days," said Skylar.

Aashi looked at her puzzled.

"You slept for three days. I'm sorry I drugged you. You needed your rest and your thoughts were going to keep you awake."

"It was a relief," said Aashi, smiling. "I *forgive* you."

Skylar laughed. "I'm glad you remember our conversation."

Aashi rubbed her stomach. She still felt hungry despite the egg she'd just devoured.

Skylar placed another plate in front of her and she got to work on the next egg immediately.

"You never told me how you met Nikii," said Aashi, keen to learn a little more about their relationship.

"Nikii and I went to school together," she said, perching on the bench top. "As you can imagine, school wasn't an easy place for me. Nikii was my only friend. That is to say she was the only person who never laughed at me. Not once. Not that I was her only friend, of course. Everyone loved her."

It was hard to imagine Skylar as a schoolgirl. It was hard to imagine anyone as a schoolgirl really, having never been to school herself.

"I thought you said everyone's your friend now."

"Things are a little different nowadays."

"Nikii's wonderful," said Aashi. "Have you seen her lately?"

"She visits from time to time. I can always feel the earth moving when she's on her way. Like a little tremor beneath my feet. It was more like an earthquake when you were on your way."

"You were ... umm ... pretty intense."

"I'm always intense," she said, her eyes staring once more. "But that night my voice was screaming inside my head. It was as exhausting for you as it was for me."

"When did you learn to speak Hindi?" she asked, amazed at being able to have this conversation with her.

"I never did."

"What do you mean? You're speaking it perfectly now."

"Am I speaking it? Or are you understanding English? I can't explain it."

"That's a first," said Aashi, chasing the last of the spilled egg yolk around her plate with a crust and wondering about what she'd just said. She was sure they were speaking Hindi.

"Life has many firsts," said Skylar. "Many lasts as well. Now, I'll get you a towel and you can take that shower you've been wanting."

It still amazed Aashi that Skylar could read her mind. She did seem to mean well though. Perhaps she wasn't so frightening after all.

It wasn't until she was standing under the blast of warm water that a sense of dread began to wash over her. Since she woke, she'd been so absorbed with her physical needs that she'd pushed back her emotional ones.

She was going to have to return to Tara and beg for her forgiveness. As much for Tara's sake as for her own. Surely Tara couldn't hate her forever?

She'd have to keep away from Finn. That would only infuriate Tara more. But how? How could she keep away from him now she'd looked into his eyes and felt his hands upon her skin? Not seeing him was like asking herself to no longer breathe.

But if she upset Tara to the point that forgiveness was no longer an option, then Tara was doomed. She couldn't risk that.

To think she'd once taken Tara's life, just as Tara had once tried to take hers. Did the fact that they'd both caused each other such harm somehow make them even? Did she really owe it to Tara to keep away from her soulmate and forgo any chance she had of happiness in this life?

Yes. Yes, she did. She owed Tara her life and more. Tara was a good person. A pure soul. When she hurt her as Maari, she thought she was doing the right thing. She didn't understand.

She missed Tara, feeling almost like a knife were twisting in her belly. They'd never been apart before. Even when she'd been in hospital as a young girl, Tara had visited every day. She needed to get back to her. Being apart like this was doing more harm than good. Who knew what thoughts or anger were building up in Tara's mind?

She turned off the water and stepped out of the shower, wrapping herself in a scratchy, gray towel.

Her bag was in the room she'd slept in and she headed there to dress in clean clothes.

There was an envelope on the end of the bed. The handwriting on it was neat and pressed deeply into the paper. She'd seen her name written enough times now that she could recognize it. Who would send her a letter? Nobody sent letters on paper these days—especially to illiterate people.

She picked it up. It smelled like Finn. She could sense his

words contained within it. How had he known how to reach her?

She slid the letter from the envelope, spreading it out on her lap, desperate to know what secrets it contained. If only she could read. Perhaps Skylar would help her?

She dressed, pulling on whatever clothes her hands fell on first.

"Skylar," she called, heading down to the kitchen.

"In here," came the reply from behind her.

She turned and headed back the way she came.

Skylar was seated in the room of candles—the room she'd sat in when she first arrived.

"You want me to read you the letter?" she asked, holding out her hand.

Aashi nodded and handed it to her as she sat down in the vacant armchair.

"Don't look so panicked," said Skylar. She took a deep breath and began to read...

Dear Aashi

I'm not sure how much of this you'll understand. I'm told your English is not as strong as Tara's. Hopefully you understand enough for this to make some kind of sense.

Tara won't speak to me and I don't know where you've gone. Nikii says you're giving us some space, but this doesn't make any sense. Why do we need space? She won't tell me where you are, but she must know as she's agreed to pass this letter onto you. I hope it finds its way into your hands.

I know we've only spent a few moments in each other's company, but something happened in those moments and I know you felt it, too. It was like my heart beat so hard that it had to stop to catch its breath. I know this sounds crazy. But if you didn't feel the same then why would you have blacked out like that? Is it possible you felt it even stronger than me? That's hard to imagine.

I didn't want to leave you lying there on the sofa. I wanted to stay by your side. Gerard convinced me to leave. I thought maybe if I didn't then you'd never wake up. I returned only an hour later, but you'd already gone and nobody will tell me where you are. I knew I shouldn't have left you.

When I met Tara all those years ago, she affected me deeply. I felt connected to her in some way. I can only think now that she must have felt a different kind of connection to the one I felt. A romantic one perhaps? What I felt was more like how a brother might feel for his sister and it pains me that she may think I led her to believe anything else. She's felt enough pain in her life already. I don't wish to cause her more.

I've looked at Tara's photo every day and over the years I became sure we shared something profound there on the streets of India. I always wanted to find her again so I could help her in some way.

Then Bakul found me. He was fierce, loyal and determined to find his sister. And you. I didn't even know about your existence, yet when he mentioned your name, I felt a familiar pull in my heart. You see, all my life I've been sure I would one day find my one true love—the person who was put on this earth especially for me. No other woman was ever right for me.

Until I met you.

It's you, Aashi. I know it is. And I know you feel it, too. Why have you run away? You can't disappear the moment I've found you. Together we can make this right with Tara. She'll understand.

My heart will never change. It belongs to you. Come back to me.

Finn

"Well, isn't that sweet?" said Skylar. "Here he was worrying about your English and all this time he forgot you couldn't read."

Aashi blushed. "I can read a little," she said, wondering why she bothered to lie. Skylar knew the truth. "Did you interpret it for me?"

"Language doesn't exist in this room." She waved her hands around as if that were supposed to make sense. "Would you like me to read it again?" Aashi nodded and this time as she heard Finn's words, she burned each of them into her mind to go over later.

The letter was beautiful. The most romantic set of words to ever be written on a page. And they were for her. If only she were free to take these words and cherish them in the way they deserved. To cherish Finn in the way he deserved.

He was right about so much. She *had* felt the emotion of their meeting even more acutely than he had. She *had* been put on this earth to be by his side.

But he was wrong about one thing. One very big thing. They could *not* make this right with Tara. She'd never understand.

"Why are you fighting this?" asked Skylar, a harsh edge creeping into her voice. "It's what he wants. It's what you want. It's what the Author wants. If you don't go to Finn then the Author will be forced to put Tara to another test. And who knows how difficult the next one might be."

"Why would he do that?" Aashi was horrified. What test could possibly be more difficult than the one he'd already set for her?

"He's testing her forgiveness in the harshest way he knows how. If you stay away from Finn then of course she'll forgive you. He'll be forced to set another test."

"No. That can't be true."

"Do you forget who you're speaking with?" asked Skylar.

"I'm sorry, Truthseeker. It just seems so cruel. I never thought of the Author—the Creator—as cruel."

"You never thought of him as cruel? With the life you've lived, that's a surprise. But you're right. He's not cruel. His actions are always just."

"How is this just? Hasn't Tara been through enough?"

"A deal is a deal. He promised to forgive her if she learned to forgive you. He cannot back down from this. Without his word he's nothing."

"So, I have no choice but to do what Finn says and return to him to ask for Tara's forgiveness together."

"If you love Tara that's exactly what you'll do."

Aashi placed a hand on her beating heart. She could feel the excitement building within her. Was she allowed to give herself to the man she loved? Could she finally tear down the walls she'd built to keep him out? Could she dare to dream of the future she longed for without it being a betrayal to her sister?

"Go to him," said Skylar.

Aashi knocked on the door and waited. Her stomach tied in knots at the anticipation of seeing Finn again.

The door didn't open, so she knocked again. Was it the right address? She'd shown the return address on the envelope of his letter to several people in the street and they'd all pointed her in this direction.

She held up the letter and studied the shape of the number at the start of the address, comparing it to the brass number on the door. They looked the same.

Disappointment gripped her. Where was he? Why wasn't he waiting for her?

She slumped on his doorstep and leaned against the coolness of the brick wall.

The sky grew dark and soon night fell. She wrapped her arms around herself and shivered, feeling as if she'd done this before.

The cold brought back a memory of waiting for Finn in a life gone by. Of being cold—so cold—and wishing he were by her side. A life where she was Maari and he was Nax and their love was a force so powerful that without it she lost the will to live.

She began to shiver, knowing she should stand and walk away. She could return tomorrow.

But she knew her heart wouldn't last until then. If she didn't see Finn now, it felt like it would stop beating all together. She needed him by her side. To feel her life force wrapped in the energy of his own. Their souls intertwining, merging, caressing each other with gentle care.

Pain shot into her hands and feet as snow began to fall. The cold was threatening her, beating her down.

She closed her eyes and felt heat on her lips. Her cheeks. The center of her soul. It was a burning heat made from passion and love.

Finn knelt before her, his lips pressed to her own, her face cupped in his hands. She parted her lips and returned his kiss, reaching for him with every cell of her body. It was a kiss continued from a time long gone in a place far away. A kiss that would continue long into future when time was no more.

"You came back to me," he said.

Her English may have been poor, but it was enough to understand these words.

"I never left," she said.

PART V

VIKRAM

CHAPTER SEVENTEEN

From Vikram's kitchen window he had a view of the village. He kept his curtains closed, fighting the urge to look down upon the sea of human misery. A sea that had once been his home. If he looked at it, he might be tempted to return.

Although the village was a life of hardship and despair, it was also the home to some of his happiest memories. They were memories he missed with a desperation that sucked the air from his lungs.

He had to remind himself it wasn't the memories he missed. It was the two skinny girls with skin so stained with dirt that the whites of their eyes shone at him like the stars in the sky. Two girls who were so ingrained with each and every memory, that he had no idea how to pull them apart.

Aashi.

The girl with a spirit that was impossible to crush.

And Tara.

The girl who never once failed to impress him with her determination and the love she showed her sister. As she'd grown into a woman, his feelings for her had confused him.

He'd had to build new walls around his heart to prevent him from reaching out to her and drawing her close.

Not that any of that mattered now. The last time he'd spoken with Bakul, he'd said she was in love with the man who'd taken that heartbreakingly beautiful photo of her. He wondered what the man saw when he looked at that photo. A girl to feel sorry for? A girl who needed saving? A girl struggling to survive?

How wrong he'd be.

Bakul had left him with a copy of the photo and when he looked at it, he saw a different kind of girl looking back at him. One who was strong. A fighter. A girl who'd survived against the odds, determined not to let the world drag her to the depths of hell. She was intelligent, resourceful and fierce. He admired her like he'd never admired another.

He was reluctant to use the word *love* when he thought of her. He'd sworn long ago he'd never love again. This life would hold many things for him, but love wouldn't be one of them. He'd walk through this life alone. Love led to pain. He'd had enough pain already.

He sat down on the small, second-hand sofa he'd purchased not long after he'd moved into the apartment and stared at the clock that hung on the wall, watching the seconds tick by. Each time that thin, red hand moved forward he felt a second closer to death. That was another second of his life taken care of. Another second he no longer needed to worry about. It was a slow march to the grave.

He wasn't sure how old he was exactly. He'd lost track of that years ago. He guessed he was in his late twenties, aware that those around him often mistook him for being older. When the girls had arrived in the village, he'd been only little more than a boy himself.

Although the world hadn't blessed him with a happy life, it had at least blessed him with a strong body that'd grown exactly at the time he'd needed it most making him look like a man long before he was.

His skin was dark—several shades darker than Tara and Aashi's. He liked it that way. It'd made him feel invisible in the village, camouflaging him with the night's sky. He was taller than most, too, a result of genetics more than the meals his mother had cooked him as a child. He'd let his hair grow since leaving the village and it now hung to almost the length of his collar. He was proud of his new sleek mane, more because of what it represented than how it looked. In the village he'd had to keep it cropped short. It was easier to keep clean and meant he could avoid the frequent outbreaks of lice that plagued his neighbors. But now, he was free to let it grow and he relished the way it changed his appearance.

His physique had filled out now that he was able to buy his own food and he liked the way his biceps had expanded. He'd kept up his nightly exercise routine and felt stronger than ever. He had to stop himself from admiring himself in front of the bathroom mirror. Vanity wasn't a trait he wished to acquire as part of this new life.

He ran his hand across the soft fabric of the sofa, feeling grateful and embarrassed at the kindness Bakul had bestowed upon him. It'd been hard to accept money from him. He'd said no at first, accepting only the phone that he'd given him as a way for the girls to keep in touch.

He soon found out the phone was more of a means for Bakul to ring him and hassle him about taking his money to get himself out of the village. Bakul had explained to him over a number of phone calls that English money was worth a lot more in India. He was so insistent that Vikram had nearly thrown away the phone so he'd stop badgering him about it.

He could never have done that. The phone was the last remaining lifeline he had left to Tara. Even though he never spoke to her on it, he'd sleep with it by his side, knowing it had the ability to connect him to her if he ever chose. That in itself warmed his heart in a way he'd promised himself nothing ever would again.

How had he managed to let her slip in under his guard?

He'd eventually taken Bakul's money as a loan. He knew that moving from the village and taking up residence in the apartment almost guaranteed him the ability to find work—work that would enable him to earn a wage and pay Bakul back all his money with interest. It would take many years, but he'd do it. He wouldn't leave Bakul out of pocket.

His instincts had been right, quickly landing a job as a cleaner at a large shopping mall nearby. The other cleaners spoke of the work like it was difficult. A few of them seemed to think it was demeaning. How little they knew about the world.

They should try eating a burger from a rubbish bin then spending the night running from their house with a pain in their gut that threatened to rip the life from their body. Or perhaps they should try having to approach a stranger and beg them for some of their change or wash themselves in front of crowds of women and children. There's no dignity in any of that. Having a paid job, sweeping floors and picking up trash wasn't difficult and it certainly wasn't demeaning. The only challenging aspect was turning off his reflex to put various pieces of trash in his pocket instead of the bin. There was no need to do that anymore.

It wasn't entirely the promise of finding work that had eventually convinced him to accept Bakul's money. It was the need to leave the village.

Without the girls living next door, life quickly became unbearable. He'd thought he felt alone before, but with them gone he felt incredibly lonely. The faces that surrounded him seemed blank. They held so little interest for him that it was like they failed to exist at all. He was living in a village of ghosts.

One sleepless night he went to the girls' house and lay on the floor. Moonlight streamed through the gaps in the roof, lighting up the rainbow that arched across the walls. But the rainbow failed to fill his heart with sunshine. Instead, it was like a storm that raged inside him, churning his guts until he felt like he would vomit.

He quickly returned home vowing never again to return. The house wasn't the same without the girls. It was like a body once a soul has taken for the skies. Empty. Hollow. Nothing but a painful reminder of what once was.

It was that night he decided to take Bakul up on his offer. He'd get out of the village, find work, pay him back then put money aside to see him through old age.

Bakul had other plans for him, of course. He wanted to move him to London. He'd tried telling Bakul this would never happen. It would be like moving to Planet Mars. He couldn't do it. He wouldn't. He denied within himself that his decision had anything to do with having to witness Tara in love with another man.

He was glad she loved someone else, for if she loved him in return then it would be impossible to keep his heart closed. She held a key she was unaware was in her possession. It was better that way.

Thoughts of his own sister began seeping into his mind.

He stood with urgency, picking up his keys and leaving the apartment. He had to go for a walk to distract himself. He wouldn't think of his sister today. He wouldn't think of her any day. She was dead and so too should be her memory.

"Sweet, Lali," he whispered, unable to push her from his mind. "I'm sorry."

Life soon became monotonous for Vikram and he found himself a second job, hoping it would fill the empty hours of his day. Treacherous hours that if not filled with work would soon be filled with memories. It also meant he'd be able to pay Bakul back sooner than he'd first calculated.

The job was at the fish market. His task was to slice the fish open and rip the guts from their lifeless bodies. He looked at each fish before he brought his knife to its belly, seeing himself reflected in its eyes. He, too, had started life with a promise. He, too, had been ripped from his existence against his will and had his guts torn from him. The only difference was that this fish no longer suffered.

From where he stood at his workbench, he could catch glimpses of the customers being served. They held little interest for him. More ghosts walking the earth, failing to connect with his closed-off soul.

He ignored these customers, just as he'd ignored his neighbors in the village. They weren't important. He focused on his job, blocking the sounds of the market from his ears.

It was because of this attitude that he found it hard to understand how this one particular customer had penetrated the bubble that surrounded him.

It was a man's voice. A man's voice he'd hoped never to hear again.

He froze, knife pointed in the air, fish dangling from one hand.

Fear washed over him.

His hands began to shake, the fish quivering like it was made from jelly.

The man laughed at something that was said about the fish he'd just bought.

Vikram steeled himself and turned to look at him.

His hair was gray now, his face hollowed with age. He still wore expensive clothes and thick gold jewelry, forever advertising his success to the world. Little did he realize there were other ways to judge success than the amount of money you held in your hand.

Vikram dropped the fish. He didn't drop the knife.

This was his chance. He could take his knife and gut that man like the pile of fish that lay before him. Only this was a gutting he'd enjoy. This man didn't deserve to live. This man didn't deserve the air that was filling his lungs.

How dare he stand there laughing after all he'd done. Lali wasn't laughing. She no longer had a mouth to laugh with. Her pretty, little mouth would've turned to dust in the ground by now.

He took a step towards the counter. A few swift movements and it would all be over. He wouldn't even know what happened to him. Unlike Lali. She knew. Oh, how painfully she knew.

"Back to work," his supervisor said, grabbing him on the arm.

He turned, shifting his gaze for only a moment from the evil that stood before him.

It was a moment long enough for the man to disappear.

"See someone you know?" his supervisor asked.

Vikram nodded, returning to his workbench.

"My father," he said, picking up a fish and slicing it in half with one stroke of his knife.

Vikram arrived home that night aware of the stench that followed him. It wasn't the smell of fish guts that overpowered him. It was the smell of fear.

Fear of what he would've done if not woken from his trance by his supervisor. Or was it the memory of the fear that man had ensured was branded into his soul?

The mere sight of him had almost caused him to lose control.

He ripped his clothes from his body and stepped into the shower, not waiting for the water to warm up first.

Cold water hit him with force, shocking him back to the present.

It washed the fear from him and he stood there as the water ran down the drain, taking his stench with it.

Of all the luxuries living in an apartment brought him, this was the one he appreciated the most—the ability to clean himself whenever he felt the need. He must've taken at least twelve showers a day when he first moved in.

He soaped himself, becoming entranced by the bubbles as they slid from his skin.

Satisfied he was clean, he stepped from the shower and threw his clothes into the empty bathtub. He'd deal with them later.

He dressed in a pair of black pants, leaving his torso bare. It was hot and the air-conditioning in his apartment had ceased the day he'd moved in. He'd not bothered to have it repaired. He was used to the heat and couldn't justify the expense when his debt to Bakul stretched before him. It didn't seem fair.

The clock told him he had one hour before starting work at the mall. He lay down on the sofa and placed his hands on his stomach, concentrating on the rise and fall of each breath he took.

He should've killed his father while he'd had the chance. It'd be worth spending his life in prison just to have seen the look in his eyes as the life drained from his cowardly face.

There was a knock at his door. He jumped, feeling for a moment like he'd been caught out for his evil thoughts.

It wasn't a gentle knock. It was more of a pounding. Had

his father seen him at the market and come to find him? He hoped so. They had unfinished business.

He went to the kitchen and took a knife from the draw.

The pounding came again.

He opened the door a crack and peered out, holding the knife behind his back, ready to strike if the opportunity presented itself. He wouldn't let this chance go by again.

"Hello, Vikram."

This time he dropped the knife.

"Tara," he said, opening the door. "Tara."

He couldn't believe it. There she was, standing before him. It was really her. She looked different. The hollows in her cheeks had rounded out, her hair was shiny and clean and her clothes were so…new.

She stepped toward him and wrapped her arms around his waist.

She smelled different, too. Like honey and strawberries and coconut. He put his arms around her tentatively at first. Then he found himself gripping her, pulling her close as he breathed in the scent of her, the feel of her, enveloping himself in her essence.

"Can I come in?" she asked, breaking away. Her cheeks contained a blush that hadn't been present before. Had she felt that moment as much as he had?

He nodded, stepping backward and holding the door open.

He felt the knife beneath his feet, and he kicked it aside, hoping she hadn't noticed.

"You look fantastic," she said.

A blush spread to his cheeks now. He wanted to return the compliment. He wished he knew how. It had been so long since he'd had anything resembling a normal conversation with anyone the words were unable to find their way out.

She set a bag down at her feet and stood surveying his small apartment. It was only the one room that served as both bedroom and living room. There were two internal doors—one that led to his small kitchen and the other to his bathroom. He was confident Tara wouldn't judge him poorly for this apartment. She knew as well as he did what luxury it was.

"It's wonderful," she said. "A little bare, but wonderful."

He looked around, seeing the apartment for the first time through her eyes. It was bare. The gifts the girls had made him in the village sat in a bag in the bottom of his cupboard, too heartbreaking to display. There wasn't a painting or an ornament or an object of beauty to be found. Apart from the one that stood before him now. He'd forgotten just how beautiful Tara was. She was a shining jewel in a field of pebbles. No other woman could compare.

"Why are you here?" he asked, reaching for his shirt and pulling it on, feeling shy of his bare chest. It didn't seem like good manners to speak to her half undressed.

"Can I stay with you for a little while?" she asked, ignoring his question.

"Of course," he said, his heart leaping in his chest. "But why? Where's Aashi? Is she all right?" He'd never known her to leave her sister. He began to panic. Tara wouldn't leave her.

"She's okay. She's good, actually. Let's just say she doesn't need me anymore."

He raised his eyebrows. That seemed unlikely. Tara and Aashi were like two halves of the one person.

"You're different," she said.

"My hair's longer." He cursed himself. That wasn't what she'd meant.

"It is, but it's more than that. You're different on the inside, too."

"A lot has happened."

She sat next to him on the sofa. He shifted away slightly, aware of her close proximity and what it was doing to him.

She noticed and frowned.

"Sorry," she said.

"I'll get you a drink." He got up and walked to the kitchen.

He took a glass from the cupboard and realized he'd failed. He'd promised to never love another and yet when he looked at Tara, he knew with every cell in his body that he loved her. Pretending otherwise was useless.

He poured some iced tea into the glass and brought it to her, pulling a chair over toward her. The sofa seemed too intimate. It was important to keep his distance.

"I have to go to work," he said.

"You have a job?" she asked, taking a sip of her tea and licking her lips.

He tore his eyes from her mouth, fighting the desire to lean forward and kiss her.

"I have two jobs," he said.

"That's impressive."

"Why are you here?" he asked again. It didn't make sense. Bakul had said she was happy.

"I missed India. It's my home."

He pushed down his disappointment and scolded himself. What had he expected? That she'd come back for him? That was ridiculous. She saw him as a brother, not a lover. He was her protector. Her friend. She wasn't here for him. He should've built a stronger wall. He could feel his heart breaking already, only moments after being released.

"Don't you want me here?" she asked, misreading his face.

"I do. Please make yourself at home," he said, pulling on his shoes and opening the door to the apartment. "You're welcome to stay as long as you like."

He caught a glimpse of her surprised expression before he closed the door behind him.

He'd be early to work, but that didn't matter. He couldn't stay in the apartment any longer. Tara's presence both caressed and tortured him.

Some days it felt like the world turned faster than others. Today was one of those days. First seeing his father and now Tara. The person he hated the most in the world followed by the person he loved the most. It was too much to take in.

He just hoped the world didn't turn any faster or he was afraid he might fall off.

CHAPTER EIGHTEEN

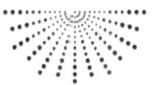

*T*ara was sleeping on the sofa when he returned. Her tiny frame curled up, making the sofa appear larger than it was.

She was wearing pink pajamas, her hair pulled back into a ponytail. She was frowning. Whatever she dreamed of was troubling her.

He fought the urge to sit by her side and stroke her forehead, telling her that everything was going to be okay. Clearly, it wasn't. Something had brought her back to India. Something she wasn't willing to tell him about. He wouldn't press her. He knew what it was like to have secrets you were unwilling to part with.

In all the years she'd lived beside him, he'd never seen her sleep. It made her look younger. An innocence etched itself across her face. It reminded him of the day he'd first seen her.

He'd noticed her and Aashi walking through the village, searching for a patch of land to call their own—an impossible task for two young girls new to the village. He remembered staring at them, fighting his fascination. They were just like any other girls in the village.

But the more he'd watched them, the more he'd realized they were nothing like the other girls in the village. They reminded him of someone else.

Lali.

Aashi reminded him of his sister. She had the same glint in her eyes despite the hardship being forced upon her.

And Tara...well, she reminded him of himself. The way she clutched her sister's hand, determined to protect her despite the odds of achieving anything of the sort being stacked against her.

He'd wanted to take them into his home himself, but that would never work. Apart from the fact his mere presence as a man would scare them half to death, it would kill him to have to look at Aashi's face while she slept, all the time thinking it should be Lali who lay beside him.

So, he'd returned to his home and put together a food offering for the old woman who lived in a cardboard box next door. She wasn't long for this world, anyone looking at her could tell that. She'd been easily bribed to share her home. It was the best he could do to help the girls.

Tara had seemed so proud of her efforts to find shelter. He knew he'd never tell her otherwise. He also knew he'd watch over them, protecting them in the way he hadn't been able to protect Lali. He'd failed her. Perhaps if he succeeded in protecting these two girls then the universe would forgive him. Perhaps he'd even be able to forgive himself.

Then Tara had come to him with the orange. Her dark eyes had been filled with desperation as she'd beseeched him to protect them from the dangers that lurked in the village.

He'd accepted the orange, wanting her to feel she'd arranged their safety herself. It was another thing he knew he'd never tell her—that her safety had already been assured.

When he'd heard Aashi crying for her orange and Tara trying to keep her quiet in case he heard, he'd been unable to stay put. He'd rolled the orange into their box, aware that he was rolling a little piece of himself in there with it—a little piece that he'd kept stowed away until then. A piece that he'd spent every day since trying to get back.

And now here she was, robbing him of more pieces of his heart. The very sight of her was making him crumble.

He tore himself from the room and went to freshen up, only to find his clothes from the fish market clean and hanging to dry on the makeshift line he'd set up over the bathtub.

Tara had been busy. He blushed at the thought of her handling the stench of his clothes, consoling himself with the fact that as a previous inhabitant of the village she was used to stench. She'd probably barely noticed the smell. Compared with the rubbish dump they'd lived beside for so many years, his clothes had practically smelled like rose petals.

It was a kind gesture—even if it was unnecessary—and he tried to feel grateful rather than embarrassed.

He washed his face and changed his shirt, worried that if he took a shower he'd wake her. She looked like she needed her sleep.

His stomach groaned. He scowled. He used to be able to go days at a stretch without food and now if he didn't eat every few hours his stomach would complain loudly.

He crept into the kitchen and took a tub of yogurt from the fridge, leaning on the edge of the bench as he ate it.

The urge to open the curtains grew and he relented, pulling them aside. It was midnight and the village was shrouded in darkness. He could only make out shadows, yet his memory filled in every line. He knew the village as if it were a part of his own body.

It was strange to think that only months ago, he'd been down there in the darkness—Tara and Aashi by his side. He missed it. It was hard to admit, but he'd enjoyed protecting the girls and having them rely on him for their wellbeing. The knowledge that they needed him was all that kept him going some days.

And now? Well, nobody needed him now. He'd had to push suicidal thoughts from his mind many times since leaving the village. It was a struggle to come up with reasons to continue on.

He'd always known that one day things would change and he was grateful to Bakul for rescuing the girls and assisting him to drag himself out of the village. But all the same, it'd been an extremely difficult day for him, the day Bakul had turned up looking for his sisters.

He'd had to push down his selfish grief at losing them and focus on being happy for the second chance at life they were being given. Not that it was really accurate to think of it as a *second* chance, given they were never really given much of a chance to begin with.

He put the empty yogurt tub in the sink and started as he felt a soft hand on his arm.

"You're back," said Tara, smiling.

He shuffled across slightly, wanting some distance from her. He needed to control his emotions. Standing too close to her made his brain both freeze up and melt into puddles at the same time.

"Did I wake you?" he asked. "I'm sorry."

"No. I would've woken anyway. I'm jetlagged. My brain doesn't know what time it is."

"Go back to sleep."

"Come and talk to me." She reached for his hand and led him into the living room.

He was going to need to be more open with his words,

not just his heart. He already felt like his heart had forced its way over the wall of the cage he'd built, desperate for the freedom to love once more. He'd been able to hold Tara at a distance in the village, but now he didn't know if he was going to be able to contain himself.

"Vikram?" she said, sitting beside him on the sofa.

"Yes?"

"Please don't be afraid of me."

"I'm not afraid," he said, wondering how she knew his heart was gripped with terror.

"You're shaking. It's only me."

"Only you," he said, shaking his head. "Tara, why are you really here?"

"I don't want to talk about it." She looked upset. "I thought you of all people would understand that."

He stood, raking his hands through his hair. The room was alive with secrets. He could feel them dripping from the walls. His secrets. Her secrets. They were suffocating him. What was the point of them? Why couldn't he talk about his past? Why couldn't she speak of her present?

He doubled over with the pain of it all.

"Vikram! Are you all right? What's happening?" She was at his side now.

"I can't do it anymore." He looked deep into her eyes, imploring her to understand.

"What can't you do?" She reached for his arm.

He pushed her hand away, more roughly than he intended. He hadn't meant to use his strength against her.

"I don't understand," she said, tears pouring down her cheeks.

"Tara. I love you. I've loved you since the moment I first saw you and I'll love you until the day I die. I love you so much I don't know how to live without you and I certainly don't know how to live with you either."

The words tumbled from his mouth and he felt all the walls in his heart collapse.

Her hand fluttered to her open mouth, her eyes wide with shock.

"You love me?" she said. "I didn't think you loved anyone."

"It's impossible not to love anybody. Believe me, I tried."

"And Aashi, too? Do you love her?" A strange expression crossed her face. He nodded. "Yes. She is my sister who came back to me."

"You had a sister?"

"She's dead now." His voice was little more than a whisper. It was the first time he'd admitted out loud that Lali was dead.

"But now you have two sisters," said Tara, reaching out for him only to withdraw her hand before making contact, afraid perhaps of being rebuffed again.

"Now I have one sister," he said. "Aashi. You, Tara, are not my sister. You are so much more."

This time he reached for her, pulling her into his arms. A weight lifted from his shoulders. It didn't matter what her response was. It didn't matter if she loved him in return. All that mattered was that she knew how precious she was to him. How highly he thought of her.

She tilted her head toward him and he bent down, placing a gentle kiss upon her lips.

Her lips stirred in response and he found himself deepening the kiss, his arms wrapping more tightly around her waist. Joy surged in his heart, racing around his body in rapturous waves. He became lost in her, relinquishing all his strength and power into her hands.

"Stop it. Vikram!" She was pushing him away, breaking the spell, crushing his spirit.

He realized she hadn't been kissing him at all. It was a

kiss coming from his lips alone. He'd been forcing himself on her.

"I'm sorry," he said, his eyes filling with horror.

"It's okay," she said, backing away. Her arms were crossed. She looked confused. She looked afraid.

"What have I done?" he said, falling to the floor, cupping his head in his hands. He'd made her afraid of him. He'd become the very person he hated most in this world.

He'd become his father.

"Vikram, I said it was okay. Please get up." She crouched beside him.

"I'm sorry," he said again, avoiding her eye, not sure if he'd ever be able to look at her again.

"You took me by surprise, that's all. Please get up. It's okay."

He took her outstretched hand and once more she led him to the sofa.

"Please tell me about your sister," she said.

He was unsure why she asked. Was she changing the subject to protect his feelings? Or did she feel this was the one time she could ask without him refusing her an answer? He could hardly deny any request of hers after what he'd just done.

"Tell me," she said again. "I want to understand you. I can't do that if you don't tell me where you came from. You're a mystery to me. How did you end up in the village?"

He hesitated. He had nothing to lose by telling her. Or perhaps he had everything to lose. He couldn't tell. The world seemed so much simpler when he'd remained silent.

"My sister's name was Lali," he said, keeping his gaze ahead, staring at the clock instead of her. "She was my twin. First, we shared a womb. Then we shared a closeness I cannot describe to you."

"What did she look like?" asked Tara.

"Like Aashi. Beautiful. Happy. A light shone from her. Being near her was like coming to life."

"Did you have other siblings?"

"No, it was just the two of us. I have many half siblings, however I never met any of them. My father loved many women. Either that or he never loved any of them at all. I was never quite sure which it was. He had wives all over the country. He was a wealthy man. We wanted for nothing."

"Was he a good father?"

"I thought he was. Always smiling. Always bringing us gifts and swinging us in the air above his head. We were happy to see him. It wasn't until I was older that I noticed the dread his presence cast upon my mother."

"Was she jealous of his other women?"

"It was the opposite. She was happiest when she knew he was with one of them, as it meant he wasn't under the same roof as us."

"Was she afraid of him?"

"Yes, but not for herself."

"I don't understand. You said he was good to you."

"It was Lali she was afraid for. My mother saw things my innocent eyes were blind to. She saw the way my father looked at Lali. He looked at her in a way a father should never look at his daughter. Do you understand what I'm saying?" He dragged his eyes to her face, only to see a look of despair move across her eyes.

"My mother would make excuses for him not to visit and I'd get angry with her. I didn't understand. If I understood then of course..."

"Of course," she soothed.

"This drove a wedge between my mother and me. I resented her for keeping us from our father and she resented me for not understanding what it was impossible for me to understand. As we grew older, I saw my father favoring Lali over me. He'd take her into his bedroom to tell her stories. Stories I wasn't allowed to hear. I was desperate with jealousy, wanting him to tell me stories too."

"Oh, Vikram."

"I became more angry with my mother. I thought she'd told him lies about me to drive him from my side. I blamed her. She never told me the truth about him. She knew he was a monster, but still she never spoke a word against him. She sat there with me in the kitchen while my father was with Lali and she never once tried to stop him." His voice broke with pain.

"It's okay. You don't have to tell me any more."

"No, I need to." Now that he'd started, he had to finish. If Tara was ever going to love him in return she needed to know where he'd come from.

She nodded, waiting quietly for him to continue.

"I began to notice Lali withdrawing into herself, reminding me more and more of my mother with each year that passed. It was like a gray cloud hovered over her, stopping any sunshine from reaching her heart. She dreaded my father's visits and I was upset with her. In my mind, our father was bestowing upon her the great gift of his attention. A gift I yearned for. I thought she was ungrateful. How little I knew."

"You couldn't have known. You were young."

"One day, I decided I'd had enough of sitting quietly by. I wanted to hear my father's stories, too. It was unfair. So, when my mother left the room to take a phone call I ran upstairs, preparing to beg my father to love me."

"Oh no, Vikram."

"I burst into the bedroom and ... and ... and ..." He was crying now. Great big tears were rolling down his face and he was powerless to stop them. How could he possibly describe what he'd seen? The scene that had lain before him had changed his life forever. Most people have no idea of when they grew up. It's more of a process than an actual moment in time. But not with him. It happened to him the moment he'd opened that door.

"He was on top of her. She was lying there, her face twisted in pain. I remember I screamed and she turned to look at me. Her pain was replaced by horror. She was embarrassed, Tara. This mongrel that I called my father was practically tearing her in half and *she* was the one who was embarrassed. And do you know what he did? Do you know what that animal did?"

Tara shook her head.

"He smiled at me. He didn't even stop what he was doing. He just looked at me, smiled and asked me to close the door on my way out. So, I jumped on top of him, tearing at his back with my nails, beating him with my fists, yelling at him to stop."

"And did he?" asked Tara, clearly afraid of the response.

"He had no choice. He flicked me from his back like I was a fly. I continued to throw punches, my hatred for him far outweighing my fear. But I was young. Skinny. Weak. My hardest punch barely left a bruise. I saw his face turn from a smile into a look I cannot describe to you. He raised his hand, bunching it into a fist and he slammed it into my skull. He could've killed me. In many ways he did."

"What happened to Lali? What did he do to her? Please tell me he didn't hit her too."

"He didn't get the chance. My mother got to the door just in time to see her run from him."

"Did she get away?"

"No. He stood between her and the door. It was to the balcony that she ran. She threw herself off. Her neck broke on impact. She died instantly. My sister died and it was all my fault."

"How could you say that? It wasn't your fault. You tried to protect her."

"I shamed her. She couldn't live with the shame of knowing that I knew. That's why she jumped."

"You can't know that. It seems to me she jumped because she was afraid of your father."

"What could he do to her that he hadn't already been doing for years?"

"Maybe she'd had enough. There's only so much a person can take."

"I shouldn't have gone upstairs."

"Don't blame yourself for this. You had to go upstairs. What other choice did you have? To stay downstairs like your mother and pretend nothing was going on?"

"How could she do that, Tara? How could she let him do that to her daughter?"

"She was scared? Don't you see? She didn't know what else to do."

"I can't accept that."

"So, you're angry with yourself for taking action just as you're angry with her for staying silent? You can't win."

"Of course, I can't. There are no winners in this situation."

"Is that when you ran away to the village?"

"Three days later I left. It was the day of Lali's funeral. I couldn't stay in that house. With her. With him. With myself. I needed to go somewhere he'd never find me. Somewhere I'd never have to see his face again. This is why I am the man I am today."

"I'm sorry these things happened to you, but you shouldn't be sad to be the man you are today. You're noble. Kind. Brave. I've always admired you."

"Thank you." These were beautiful words. He hoped she meant them.

"No. Thank *you*," she said.

"For what?"

"For sharing yourself with me at last. Everything about you makes sense to me now. It's like I've just met you for the first time."

He nodded, feeling shy once more, as was becoming his way in her presence.

"I love you, Vikram." She reached for his cheek, turning him to face her.

"You don't need to say that."

"It's true. I love you. I'm not sure it's in the way that you love me. Not yet. Can you please give me some time?"

He nodded. Was it possible she'd ever love him the way he wanted her to?

"I'm sorry I kissed you," he said.

"You're not like your father," she said, understanding his grief.

"I know that."

"Do you?"

He offered her a weak smile. For someone who claimed to feel like she'd only just met him, she certainly knew him well.

"I ran away from London," she said, matter-of-factly.

"You don't need to tell me, just because I told you."

"Yes, I do. I ran away because I thought I hated Aashi."

"What?" He was surprised. No, he was shocked.

"Bakul has probably told you that I was in love with a man? The photographer, Finn."

"Yes, he mentioned it only briefly." Bakul had mentioned it more than just briefly, however he didn't want her to feel she'd been discussed behind her back.

"It turns out that he loves Aashi, not me."

"Oh." He wasn't sure what to say. His initial reaction was that this man must be mad not to have fallen desperately and hopelessly in love with Tara, but he held his tongue fearing this would make her uncomfortable.

"It hurt," she said. "A lot."

"Does Aashi love him?"

"Yes. In fairness to her, she tried to keep away from him, but it was no use. There's a strong connection between them. Everyone could see it."

"Why did she try to stay away from him?"

"To protect me."

"And you're mad at her why? I'm not getting this."

"I'm mad at her because he loves her and not me." She smiled as if realizing how ridiculous this sounded.

"We can't help who we love," he said, trying not to feel glad that Finn hadn't returned her feelings. Jealousy was a dangerous beast.

She nodded, accepting his words.

"Does Bakul know where you are?" he asked.

"He does. I convinced his parents to send me back here. I told them I was worried about you, but they knew the truth. It would kill me to watch Aashi with Finn."

"Does Aashi know?"

"No. I asked them not to tell her until after I'd left. She went away for a little while to stay with a friend of Nikii's. I left before she returned."

"You can't run from your problems like this."

She raised her eyebrows at him.

"We're more alike than I realized." he said.

"We're a disaster." She smiled.

"A catastrophe," he added.

She reached for his hand and held it in her own.

He stared ahead, too afraid once more to look at her in case the spell of this moment were to break.

"That's an ugly clock," she said.

They laughed, their laughter quickly turning from stifled giggles to uncontrollable hysteria.

He clung to her hand in the same way a drowning man would cling to a piece of driftwood floating by. No matter how dark his life had been or was still yet to become, he had this moment in time to hold onto. It was a light he could turn on inside his mind to brighten his path and remind him that there is good in this world.

CHAPTER NINETEEN

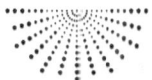

*T*wo weeks slipped past. Anxiety began to grip Vikram tightly around the chest. He was enjoying Tara's presence too much. When she eventually decided to forgive Aashi and return to London—as he knew she would—he'd be ruined.

He'd insisted she sleep in his small bed in the corner of the room, while he took the sofa. Most nights he ended up sleeping on the floor where he could stretch out. In truth, he'd slept on the floor most nights even before Tara's arrival. He'd gotten used to it over the years. It seemed unnatural to sleep on a surface so soft.

He hadn't tried to kiss her again. Nor had she reached out for him the way she had the night their secrets were shared. She seemed nervous around him and he felt embarrassed for having bared his soul to her only to have her tell him she loved him as a friend.

His two jobs continued to take up most of his time, leaving him only few precious hours to be with her. It seemed a waste to spend these sleeping and his bones soon became weary.

"You work too hard," she said to him one day when he returned home to find her sitting at the small kitchen table.

"I have a debt to pay," he said taking a seat beside her.

"Bakul doesn't want the money back."

"But I want him to have it back. He worked hard for that money."

"You're very stubborn," she said, poking her tongue out at him.

"Don't you want to pay him back, too? For everything he's done for you."

"Of course, I do. And I will when I…"

"When you return? Is that what you were going to say?" he said, fear gripping him. The moment had come. She was going to tell him she was leaving.

"Come with me," she said.

"I don't have the papers."

"We'll get you the papers."

"India is my home."

"I am your home," she said.

Hope lit his eyes. Was it possible her heart had warmed to him?

She reached for his hand across the table. Her hand was soft. He squeezed it gently.

"I'm so sorry," she said.

His hopes fell. She was letting him down.

"It's okay," he said. "I understand."

"No, you don't. I'm saying sorry for not noticing you in the village. It was like I was walking around with a blindfold on. I spent my life loving someone I met once for five minutes when all the time the man I should've loved was standing right in front of me. How did I not see you?"

"I didn't want to be seen." It was true. He'd never stepped forward to tell her how he felt. He'd melted into shadows and hidden himself away, believing he was protecting himself when in fact it was a punishment.

"My eyes are open now," she said.

"When are you leaving?" he asked, not daring to believe what she was saying. Had she noticed him at last when it was too late? Why hadn't he stepped forward before?

"I never said I was leaving."

"You asked me to come with you?" He was confused. He was sure she'd said she was leaving.

"That's right. I asked you to come with me. You said no. That means I'm not going. I'm not leaving you, Vikram. I'm never leaving you again."

She stood and stepped towards him, taking a seat on his knee.

His heart pounded in his chest as he smelled the sweet essence of her soul. The hair prickled on the back of his neck as waves of desire crashed over him.

Still, he wouldn't kiss her. It had to be from her. He wouldn't make that mistake again.

She leaned down and pressed her lips to his. He hesitated.

"I've always loved you," she whispered. "I just didn't realize it until now."

His hands slid to the back of her head and he pulled her face towards him, eliminating all space between them. He kissed her in a way he'd never kissed anyone before. He'd already opened his heart to her and in this kiss, he opened his soul. He loved her more than he'd loved her before. More than he'd ever love another. She was beautiful. She was powerful. There would never be another like her.

Vikram had never known such joy as that which lay within the weeks that followed.

Being close to Tara reminded him of a time long ago when there'd been another half to his soul. When he was talking to her, laughing with her, walking by her side he remembered what it'd been like when Lali was alive.

What comfort there was in having someone to share your life. Someone who was on your side without question or condition. His love for Tara grew impossibly deeper. It also opened up a part of him he never expected—a longing to make peace with the world.

He'd spent so much of his life angry and fearful. He realized now that by being that way, he'd given his father complete power over his life. This was a power his father didn't deserve.

If he were ever to move on and be the man that Tara deserved to have standing by her side then he needed to let go of his pain. It became more and more clear to him what exactly he needed to do.

"I want to see my mother," he said over breakfast one morning.

Tara looked at him in surprise then smiled.

"Do you know where to find her?" she asked.

"I could try our old house."

"Would you like me to come with you?"

He nodded.

"Would you like to go now?"

He nodded again.

"Come on then," she said, dropping her half-eaten piece of toast.

He knew she'd understand.

The train that took them to the other side of the city seemed to travel at an impossibly slow pace. Now that he'd decided to see his mother, he was anxious to get to her.

He'd held his grudge for too long. She'd loved Lali, too. Tara was right when she'd said his mother had been frightened. Who knew what his father had done to her. Who knew what he'd threatened to do to Lali if she'd tried to stop him.

In his grief at losing his sister, he hadn't stopped to see things from anyone else's point of view.

His mother not only lost her daughter that day. She also lost her son.

He led Tara through the winding streets in silence.

She didn't ask him what he planned to say or hoped to find, instinctively knowing he needed to be left to his thoughts. It was enough that she was there, holding his hand, ready to catch him if he were to fall.

The street was as he remembered. His house wasn't. It looked smaller. More ordinary. Less like the hell he'd turned it into in his mind.

He glanced up at the upstairs balcony and a sick feeling filled his gut.

Tara squeezed his hand.

"I'll wait here," she said, urging him forward.

"No. Come. Please." He wasn't sure he could do this without her. It was because of her that he'd even gotten this far.

He knocked on the door, preparing for a stranger to answer. It was unlikely his mother still lived here. Or if she did, why would she be home, waiting for a visit she must surely have given up on many years ago?

The door opened a crack. He felt eyes upon him.

"Hello?" he said.

The door opened wide. His mother stood before him. Her hair was gray, her face filled with wrinkles. Two deep scars ran the length of one cheek. It seemed she had aged a decade for each year that had passed.

"My son," she said, reaching out her arms. "I knew you'd come home."

He stepped toward her, unsure of how he felt. Unsure as

to whether this was a giant mistake. She was like a stranger to him.

She wrapped her arms around him, burying her face in his chest. He could feel the dampness of her tears soaking through his shirt.

He placed his arms around her and a wave of recognition flooded through his body. This was no stranger. This was his mother. This was the woman who'd loved him as a boy and loved him now as the man he'd become.

The love that had grown in his heart for Tara expanded to allow his mother in. He'd been a fool to have waited so long.

"Mother, this is Tara," he said, placing an arm around her shoulder as he broke from her embrace.

"Your wife?" she asked.

"Not yet," he replied.

Tara gave him a crooked smile and stepped forward.

"Thank you for looking after my boy," his mother said, pulling Tara into a warm hug.

"I promise you, it's him that's always looked after me," she said. "Your son is a good man."

"Come in," she said, stepping aside.

Vikram paused.

"Is he here?" he asked, worried for the first time that his father might be home. He was ready to forgive his mother—and ask for her forgiveness himself—but he wasn't sure he'd ever be ready to do the same for his father.

"Who?" she asked.

"Him."

"Oh, him." She waved her hand in the air. "No, he left the same day as you."

They followed her into the house and sat on her sofa, while she sat nearby on an armchair. If the house had seemed to have shrunk on the outside, it had done the opposite inside. All those years of living in the village had left him feeling the vastness of even the smallest spaces. The house he'd grown up in as a boy now seemed enormous.

He looked at his mother, sensing the well of pain that was bubbling to the surface of her eyes.

"I'm sorry," they both said in unison.

"I tried to protect her," she said.

"I know," he soothed.

"I tried to protect you, too."

"I know."

"You thought I was angry with you. I wasn't. I was never angry with you."

"Mother, I know."

"I'm sorry," she said again.

"Please stop," he said. "I'm sorry I left you. I should've stayed."

She looked at him, neither agreeing nor disagreeing. He felt Tara's hand on his thigh as she sat silently beside him. He was grateful for her presence.

"What happened to your face?" he asked, unable to tear his eyes from the two scars that marked his mother's cheek so vividly.

"Nothing," she said, her hand leaping to her cheek.

"What happened to your face?" he repeated. "Enough silence, Mother. Enough secrets have lain between us."

"Your father," she said, dropping her gaze to the floor.

"He did this to you?"

She turned her cheek to face him.

"This one was for Lali," she said, running the tip of her finger the length of one of the scars. "And this one was for you."

A gasp leaped from his throat.

"It's not your fault," she said. "None of this is your fault."

"But it is," he said, wringing his hands in his lap.

"It's not," said Tara. "Listen to your mother. She's right."

"Thank you," said his mother.

"It's not your fault either," said Tara.

His mother smiled sadly at Tara. "You are young," she said. "Life is simple when you're young."

Tara nodded politely. Vikram wanted to tell his mother that she was wrong about this. Nothing had been simple about his life or Tara's when they were young. Just as there was nothing simple about it now.

He held his tongue.

Instead, he knelt on the floor at his mother's feet and held her hands, his eyes level with her own.

"It's not your fault," he said.

"I'm sorry," she said.

"I forgive you."

"I'm so sorry," she said again.

"I forgive you." He searched her eyes deeper still, realizing that the forgiveness he'd come here seeking was of little importance compared to the forgiveness he could offer himself. "Mother, I forgive you."

He reached for her, embracing her once more. This time her tears were angry sobs that raged from deep inside her. Sobs that only he could comfort. Sobs that only he could understand.

"I'm proud of you," said Tara as she lay in his arms that night.

"It was time to forgive," he said, feeling a lightness upon his chest. "And to be forgiven myself."

She squeezed him around the waist.

"Is it your time, too?" he asked.

"My time?" she asked, lifting her head to look at him.

"To forgive Aashi."

Her head returned to his chest.

He didn't want to think about what that response meant. If she refused to forgive Aashi then that could only mean one thing—she still loved Finn.

"Do something for me," he said.

"What?" she asked, sounding anncyed.

"Picture Aashi in your mind—"

"Enough about Aashi," she snapped.

"Just do it. Picture her in your mind and tell me what you feel."

"Angry," she said.

"What else?"

"I miss her. Are you happy? I said it. I miss her so much it hurts."

"Then I'll ask you again. Is it your time?"

She sat up on the bed and crossed her legs.

"Okay, Vikram, this is what we're going to do." She loomed over him, her voice in full command. He liked this side of her. It was exactly the side of her that had made him fall in love with her to begin with. She knew how to take control of a situation.

"Yes, boss. Tell me," he said.

"First we're going to get married. Okay?"

He nodded in surprise. Was she serious? He'd love nothing more.

"Then we're going to sell this apartment and repay Bakul. We'll keep only a small amount to take ourselves to London for our honeymoon. Okay?"

"But where will we live?"

"I'm getting to that. When we're in London I'll sort things out with Aashi. I can't hate her. I don't even care about Finn anymore. Well, I mean I do care about him, but not like that. I have you now."

"But—"

"Hush! After our honeymoon, we'll return to India. We'll

live with your mother. She's been on her own for far too long."

He wasn't sure what to say. What she was saying made sense. It made so much sense he found himself wishing he'd thought of it himself.

"Well, aren't you going to say anything?" she said.

"Am I allowed to talk now?"

She nodded.

He got up from the bed and shuffled in his drawer looking for something. He found it and dropped to one knee before her.

"Tara. I—"

"What are you doing?" she asked.

"It's your turn to hush now. Tara, you are a surprise to me every day. I thank the universe for sending me to the village, for I am thankful that the village led me to you. When I met you, I was half a person. You have made me whole. I love you with all my heart. Will you marry me?"

He opened the small box he held in his hand and presented her with the thin gold band he'd purchased only days before. He wished he could afford a diamond or another precious stone. One day he would.

He'd been waiting for the right time to ask her. Instead he'd waited too long and she'd asked him herself. He couldn't let her get away with that.

She leaped from the bed as she threw her arms around him. They fell back onto the floor, her body pinned on top of his.

"I will marry you," she said, between the soft kisses she lay upon his face. "I will marry you and I'll be the happiest girl in the world."

"Are you going to put it on?" he asked.

"What?"

"The ring, of course."

"Oh, yes," she said, reaching for it and lifting it from its case.

She handed it to him.

"You put it on," she said.

He took it and slid it onto her finger.

"I'm sorry it's so…"

"It's beautiful," she said, kissing him on the tip of his nose.

"You're beautiful," he said.

"Well, you certainly make me feel like I am."

He decided at that moment to make it his life's mission to do more than make her feel like she was beautiful.

He'd make sure she knew it.

EPILOGUE

The Soulweaver stood by the window. Not that he had legs to stand on or a body to carry his soul. He'd long since relinquished the simple earthly pleasure of having blood in his veins.

He no longer thought of himself as Shen, despite the knowledge that was once the name by which he was known. He'd had many names, one to go with each of the bodies he'd resided in.

And now he had no name. It'd been an unexpected freedom in having his spirit set free.

His work as the Soulweaver was difficult. Progress toward restoring the planet to peace had been slow and he'd found himself understanding the actions of the soul who'd held this job before him—a soul who'd lost her confidence in the world. A soul who now stood in this very room.

Aashi. Maari. Mother. It didn't matter what name he called her— her soul was the same.

He looked at her, seeing not her body, but the light contained within. Her journey had been an interesting one. He hadn't expected to see her again once the Author sent her to Neron. It had been a surprise to find her placed in his care once more.

She'd impressed him with her strength, her compassion and her ability to love with all her heart. Her life had been filled with both joy and sadness. Her greatest sadness hung over her now.

Aashi's sister had turned her back on her. And although she'd found her soulmate to soothe her troubles, the separation from Tara wasn't a trouble that could be soothed. She worried for Tara's soul.

He also worried for Tara's soul. This was the soul he was connected to as his mate. The soul that was supposed to stand by his side for eternity, weaving lives and shining light.

But her light had flickered. It was only for a moment, but it was long enough to change the course of her journey.

Somehow, as a Soulweaver, she'd been able to hold onto a piece of herself that was supposed to have slipped through her fingers. Her love for the soul once known as Nax was strong. Stronger than either he or the Author had realized.

Unbeknown to him, she'd kept an eye on him and been disturbed by what she'd seen.

He wished she'd kept her eyes on the earth instead of the sky. Her actions had torn her away and he missed her with the kind of pain a Soulweaver was not supposed to feel.

The Author hadn't given him a chance to weave her soul, but that hadn't stopped him from sending her a light to keep her safe. He'd sent her Vikram.

Finn came into the room. He put his arms around Aashi. Bright sparks surged from their bodies and raced around the room, swirling in circles like a tornado. They were orange, then blue, then green, then purple.

They were sparks only the Soulweaver could see, but he knew both Finn and Aashi could feel them. This is what had bound them together in their last lifetime and this was what bound them now.

The front door opened and in came Nikii and Gerard. Bakul was behind them talking to Vikram. Last of all was Tara.

The room hummed with the energy of the seven souls who stood in silence.

Tara and Aashi ran to each other, tears falling from their eyes. They were tears filled with words they had not yet had the chance to say. Words of regret. Words of sorrow. Words of pain.

But shouting louder than all those words combined, were words of forgiveness.

Tara wrapped Aashi in her arms in the same way she'd done as a child and a hush fell across the room. These two strong and brave women had survived against the odds because they'd had each other. It was a bond that had been damaged but not broken. One that was sure to be rekindled, not just in this lifetime but in many more to come.

The Soulweaver felt an enormous sense of relief. Tara's soul was safe. Perhaps one day the Author would return her to his side and the empty hole he felt inside him would once again be filled with her light.

Before he left, he poured blessings and love into each of the beautiful souls that stood before him.

He would see them all again before long.

Right now, he had more work to do.

THE END
Ready for the next lifetime?
Check out Book 3, The Shadowmaker, now
http://mybook.to/hcshadowmaker

THE SHADOWMAKER

BOOK 3 THE SOULWEAVER SERIES

Two strangers. Two planets. One epic conclusion.

Forced to leave his family behind as Earth is destroyed, Buzz finds himself hurtling away from everything he knows and loves. Alone. Frightened. But alive.

He lands on a deserted planet. A place so similar to Earth, yet so very different. Just as he wonders how he'll survive, a girl with a familiar soul emerges from a civilisation deep under the ocean and changes everything once more.

Without so much as a language in common, Buzz and Nahlah must learn to thrive. Together, they create a new kind of world to live in - one that not only binds them but draws others to their side.

It's here that two worlds will finally become one. As hearts merge and threaten to break, souls will entwine, and we discover if the power of soulmates is greater than the power of time.

Grab your copy now!

http://mybook.to/hcshadowmaker

ALSO BY HEIDI CATHERINE

The Kingdoms of Evernow
Five kingdoms. Five senses.
One secret that will change them all.
The Kingdoms of Evernow (Prequel)
The Whisperers of Evernow
The Alchemists of Evernow
The Empress of Evernow
The Guardians of Evernow
The Angels of Evernow

The Soulweaver series
Two girls. Two lives. One soul.
The Soulweaver
The Truthseeker
The Shadowmaker

The Sovereign Code
Humans saved bees from extinction...
and created the deadliest threat we've seen yet
Harvest Day
Hive Mind
Queen Hunt
Venom Rising
Sting Wars

Elemental Games

Elemental powers. Deadly games. No escape.

Elemental Games

Elemental Uprising

Elemental Wars

Elemental Solution

The Thaw Chronicles

Four tests. Seven days. Nine teens.

Only the chosen shall breed.

Burning (Prequel)

Rising

Breaking

Falling

Reckoning

Extant

Exist

Exile

Expose

Tournaments of Thaw

Conquer the Thaw

The Oasis Trials

The Oasis Deception

The Last Oasis

WANT TO STAY IN TOUCH?

Heidi loves to connect with readers, so please say hello on social media, leave a review on Amazon or Goodreads, or visit her at www.heidicatherine.com

f facebook.com/HeidiCatherineAuthor
⊙ instagram.com/HeidiCatherine
♪ tiktok.com/@heidicatherineauthor
a amazon.com/author/heidicatherine

ABOUT THE AUTHOR

Heidi writes fantasy and dystopian novels, which gives her a chance to escape into worlds vastly different to her own life in the burbs. While she quite enjoys killing her characters (especially the awful ones), she promises she's far better behaved in real life. Other than writing and reading, Heidi's current obsessions include watching far too much reality TV with the excuse that it's research for her books.